BLADES OF HAVOC *book one*

Shotgun Spin

Book 1 in the Blades of Havoc series

First Digital Edition, 2023

Cover design: The Pretty Little Design Co.

Ebook ISBN: 978-1-998752-14-0

Paperback ISBN: 978-1-998752-15-7

ONE

Luciana

MOST OF MY mother's gangster minions had obviously never considered that a skate could be a lethal weapon. Even with two of them dangling over my shoulders as I headed out of the house, the lackeys standing guard in the front rooms had to make their teasing remarks.

"There goes the Ice Princess, off to her frozen castle," one of the guys said from the living room doorway, with a salute that could have passed for respectful if he hadn't been smirking at the same time.

"When are you going to start ruling around here, chica?" another called out from across the foyer.

I paused to shoot a glower at the second guy. No doubt they'd have said a lot worse if I *hadn't* been the daughter of their boss, the Deadly Rose, one of the most powerful crime bosses in the world.

But Mom had taught me plenty of lessons as her heir apparent, including that I should never let anyone intimidate me or get the upper hand, not even for a moment.

"Si yo te gobernara, te estarías comiendo tus bolas," I replied. *If I ruled you, you'd be eating your balls.* After I sliced them off with the blade on one of these skates, maybe.

I kept my tone firm but even. Maintain control, show only confidence.

The criminal underworld wasn't an easy place to survive for anyone, but it was twice as hard when you didn't have balls at all. At least not the literal kind.

Mom liked to say we Cordova women had to make up for it by making our metaphorical bolas twice as big. She'd also insisted on me learning Spanish, though I'd never even gotten to meet my great-grandparents who'd emigrated from Mexico.

Every piece of knowledge you collect and every skill you cultivate gives you that much more of an advantage, she'd said. Funny how she didn't apply that philosophy to my figure skating.

At five foot one, I was nearly a foot shorter than the dude who'd shot his mouth off, but he knew his place well enough to shrink at my retort, ducking his head while the others chuckled. Rafael emerged from the shadows of the hallway to flank me, and suddenly all of the house guards had much more important things to focus their attention on than the nineteen-year-old mafia princess in their midst.

"Ready to go, Lou?" my bodyguard asked in his typical low, subdued voice.

Rafael could have won awards for his poker face. Even the short coils of his wiry black hair stayed perfectly still with the turn of his head.

I'd never seen him show any emotion except the few times some prick had hassled me enough that he'd felt the need to turn on some real rage.

It was a little annoying how quickly the asshole underlings got their act together when they had to face a man instead of just me, even though I had a gazillion times more authority than he did. But I was used to it.

"I think so." I cast a quick glance around before I strode on toward the front door, half expecting a random flunky to come running with a message that the Deadly Rose needed me for some important task right this minute.

Mom had never been particularly enthusiastic about my dedication to my skating, but in the last few months it'd felt like she was outright interrupting my training sessions more and more.

No one charged over this time, though, so I made it out the door unhindered.

The dry summer air hit me with a smack of heat even this early in the morning. I wasn't going to need the sweatshirt packed in my duffel bag until I reached the chilled air of the indoor arena.

I walked around the white-washed walls of our

sprawling mansion, enjoying the brief glimpse of the Colorado River I got before I reached the garage.

Rafael didn't make any comment when I headed for the driver's side door of my Mini Coop. As soon as I'd gotten my license, we'd had the argument about who got to be behind the wheel, and he hadn't been able to deny that he'd have a much easier time protecting me in an emergency if he wasn't having to steer at the same time.

I slipped my small frame into the driver's seat easily. Rafael had to fold his tall, brawny form in beside me a little awkwardly even with the passenger seat pushed all the way back.

But he fit just fine once he was inside. And, I mean, he was *fine* in general. I couldn't help admiring his burnished brown skin and broad, muscled shoulders for a second before he flicked his intense burgundy gaze toward me and I jerked my eyes away.

There wasn't any point in looking for more than a bit of eye candy anyway. I'd already tried to hit that once when I was sixteen—and really should have known better, considering that Rafael's stoic discipline was one of the qualities I admired about him beyond his looks—and again once I was eighteen and totally legal.

He'd still turned me down the second time, with his usual calm reserve, and no amount of flirting had changed his mind, despite the hint of a smolder I thought I caught in his gaze now and then. I'd decided it was better to stop before I crossed the line between persistent and pathetic.

I was reaching to start the engine when my phone chimed with a text alert.

Oh, God, it'd better not be Mom calling me away for a mission after all.

I pulled the phone out of my pants pocket and flicked it on. One glance at the words that popped up on the screen had me frowning.

The message wasn't from Mom but from Coach Balakin, the man I'd been about to drive to meet at the arena.

I'm sorry to end things like this, but I can't watch you cling to this unfortunate dream any longer. You haven't progressed to the level you'd need to truly compete, and I don't think there's any point in continuing to coach you. Let's end this here, and you can move on to other dreams.

I stared at the sentences until they blurred together.

Rafael leaned toward me. "What's the matter?"

"I—I don't know. This doesn't make sense."

The bottom of my stomach had dropped out as I'd read Balakin's dismissal, a burn of shame and frustration forming in the back of my throat.

He'd been my coach since I'd first started training seriously when I was five, and in some ways the message shouldn't have been a surprise. He'd always said I wasn't quite there yet, not quite skilled enough that there was any point in entering competitions.

At nineteen, my time to reach that point was running out.

But getting this message right now felt wrong. Just a couple of days ago, Balakin had pulled me aside and told me, in a weirdly urgent voice, that he thought *he* was holding *me* back from what I could really achieve. That maybe I should find a new coach who could let me really take flight.

He'd seemed so twitchy when he'd said it that I'd asked him if everything was okay, and he'd covered it up with a nervous-sounding chuckle. I'd had no idea how to take that statement.

It was the total opposite of what he was saying in this text, though.

I swallowed the lump of emotion that'd constricted my throat. "Something strange is going on. I need to talk to him properly."

I tapped out a quick message telling Balakin to wait for me at the arena so I could hear him out and then shoved the phone back in my pocket.

The rest of Rafael's expression stayed typically reserved, but something flashed in his eyes. "If he said something that upset you—"

"I'm sure he didn't mean it like that," I insisted. "That's why I'm going to find out exactly what he did mean. I don't need you to protect me from my coach."

Rafael's jaw flexed, but he didn't push. If I *had* needed protection from the man I'd spent more time with than my own family for the past fourteen years, I had no doubt that my bodyguard would have leapt to my defense without a second's hesitation.

I drove along the outskirts of Austin to the small arena where I'd done most of my training for years. It was safer going someplace that wasn't very busy—easier for Rafael to keep an eye out for threats, less chance of anyone who might have a beef with my family even knowing I was there.

My body moved through the motions automatically. My heart was thumping heavily in my chest with a mix of apprehension and swelling grief.

What if the message was real? What if Balakin had just wanted to get out of coaching me without hurting my feelings the other day, and he'd been nervous because of how sick he was of trying to bring me up to par?

I gritted my teeth and focused on the road ahead. It didn't help anything thinking like that.

All that mattered was what Balakin would say when I could look him in the eyes. If he really felt that way, then I'd accept it.

The parking lot outside the dingy arena building was empty other than Balakin's blue Honda. At least he was here.

I hustled into the building, heading straight down the hall to the rink, where we usually met up. "Coach? I'm here. I don't want to argue with you—I just—"

I stalled in my tracks a few feet from the scuffed boards that surrounded the ice. A stark red smear had just come into view, standing out against the pale surface beyond.

My pulse hiccupped. I threw myself the rest of the way to the boards.

My hands hit the plexiglass, and a cry burst from my throat.

Coach Balakin lay sprawled on the ice at the base of the boards, his head lolled to the side. His pale eyes stared blankly.

His sweater was drenched with blood from multiple stab marks that'd broken through the fabric. The crimson fluid splattered his hair—once blond and now pure silver —and the waxy-looking skin of his face.

Above his head, someone had streaked more blood across the ice to form the words *Death to the Rose.*

"No," I mumbled, as if I could argue my coach back to life. "No, no, no. Why would anyone—how could they—?"

I'd seen dead bodies before. I'd killed more than one man myself. But that'd been in the other part of my life. The most violence I'd encountered while skating was a bruise from a badly landed jump.

Balakin had nothing to do with my family's criminal operations. He'd been patient and kind—he had a wife and two grown kids and a new granddaughter he'd been so pleased about last year...

Rafael grasped me by the arms and tugged me away, turning me in the same motion so the corpse was no longer in my view. "Come away from there, Lou."

He sounded strangely gentle.

I bit my lip, willing back the tears that burned at the back of my eyes, and clutched on to the anger that was rising up alongside my sense of loss.

"We have to find whoever did this. We have to find them and make them *pay.*"

"We'll do that," Rafael said in the same steady tone, but I could tell from the slight roughness that'd crept into his voice that he was pissed off too. "We'll take care of this. I need to make a couple of calls. But you shouldn't have to keep looking at him in that condition."

Maybe I should. It was my fault, wasn't it?

Death to the Rose.

This had something to do with my family's connections. Balakin had put so much time into training me when I'd never even been all that impressive, when I'd had to badger my own mother into letting me—

A chill swept through me that had nothing to do with the artificially cooled air. My heart skipped a beat.

I didn't want to even consider the possibility, but now that it was in my head…

I pushed away from Rafael. "I need to get back to the house. I need to talk to my mother."

It was evening before Mom answered my request to speak to her and summoned me to her home office. Apparently she'd been out of the house all day, although it was hard to tell for sure.

The Deadly Rose came and went at her pleasure, answering to no one.

The first confirmation that something was off was the fact that when I came into the grand room with its antique desk and bookcases, Mom sprang up from her chair and stalked over to wrap me in her wiry arms. She was tall enough that her chin rested against my forehead with the embrace.

The hug only lasted for a couple of seconds, but Mom rarely touched me at all. When she did, it was usually a poke or a smack to correct my position or to chide me for a mistake.

"I just heard," she said in her crisply smooth voice. She stepped back, giving my cheek a slightly patronizing pat that felt more in character. "I'm so sorry, Luciana. I know he was important to you."

I gazed back into her eyes, which were the same dark brown shade as mine. Her face had turned gaunt with middle-age, but she still looked elegant as ever with her bold but classically styled make-up and her black waves that she carefully dyed the gray out of.

We shouldn't have *to worry about being judged by how attractive we are, but we will be. So we do our best to turn that prejudice toward serving our purposes.*

Everything Mom did was part of a strategy. What was the purpose of the mask of mild sympathy she was showing me now?

"I don't understand why someone would have killed him," I said. "He never messed with anything criminal."

Mom tsked her tongue. "Plenty of our enemies might not have realized that. Most likely, though, they went after him because of his connection to you. They were looking to strike a blow at us. Maybe they hoped they'd get information out of him and killed him when he'd given everything he knew."

"He didn't know *anything* except how well I can move on the ice," I protested.

"Yes. It is unfortunate." Mom folded her arms over her chest. "I suppose we should take this as a sign that it's time you took on more responsibilities within our actual business. You can help me with keeping the lowlifes who'd attack us like this in line."

There it was. My heart sank.

She didn't even sound upset, just briskly business as

usual. Because the horrific murder played right into her plans.

Wasn't that convenient?

I studied her expression as I prepared my next words. "What if I want to keep skating?"

Mom waved her hand dismissively. "I'm sure you'll find time to get out on the ice here and there. But the schedule you've been keeping—there've already been conflicts. And wasn't Balakin saying that you'd reached your limits anyway?"

I hadn't been totally sure before that moment. I hadn't *wanted* to be sure.

But I hadn't said anything about the text Balakin had sent me to anyone. How could Mom say that with so much confidence if she didn't know about it for other reasons?

Like, because she'd ordered whoever had actually written that text to send it on Balakin's phone after they'd slaughtered the poor man.

That would be a perfect strategic move, wouldn't it?

Mom didn't have to be the bad guy, ordering me to give up my aspirations. It was the coach telling me I'd reached the end of the road, a coach who was now gone so his supposed last words to me would stand unchallenged.

It was awful, but also completely on brand for the woman in front of me.

My stomach lurched queasily. I held on to my composure with the iron fist she'd beaten into me.

Part of me wanted to throw her deception in her face. But what purpose would *that* act serve?

If she realized I was on to her, she'd only up her game.

"I guess he was," I said, playing along with the rouse. "Are we going to find the people who murdered him?"

Mom's reaction was only further confirmation. If she hadn't intended this outcome, she'd have been furious about the violation, the direct threat aimed at her in the bloody message on the ice.

Instead, she simply said curtly, "They'll be tracked down and dealt with. We have men on it already."

"Good," I said, letting just a hint of my own anger color my voice, even if I couldn't fully direct it at its real target.

Then I exhaled as if in exhaustion. "It was so sudden—I know I shouldn't be shocked by something like this, but I'm still a little shaken up. I think I'm going to turn in early."

Mom nodded, not bothering to express disapproval of my admission of this small weakness when she thought she'd gotten what she wanted. "Nothing wrong with taking a little time to gather yourself while you have the chance."

I couldn't get out of her presence fast enough, but I forced my steps to stay measured until I'd shut the door of her office and was heading down the hall. Then I hustled the rest of the way to my bedroom at the back of the house.

The funny thing—in a sick way—was that I'd already been prepared for this moment. I just hadn't expected it to play out quite like this.

For the past several years, I'd been siphoning as much money from the family accounts as I could get away with into a hidden stash of cash as well as a secret bank account under a pseudonym Mom didn't know. I had a getaway bag packed and stashed in the attic, easy to grab from the trap door in my walk-in closet.

I'd been planning to leave this house and Mom's expectations behind eventually. I might have done it already if I hadn't kept convincing myself that I should hang in there a little longer, build up my nest egg a little more…

And I hadn't decided how I'd handle the issue of Balakin and my training, since obviously Mom could find me through him.

Little did she know that with her vicious gambit, she'd swept the main factor keeping me with her into oblivion. There was nothing left in this city that I really cared about —nothing I couldn't just as easily find someplace else.

Mom had taught me how to survive in a man's world, how to stand up for myself and take control of my life. And for the first time, I was actually going to enjoy putting those lessons to use.

I stuffed my skates into my training duffel along with a few other items I couldn't bear to leave behind that weren't in the emergency bag. Then I swapped my black-and-white striped leggings and hot pink muscle tee for an all-black ensemble.

For a second, I imagined how Balakin would have clapped to see me wearing more typical workout gear rather than sticking to my preferred style at the rink, and a fresh pang of grief rippled through me.

He would have wanted this escape for me too. He'd been trying to tell me that when we'd talked two days ago, hadn't he?

Had Mom been putting pressure on him to cut me off, and he'd defied her? That would explain his nervousness.

But God, how he'd paid for it.

I blinked hard and sank onto my bed, pulling my knees up to my chest.

I couldn't leave just yet anyway. There was too much activity in the house; the sun hadn't even finished setting.

I waited until midnight. Then I grabbed all my things, popped out the screen in my window, and shimmied down to the roof on the back porch.

From there it was an easy drop to the backyard. My sneakers only made a soft thump in the grass.

A couple of men patrolled the expansive yard, but I'd timed my departure well. I slipped through the night toward the hedge between our grounds and the neighbor's.

I already knew I could squeeze between the tall, conical bushes and—

I'd almost reached them when a brawny shape stepped out from behind one of the trees. I jerked to a halt, clutching my bags, narrowing my eyes at Rafael.

"Where the hell are you going?" he demanded under his breath, his gaze flicking to the house behind me.

If he raised the alarm, I'd simply have to run.

I stared back at him fiercely. "She killed him. She killed Balakin. I can't live under her roof for one more day. I'm leaving, and you'd better not try to stop me."

I couldn't tell whether my accusation startled him. Rafael gazed back at me for a beat, and then he said, "I'll come with you."

I blinked. "What?"

His voice left no room for argument. "You should have someone with you who's got your back."

Rafael had watched over me for almost a decade, since Mom had given him the assignment. I still wouldn't have expected him to throw in his lot with me that far.

If she found out—*when* she found out that he'd betrayed her…

But I could tell from the tension in his face that he knew the consequences of his decision at least as well as I did. The longer we stood here, the more likely it was that we'd get caught right now.

And the thought of having a little company while I threw everything else in my life away did give me a tiny rush of relief.

"Okay," I said, pushing past him. "Just make sure you keep up."

TWO

Luciana

THE ENGINE of the faded blue Mercury Grand Marquis grumbled more than it rumbled, but that fact didn't shake my sense of satisfaction as I leaned back in the creased leather seat behind the wheel.

The car was mine—all mine, in a way I couldn't say my old ride really had been. And thanks to the cash I'd been secreting away for the past two years, Mom could never trace the purchase.

Rafael and I were traveling completely incognito, which was a necessity, honestly. I could only imagine the rage that'd flared behind Mom's eyes when she'd realized I'd flown the coop.

In the passenger seat next to me, Rafael stretched out his legs and frowned at the glove compartment. Or maybe at the base of the windshield. It was a little hard to tell.

My bodyguard had frowned at the car a lot when I'd picked it out from a buy-and-sell website. But after peeking at the engine and taking a test drive around the block, he'd stepped back while I handed over the wad of hundred-dollar bills.

We'd put a lot of miles on it in the past couple of days, and it hadn't failed us yet. So I figured I'd earned my satisfaction.

Rafael rolled his shoulders. "We should make a pit stop soon. Get the joints moving before they totally stiffen up."

I made a face, but I had to admit my back was pretty achy. "I guess sleeping in a car for two nights will do that to you."

We hadn't wanted to risk getting rooms in motels along our way, even paying cash. And it hadn't seemed safe to stop driving for very long, period. During the nights, we'd taken turns napping in the back seat while the other drove.

But the bright sunlight streaming over the lush forest on either side of the narrow country road lifted my spirits all the same. "We're almost there, though. Why stop now?"

Rafael took out his phone and squinted at the GPS as if verifying my statement. His frown deepened. "Are you sure a place like this is going to be safe enough? It's not really your typical scene."

I snorted. No, Hobb Creek—a tiny town that was barely a speck on the map of Ontario, Canada—was the exact opposite of the chaotic city where I'd grown up. But that was what made it perfect.

"There's no chance Mom will bother looking there," I said. "There are only three thousand people—pretty much impossible any of them will know about the Cordovas and recognize me. Especially when it's over a thousand miles from home and across a national border on top of that."

"We're going to stick out."

"Not if we pretend like we're normal people. I think I can manage that. Can't you?"

Rafael glowered at me, which didn't have the effect he was probably going for. Instead of feeling chagrined, my body temperature rose by about five degrees.

The man was smoking-hot, what can I tell you?

"You'll be bored out of your mind," he said. "What are you going to do with yourself for days on end?"

"I don't know, I think I could use a little peace for once. And there's the skating rink."

Rafael let out a snort. "I doubt that's anything like you're used to either."

I resisted the urge to punch him. "I *shouldn't* be skating anywhere like I used to. Mom will have her people monitoring all the nice rinks in the major cities—that's the first place she'll look. And I picked Hobb Creek specifically because for such a small town, it's got a pretty nice arena. It's not hyped up in a way Mom would notice, but I found a few people talking about how good it is on more obscure sites online."

Rafael simply sighed. "And this house you're thinking we'll rent. It just happened to be available immediately?"

"It looked like the owner has been trying to rent it for a while." I shot my bodyguard a pointed look. "Which is another good thing, because it shows that this town isn't a happening spot in high demand. It won't be on anyone's radar, especially the Deadly Rose's."

At least, I sure as hell hoped it wasn't.

"We'll see what condition it's in." Rafael shifted his stance again, but rather than continuing his skeptical comments, he fell into silence.

His large frame looked a little squished even in the Grand Marquis' spacious seat. Although in comparison to my Mini Coop, I'd bet he considered it a step up.

He'd appreciate it more when he wasn't using it as a hotel room as well as a vehicle.

Maybe I did owe him a quick stretch break, though. My joints were starting to tingle with the need for a good stretch too.

I peered through the windshield at the tree-lined fields we were passing now, crops I couldn't identify swaying in the gentle late-summer breeze. Where would be a good spot to pull over for a couple of minutes?

What I caught sight of first made my heart leap in my chest.

I jerked straighter in my seat. "Hey! Look, there's the sign. We're here!"

Rafael's dark eyebrows rose, a gleam of relief in his burgundy eyes. "Hobb Creek, Ontario," he read. "I guess this is our new 'home, sweet home.'" His soft-yet-steady baritone held the hint of a smile tucked away in it, though it didn't show on his lips.

Typical Rafael. You could tell him he won the lottery, and I'd bet he wouldn't crack a grin.

I had to admit, it was calming having him by my side. I'd never expected him to go on the run with me.

He was still the stone-faced man I'd known since I was ten years old, but if there was one reminder of my old life that I didn't mind having with me, it was him. Nothing shook him. There was no one I'd ever been able to count on more.

He pushed himself up taller in the seat, and I let myself quietly appreciate the swell of muscles in his biceps while ignoring the itch in my fingers to touch them.

Maybe now that we'd be living together, he'd rethink his resistance to getting close in other ways.

I cruised past the sign, easing off the gas so we could get a good look at the town rather than speeding through it. "The house is on River Street. Watch for that."

Pointed rooftops came into view up ahead. We drove past a smattering of houses and then along what was clearly the main street.

Several pedestrians strolled along the sidewalks. The storefronts on either side looked quaint, but the people themselves could have fit in back in Austin just fine. They hefted grocery bags, pushed strollers, or scrolled through their cellphones.

It reminded me a little of Sixth Street, only, y'know, a trillion times more rural. A pang of homesickness rang through my chest, but it was softened by a swell of hope.

I could be happy in a place like this, couldn't I?

We drove by a coffee shop and a school where a gaggle of teens were busy in the courtyard in a very intense game of three-on-three. The next several blocks were stuffed full of small restaurants and stores, a bank, a doctor's office, and a tiny fitness center.

A large grocery store loomed on the left. We puttered

past it, saw a couple more streets of houses, and then suddenly there were only a couple of warehouses on either side of us followed by a stretch of fields.

I pulled over onto the gravel curb and squinted into the distance. I couldn't see anything beyond the fields except some more forest.

"Was that it?" I said in disbelief. "The whole town? It's only, like, fifteen blocks long!" That was barely even a neighborhood back in Austin.

Rafael cocked his head. "You wanted small, you got small. I can see why you didn't have any trouble getting us that house."

"It shouldn't be too hard to find. Did you see River Street?"

He shook his head and motioned to his phone. "It looks like it's down Maple Avenue, which is about three blocks back the way we came. Take a right."

I yanked the wheel to take the car in a U-turn, still chewing over the situation. Somehow I hadn't imagined the town being quite *this* tiny.

What if Rafael was right and I'd be going stir-crazy in a few days?

But what were my other options? The bigger the town or city, the more likely Mom would have connections there. She wasn't going to let me go easily.

The image of Coach Balakin's bloody body flashed through my mind, and my hands tightened around the wheel.

I'd have to make Hobb Creek work. The only thing to do now was to keep my head down and make sure I didn't attract too much attention.

I followed Rafael's directions and aimed the car down a residential street lined with bungalows and two-story houses with large lawns. In less than a minute, I spotted the sign for River Street.

I turned the corner, and there we were.

The bungalow looked just like it had in the pictures in the online listing, all maroon clapboard and slate-gray shingles on the roof, with a mailbox at the foot of the driveway. But the photographs hadn't captured the flecks where the paint was peeling, or the dent in the side of the mailbox, or the weeds that were warring with the grass for dominance in the lawn.

That was all cosmetics, though. I couldn't see anything actually *wrong* with the building.

A smile started to tickle across my lips as I pulled up the driveway. This was the perfect home for lying low.

The bungalow's front door banged open as we stepped out onto the grass, and a portly man with tufts of gray hair poking up from his broad head made his way towards the car. His ruddy face shone with a broad grin.

"Miss Lou? You've made it!"

He extended his hand prematurely, before he was anywhere near close enough for me to reach it. When he was finally an arm's length away, I grasped it and shook it. He pumped his arm up and down enthusiastically.

"It's a pleasure to meet you," he said. "You remember me from the phone call, yes? Dimitris Papadakis?"

I did. The man's Greek accent had reminded me of Coach Balakin's eastern European articulation. It had immediately endeared him to me. Now that I'd experienced his warm jubilance in person, I liked him even more.

"Of course," I replied. "Thank you for giving us the chance to rent the house on such short notice. We're very grateful, aren't we, Rafael?"

My bodyguard only nodded in response. His eyes were trained on the bungalow. He was already assessing the area, his gaze honing in on the door and windows like laser-sights, evaluating every route in and out of the building.

Dimitris chuckled. "I'm grateful too. But come, come. Let me show you around."

The heavy-set man ushered the two of us up the front steps. They creaked so loudly under our combined weight that I had to suppress a flinch.

Dimitris simply beamed at me. "They like to welcome you home."

"Such an enthusiastic welcome too," Rafael said under his breath.

The landlord chuckled again. "Your husband has a good sense of humor. I like that. But I've done some renovations inside for more comfort. I promise you'll love living here."

Rafael cleared his throat. "I'm not her husband. Just a friend."

He said it calmly enough, but the admission had me wincing inwardly in a different way. I searched Dimitris's face for any sign of disapproval, but he just shrugged his hulking shoulders.

"Ah, well," he said. "Whatever makes you happy. You see the living room—I should mention the air conditioning unit. Still very warm here in early September, so you'll be using her for a bit longer. Sometimes she gives a little leak now and then. Like a dog, not totally trained yet. But everything else is working perfectly fine!"

I eyed the gray unit protruding from one of the living room windows, which didn't appear to have piddled recently. I could handle mopping up an occasional puddle. No big deal.

At least it would only be water.

The space we'd come into was a tad dingy: the cushions on the narrow sofa worn in patches, scuff marks along the edge of the plain pine table. But at least it *had* furnishings.

Fresh country air flowed through the space. I sucked in a deep breath of it, and all I could think was that no one would come marching in to order me to do *anything* as long as I was living here.

Yeah, I could get used to that. Who needed a mansion when you could have freedom instead?

Dimitris showed us the main bedroom on the ground level, the bathroom with its slightly yellowed but ample bathtub, and the concrete steps that led to a second bedroom in the basement.

Overall, it was a pretty small home, but bigger than the one room I'd had to myself back under Mom's roof. And now I'd have a roof all my own.

"One tenant maybe ten years ago, he was writing a movie," Dimitris told us as we climbed back up the stairs to the first floor. "He said he never got as good inspiration as when he was living here."

"How did the film do?" I asked with honest curiosity.

Dimitris burst out into a guffaw, his great gut shaking. "Oh, it was a total flop. But I'm sure it wasn't because of the script. Now, let's get this unpleasant paperwork out of our hair, yes?"

I'd already reviewed the lease when he'd emailed me a copy. I scanned the printed version quickly to confirm the contract looked the same as the one I'd already considered, with its month-to-month agreement and other basic stipulations, and then signed it with a flourish.

As I handed over the cash for the deposit and the first month's rent, something I could only call joy sparked in my chest.

I'd done it. I'd finally broken from my chains and staked a claim on a life that was truly my own.

Dimitris thanked us with another emphatic shake of my hand, and then he waddled off with shouts over his shoulder about how we should contact him if we had any trouble. I waved him off and then hustled to the car to grab my things.

When I lugged my bags into the house, I found Rafael studying the lock on the door. I arched an eyebrow at him. "Does it meet your approval?"

"It's not awful," he said, which from him was high praise.

"You know, I hear that in small towns like this, most people don't even bother locking their doors."

Rafael's head snapped around just like I'd known it would. "We're keeping the door locked, Lou."

With a roll of my eyes, I held up my hands. "No kidding. I was just saying."

Sometimes it was way too easy to push his buttons.

He moved to the windows, inspecting the latches on them too. "I'll take the basement bedroom."

I paused. "Are you sure?" It was colder and darker, and the windows were tiny. I didn't really *want* to sleep down there, but on the other hand I could see turning it into a cool little cave.

Rafael had given up his whole life to follow me here. This wasn't *his* dream. I didn't want to make him any more uncomfortable than he already was.

But he simply shrugged. "I'd rather you were close to the exit if you need to get out in a hurry."

Well, when he put it in practical terms like that, it was hard to argue.

I hefted my bags onward to the main-floor bedroom, which had a picture window that was actually rather pretty and a double bed with a brass frame. The bedspread was a little frilly for my tastes, but I could always replace it if we stayed here long enough.

I could decide everything about how this house was decorated—with some input from Rafael, of course. The contract I'd just signed said it was all *mine*.

But the house wasn't the only reason I'd come here. As I unpacked my clothes from my emergency bag, taking a weird pleasure from adding them to the hangers in the closet, my gaze kept snagging on my training duffel.

When the urge became too much, I left the rest of my clothes and knelt by the equipment bag. I stuffed a few small items in my purse and then simply grabbed my skates.

I wasn't going to do anything hardcore on my first day

here. Just… take a quick spin on the local rink. Break in the ice.

I slung the skates over my shoulder by the laces and walked to the doorway. "I'm going to check out the skating rink."

Rafael appeared at the top of the stairs. "Of course you are. Where exactly is it?"

I could picture the layout of the town in my head now. "It's at the opposite end from here, east side, right on the outskirts. But that means it's barely any distance at all."

"Doesn't matter. I'm coming with you."

I hadn't expected anything less—and though I wouldn't have admitted it, part of me was relieved to have the company. Not that it was likely anything around Hobb Creek would offer a significant threat.

"You can check all the locks on the arena too," I teased.

I opted to take the car so that I wasn't flashing my skates all over town on my first day. Even with the slow speed limit and one wrong turn, we reached the squat gray building that held the rink in less than ten minutes.

The parking lot was empty. I guessed early afternoon in the middle of the week wasn't a very happening time for rink rentals. Or maybe people just walked over.

In a quiet town like this, I'd probably have the whole arena to myself most of the time.

A giddy shiver passed through me. I walked up to the front doors and tugged on the handle.

The door jarred against its partner—locked. I knit my brow, peering through the smudged windows, but I couldn't see any sign stating the opening hours.

Rafael peered over my shoulder. "We could always come back tomorrow morning."

"Who knows if they'll be open then either?"

Impatience was prickling through my limbs. I'd come all the way over here—I'd come almost two thousand miles to make Hobb Creek my home. I was going to see the goddamn rink.

It shouldn't be that hard. What I'd said to Rafael about small-town security was generally true, wasn't it? The lock on the door looked awfully simple.

I glanced around and confirmed there was no one within sight. Thankfully the arena was set at the back of its parking lot on the outskirts of town, so there wasn't a whole lot of traffic.

Bending down, I reached into my sock and fished out the set of bobby pins I always kept there, just in case.

"Is this really how you want to spend your first day?" Rafael asked. "Breaking and entering?"

"Oh, stop. This place doesn't have cameras, and there are no cars in the parking lot. No one will ever know. If anyone *does* catch me inside, I can just claim I found it unlocked."

He sighed but didn't argue further.

I had the door open within the next three breaths. Tucking the bobby pins back into my sock, I smiled triumphantly.

We stepped into a dim entrance way with a front office that showed no signs of life. A hallway branched off to the side where presumably the changerooms lay, but my attention zoomed in on the swinging doors straight ahead that would give admission to the rink itself.

I pushed past them and stopped at the top of the steps to flick a light switch. A thrill tingled through me.

The stands were empty. The rink shone glossy under the overhead lights that'd just flooded it.

The ice was calling to me.

Rafael drifted to the side, melding into the shadows along the top of the stands as he preferred to. I hurried down the aisle to the benches that ringed the rink.

Perched on one, I tore off my sneakers and slid my feet into the familiar encasing of my skates. My fingers moved to lace them automatically.

I pulled my phone out of my purse along with my Bluetooth speaker and found my playlist that included my warm-up music and the songs for a few of my favorite routines. With it playing, I set the phone and speaker on the top of the boards around the ice and then pushed off.

My blades glided over the slick surface. The breeze I generated with the swift movement swept around me. I closed my eyes just for a second.

This—this was where my new life, my real life, truly began.

THREE

Jasper

I WAS JUST TYING up my sneakers when an energetic knock sounded on the apartment door.

"Time to get going, lazy bones!" my self-proclaimed coach called through the wooden slab in his typical playful tone. "The day's not going to wait forever."

"I'm coming, I'm coming," I grumbled half-heartedly. "A guy's got to put his shoes on, you know. Especially when his coach insists that he needs to walk to the rink."

"All part of your training. You can never have too much endurance work."

It was hard to feel truly annoyed listening to Niko Okabe's cheery, lightly accented voice. Even harder when I reminded myself that he'd flown halfway across the world from Japan just to haul me out of my slump.

But that didn't mean I was going to somehow transform into Mr. Sunshine myself.

"As you always say," I retorted dryly, and glanced at the hallway mirror. A few rakes of my fingers through my auburn hair was enough to tame it into shape.

I fumbled around for the keys of my garage-top apartment as I swung my equipment bag over one shoulder. When I shoved the door open, Niko grinned at me from the landing on the side of the garage, just as chipper as he'd been when he'd arrived at my grandparents' door in Ottawa a couple of months ago.

He was already in his workout attire of black athletic pants and brightly colored tee, his black hair spiked in his usual style. The hot pink streak he'd dyed through it caught a flash of sunlight, nearly blinding the shit out of me.

I locked the door behind me and shoved the keys into my pocket. Niko was renting a bachelor apartment over a store in the middle of town, closer to the arena than my place was, but he insisted on joining me for the walk over every day.

Maybe to make sure I did actually walk. But he said it was so we could warm up our minds too, talking over goals for this practice session.

He strode down the stairs ahead of me, a thermos dangling from one slender hand. "It's a beautiful day."

"As I'm sure we'll appreciate so much while we're hanging out in a windowless room."

"It sets the mood." Niko wagged a finger at me. "You know that attitude is at least fifty percent of the performance."

I couldn't stop one corner of my mouth from ticking upward in the start of a smile. "Then I guess I'll be skating clear and sunny today."

Niko simply chuckled, that light but warm laugh that gave the impression you genuinely *had* brightened his day. The sound sent a weird twinge through my stomach that I didn't want to look at too closely.

It really was a gorgeous day if you were into that sort of thing, the sun beaming down over Hobb Creek like it was setting it up for a picturesque Hollywood film set. Summer was still hanging on enough that the breeze that brushed over my bare arms was enjoyable rather than chilly.

As usual, Niko started chattering away about his opinions on the progress I'd made.

"Your Lutzes have been looking much better in the last few weeks. Good height, and you've barely popped out of any of them."

"Hurray!" I said in a sarcastic cheer.

"We need to celebrate our victories," Niko insisted. "That's attitude too. Be happy with where you're at, and the audience will be happy watching you."

"When I have an audience again."

"We're getting there."

There wasn't a particle of doubt in Niko's voice. He unscrewed the cap on his thermos, took a swig, and grimaced. He managed to swallow with a bob of his Adam's apple, but he poured the rest of the white liquid contents out into one of the decorative flower beds next to the sidewalk.

"Another failed experiment?" I couldn't help teasing.

"When are you going to learn that carbonation and milk just don't go together?"

"They do!" he protested. "If you'd ever had proper Calpis… It's a crime that you can't buy it here. But if they can make it, there's got to be a way."

"Or you could just get your sister to send you some straight from Japan."

He snorted. "Then I'll never hear the end of it from Emi. I can be persistent. Better to teach a man to fish or something like that, isn't that what they say?"

"That's about right."

Niko had mentioned that he'd lived in the US for a few years as a kid while his father was stationed there for a job. He'd spent first through fifth grade in an American school, which explained why his accent was mild and his grasp of English idioms not bad. There were still a few concepts he didn't totally have down, though.

Like that everyone on this side of the ocean thought making pop out of milk was deeply bizarre.

He shook his empty thermos at me, grinning. "When I get it right, you'll see. You'll be guzzling it like you do that maple syrup you pour on everything."

"Sure, and then I'll land a quadruple Axel," I said, but my mouth had stretched into a full smile despite my skeptical tone.

Over the past several weeks, Niko and I had settled into something like a comfortable routine. He badgered me onto the ice in his upbeat way and delivered his coaching instructions with boundless enthusiasm. When my muscles were aching, we trekked back through town to grab a bite to eat, quickly hash out how the practice had gone, and go our separate ways. Then the next day we started over again.

But tramping along beside him, uncertainty still niggled at me.

If I was going to compete again, there was no one better to coach me back into the circuit than Niko Okabe. The guy was like music on the ice; he had a way with both the artistic and technical aspects of skating that I'd always admired.

I'd watched him compete for Japan and had been blown away by his ability to paint a picture through motion. I wanted to do the same more than anything in the world.

There was a reason he'd made it to two Olympic Games, earning silver at the last one.

He'd never coached before, though, as far as I knew—at least not professionally. He hadn't really explained why he'd tracked me down and insisted that he was going to whip me back into shape, only saying that he'd noticed my absence during the last sequence of competitions and decided he would see what he could do about it. That he'd been wanting a challenge.

Was that all he saw when he looked at me—a problem to solve? A difficult puzzle to work through to stretch his skills?

If it meant anything more than that, he certainly hadn't given any indication. He was cheerful and friendly, sure, but always with a professional air.

The thought made me feel prickly again, but really, did it matter?

I wanted to be out there performing in front of the

crowds again. If Niko was willing to help me get back into the headspace where I could, who was I to look a gift horse in the mouth?

This once, there was a car parked outside the arena—a light blue sedan I didn't recognize. Most of the time the staff never showed up while we were practicing. Hopefully they weren't messing with the ice.

Niko must have observed it too. Rather than fishing the spare key the owners had given him out of his pocket, he tried the door. It opened easily.

"Looks like I might not be the only one who gets to appreciate your talents today," he said, tugging it wide.

"Unless they screwed up our scheduling and we're about to walk into some six-year-old's birthday party," I muttered, but headed on inside behind him.

We found the reception area eerily vacant, just as it always was. I craned my neck down the short hallway, but the manager's office was shut up tight too. No lights shone through the tiny window.

No party, then. Maybe a janitor was making the rounds?

As we approached the doors to the rink, a lilting melody filtered past them to my ears. My heart skipped a beat.

Someone was playing music in there. And not any kids, unless Chopin was the new standard for birthday parties.

I opened my mouth to call out and ask who was there. We'd booked this time, after all.

But Niko had already reached the doors and nudged

them open. His hand jerked up to silence me as he stared through the gap.

Then he was off again, pushing right into the stands. I hustled after him, even more confused than before.

The second I burst into the rink area, my steps slowed.

The music was emanating from a small speaker perched on the boards around the rink, slightly tinny but the notes pealing clearly enough. And moving with the melody, a woman glided across the ice.

In an instant, I noted that she had a typical figure skater build: petite but muscular through her thighs and calves. Her dark ponytail streamed out behind her like a battle flag.

And man, could she *move*.

She held her hands high above her head, then leaned back as she trailed them down across the swell of her chest and out again. They curved with the rest of her body when her feet spun up in a beautiful triple Salchow.

She whirled through the air as though that wasn't one of the more difficult moves a skater could accomplish and landed it with a graceful sweep of her leg.

My mouth fell open. Her expression shifted in time with the music, the crescendo trilling higher until an entire storyline was playing through my head. The nocturne conveyed a sense of danger and romance intertwined, something so beautiful and touching that I couldn't tear my eyes away.

A pang reverberated through my chest. This was it. This was how I wanted to skate. The power and artistry I craved every time I set my blades on the ice.

The vision that never looked quite right even after all

these weeks of Niko's guidance, no matter how much he praised my progress in the video recordings he took to show me after.

As I drifted down the steps to the boards, I searched my memory, trying to recall if I'd ever seen this woman before. But no: nothing from the town, nothing from any of my past competitions.

She'd definitely have stuck in my mind if I'd seen her before. So who the hell was she, and where had she come from?

I was about to ask Niko those questions as I came up beside him at the foot of the stands, but then I caught a glimpse of his face.

Of the awe etched in his avid expression.

His bright brown eyes followed along with every leap of her powerful legs and every subtle curl of her fingers. His lips had parted as if the imagery she was creating had struck him speechless.

Had he ever looked at *my* skating like that?

Jealousy coupled with a hefty heaping of insecurity spiked between my ribs. If we compared who a panel of judges would be most impressed by, she would probably blow me out of the water, and Niko clearly knew that too.

"Wow," he breathed, rubbing salt into the wound. "She's really something."

Yeah, she was—in more ways than one. She eased to a stop at the far end of the rink, and for the first time I could see her face clearly, if only in profile.

The exertion of the routine had brought a ruddy flush into the smooth brown skin of her cheeks. The perfectly chiseled bow of her lips curled up in a tiny smile. The graceful arc of her eyebrows matched the elegant slope of her nose.

She was fucking gorgeous.

My cock twitched involuntarily, and I set my duffel bag on the bench in front of me just in case I needed it to hide my reaction. At the same time, my jaw tightened.

A woman like that would be used to everyone falling all over her. The last thing I wanted was to come across like another lovestruck schoolboy tripping over himself to join her fan club.

Shoving down the flare of heat that'd stirred inside me, I raised my hands in a slow, pointed clap.

Yes, we see you. Yes, you're oh so wonderful.

Now get over here and explain what the fuck you're doing crashing my training time.

FOUR

Luciana

I SOARED THROUGH THE AIR, as smooth and elegant as a swan on the water. The very soul of grace itself.

I was made for this.

Or at least, that's what I told myself.

The words had become a mantra, a prayer on repeat, bouncing around inside my brain while I tried to summon all the dignified calm and effortless confidence of a professional figure skater. When nerves nibbled at the edges of my mind, I reminded myself why I'd risked sneaking into the rink in the first place.

There was no one here watching, no one judging. Only Rafael's eyes would be on me right now, and he barely counted after all these years.

I could glide around for as long as I cared to, really get

acclimated to the feeling of this new rink beneath my skates.

After all, this strange, tiny town was home now. This little arena would be the backdrop for my skating from now on.

The familiar sound of my blades hissing over the ice filled my ears, chasing away all doubts. I shifted directions, pumping my legs with long, swift movements as my skates propelled me backwards.

My hands spread wide, my slender fingers reaching out towards the empty stands. A well of power had begun to course through me, surging in my veins and pulsing in my limbs.

Deep breath in, and out again.

This headspace was familiar. This was comfortable. Again, that mantra sailed through my thoughts, but this time, I knew the words were true.

I was made for this.

Sweeping one leg out behind me, I pushed up with the opposite foot and swung my arms around my slim form. I ascended like a bird in flight, the thrilling rush racing through my gut.

Pure, unfiltered bliss pumped throughout my body, pounding in my chest and bursting in my vision. I couldn't have stopped the smile from curving my lips even if I'd wanted to.

I knew in my heart that this was where I belonged. No matter what anyone said.

Landing felt more like floating. My skates met the ice again with a soft *shrrrk* before I pushed off again with one foot.

Another triple Salchow, this one even easier than the first. I might have tried for a triple Lutz if it hadn't been a few days since my last practice.

I closed my eyes when I landed this time, tilting the point of my toes and sweeping off once more. The moves felt natural, just as they always had before I'd left the only home I'd ever known.

I breezed across the ice in arcs and leaps, the blades connecting with the frozen surface almost magnetically. One, two, three, four, five…

By the time I reached the end of the routine's final sequence, my legs were screaming for a break, but giddy exhilaration still flowed through the rest of my body. I raised my hands in a graceful ending pose, fingertips reaching towards the arched ceiling.

My mind conjured the sound of applause, the adoring crowd roaring behind me. I almost let out a laugh.

Like that would ever happen.

A satisfied breath puffed through my lips. I was just about to turn towards the stands to tell Rafael that we should call it a day when a very real noise reached my ears.

Not a flurry of applause, but a single set of hands clapping in a slow rhythm that somehow didn't feel entirely complimentary.

As I spun toward the sound, another pair of hands joined the first, faster and more emphatic. I found myself staring at two men who'd come down to the boards at the other side of the rink.

Oh, shit.

How long had they been there? I hadn't noticed them as I'd been skating, but then again, how could I have? I'd drifted into that trance-like state of joy that had always come with being on the ice.

I grimaced. Maybe this plan wasn't so well thought out after all. I'd been in town for a whole hour and the first thing I did was get busted for trespassing. I could just imagine my mother shaking her head at me with disdain in her dark eyes.

At least neither of the guys appeared to be law enforcement or security. They weren't dressed in employee uniforms either, but regular T-shirts.

T-shirts that showed off a whole lot of impressive musculature on both of them, now that I was paying attention.

The bigger guy, who had to be as tall as Rafael and nearly as brawny, was the one clapping more slowly. Auburn waves tumbled across his face over full lips slanted at a skeptical angle. That didn't stop him from also being awfully delicious-looking.

The man next to him stood half a foot shorter, leaner but still plenty toned. A broad grin split his equally gorgeous face, sending a twinkle into his bright eyes that I could make out even across the distance.

A twinge of recognition shot through me, though I couldn't place it. Why did they look familiar? Had I seen them without really registering them when we drove through town?

Rafael hadn't emerged from his shadowy alcove to interrupt them, so he mustn't consider them much of a threat.

The slimmer man waved me over with obvious enthusiasm, still grinning away. He didn't look like he was about to accuse me of breaking and entering, but I wasn't so sure about his companion.

But I couldn't exactly pretend I wasn't here.

I skated over to the boards about ten feet down from where they stood and grabbed my phone to shut off the next song on the playlist.

"Great form," the enthusiastic man said before I could decide how to explain myself, his voice as cheerful as his expression. "Really excellent. Those two triple Salchows back to back, and then that ending sequence—you've obviously been training for a while. How have I not seen you on the competitive circuit before?"

I blinked at him, my brain not quite processing the compliment. Did he even know what he was talking about? He'd recognized the jump, so he obviously knew something about figure skating.

But Coach Balakin had always complained that I didn't achieve quite enough height, the angle of my arms looked clumsy. It wasn't likely all that had gotten fixed during the two-day drive to Canada.

"Thanks," I said warily, pushing a little closer across the ice. I couldn't shake the niggling sense that I should know who these two were…

Then the enthusiastic guy swept his lithe fingers through his smooth black hair, and a neon pink streak flashed beneath the rink lights.

I couldn't stop my mouth from dropping open. I hadn't fully recognized them at first because no part of my mind had been able to conceive of these two men actually being here.

But there was no mistaking them now that my brain had caught up.

"Oh my God," I blurted out. "You're Niko Okabe! And—" My gaze jerked to the grouchier, bigger guy next to him. "Jasper St. Pierre. Wow."

I snapped my mouth shut before I could babble any further, my cheeks flushing hot. I must have sounded like the ditsiest fangirl.

But I was a fan of both of them—I'd admired their routines from various championships more than once, glued to my TV screen.

Niko Okabe was known for his boldness both on and off the ice. He skated to music the judges raised eyebrows at, incorporated moves from other disciplines that raised those eyebrows even higher, and pulled it all off so well they couldn't help giving him top marks anyway.

In interviews, he never shied away from acknowledging his culturally controversial interest in both men and women. He refused to let anyone put him in a box.

How could I *not* admire that?

And Jasper St. Pierre... Despite his bulky build, he was pure artistry in motion. No one could paint a picture like he did when he whirled across a rink.

Of course, he wasn't making the prettiest picture right now with that stunning face of his getting increasingly grim.

He narrowed his stormy gray-green eyes at me. "Good job. You aren't blind."

Niko rolled his eyes at the taller guy and dipped into a jaunty bow. "A pleasure to meet you."

"What are you doing here?" I couldn't help asking.

Jasper folded his arms over his broad chest. "We should be asking you that. This is our ice time."

My cheeks flared hotter. Somehow two of the world's top skaters were training at this nice but admittedly rinky-dink arena in Nowhere, Ontario, and I'd gone and stolen their practice time.

I groped for the excuse I'd had ready, drawing myself a little straighter—though I couldn't come close to matching even Niko's height, skates or no. "I'm sorry. I found the door unlocked, and there was no one up front... I didn't think it'd be any problem for me to skate."

Niko waved off my concern and nudged Jasper with his elbow in what I took as a chiding way. "It's perfectly fine. I appreciated the chance to watch that amazing display of skill."

Right. He'd been saying something before about how great my routine had been. How well I'd performed it.

Hold up. Niko Okabe thought *I* was amazing?

No. That possibility did not compute. He must simply be acting friendly, overdoing it a little to make up for Jasper the Grouch.

"I had to take a little break from practice, but I'm glad to get back on the ice," I said, not knowing how else to respond, and then added quickly. "But I'll get off now so you can have it."

Jasper grunted as if my offer didn't come close to making up for the offense I'd committed. As I glided over to the opening in the boards, he dropped onto one of the benches and pulled his skates out of a duffel bag.

Niko was still studying me avidly. "You still haven't

told us who you are. And why have you been keeping such a low profile? If you'd even entered the US national competitions, I'd have seen you."

He really was being awfully nice to someone who'd snuck in during their ice time. I obviously wasn't going to give him my full name, but I had to answer him somehow.

"My name's Luciana," I said. "But I prefer Lou. Competing, well, I just always seem to get little injuries at the worst times."

Timing that would have prevented me from competing for years on end would have been incredibly bad luck, but Niko didn't question it. He probably didn't really think I was good enough to make it even to Regionals anyway.

My gaze slid from him to Jasper—who was studiously ignoring me while he laced up his skates—and back again. "Why are you two training here?"

I mean, the rink had been highly praised by the few people who knew about it online, but it was hardly world-championship-skater prominent. And Jasper had always competed for the US, as far as I knew, while Niko was obviously Team Japan.

I half-expected to get another brush-off, but Niko leaned his tan arms against the top of the boards with no sign of concern about my nosiness.

He tipped his head toward Jasper with another flash of his impressive grin. "It's all this guy's fault, really. If he hadn't gone and tried to disappear, neither one of us would be here bothering you right now."

"Bothering *her*?" Jasper muttered without looking up.

Niko ignored him. "If you recognize him, you

obviously know how fantastic *his* skills are. I expected to see him sweep through the last circuit, but he never showed. So I decided to make it my mission to drag him back into the spotlight. I tracked him down to his grandparents' place in Ottawa—"

Jasper interrupted with a cough. "*Stalked* me." But he didn't sound quite as irritated about it as he did when he was talking about me.

"—and found him lazing around in a slump. Since that was obviously not okay, I offered to give coaching him a try."

"More like he demanded I let him have a go at it and refused to leave until I said yes," Jasper put in, and met my gaze for the first time since I'd come closer. "But I didn't want it to be a big deal, so I asked around to find a place that would be very low key but still a good rink."

Huh. Their reasoning had been awfully similar to my own. I guessed that meant I'd made a good choice.

Jasper shot me a more pointed look and added, "So I'd better not see our faces plastered all over your Instagram or whatever."

I held up my hands in a gesture of innocence. Now that the initial shock of meeting two of my idols in the flesh was starting to wear off, my own prickliness was rearing its head in reaction to his.

"I came here to skate, not to take selfies. Or anyone else-ies."

He only scowled back at me. "And you just happened to turn up here?"

"I picked Hobb Creek for the same reason you did— seemed like a low-key place with a good arena," I said. "I needed a change of pace from the big city." That was a reasonable if vague explanation for my popping up out of nowhere, right? "Believe me, it would never have occurred to me that I'd run into you two here. I definitely won't spread the news."

"Good." Jasper turned to Niko. "Well, let's get on with it."

"Such a positive attitude, hmm?" Niko shot me a wry glance. I couldn't stop my lips from twitching with amusement, which from the glower Jasper shot me, hadn't gone unnoticed.

I snatched up my skate guards to pull them on and slipped past the boards to my own bag, even though a longing tugged at my gut to stay and watch. "I'll get out of your hair. Sorry again. If you let me know what slots you have booked, I'll make sure to work around them."

Niko's face brightened. "You shouldn't have to worry about that. There's lots of room on the rink, and we are here an awful lot. You should come train at the same time."

Jasper let out a sound that might have been a growl, but the offer made me too delirious with excitement for me to care.

"Are you serious? I really don't want to interrupt—"

"It's no trouble at all," Niko insisted. "I'd love to see what else you can do."

His gaze skimmed over my body, and warmth licked over my skin in its wake. Nothing he'd said had been overtly flirty, but all at once I had the impression that the appreciation in his gaze wasn't just for my skating.

Holy hell. Was *the* Niko Okabe attracted to me? I mean, I couldn't say the feeling wouldn't be mutual.

If he was… could anything actually happen between us? Had I fallen asleep on the ice and this was a crazy dream?

Just to make sure, I pinched myself where the men couldn't see. Nope, definitely awake.

Regardless of any other considerations, how could I possibly pass up the chance to train alongside two of the great skaters whose careers I'd been following?

A bright smile stretched across my face. "I'd love that. Thank you so much. I promise I won't get in the way."

"I'm sure you won't," Niko said over Jasper's skeptical grunt. "We're here every afternoon except Sundays from one until six."

"Then I'm sure I'll be seeing a lot of you."

Taking on training partners hadn't been part of my plan. Making friends—and maybe more?—with two very prominent skaters *definitely* hadn't been on my mind.

But they were laying low too. Practicing with them wouldn't cause any actual problems, right?

One thing was for sure: my new life had just gotten a whole lot more complicated.

FIVE

Luciana

"EVERYTHING OKAY, HUN?" my waitress asked, stopping by my little table outside the town's main café with a swish of her white apron.

I smiled up at her, taking a moment to peek at her nametag. I had learned a few useful things from my mother, one of which was that people appreciated it if you made the effort to address them personally.

"It's all been great, Beth," I said, poking my fork into one of my few remaining pierogies. The creamy goodness of the cheesy filling lingered in my mouth from those I'd already devoured. "Thank you."

Honestly, it was hard to imagine everything being *more* okay than it currently was. Over the last couple of days, I'd joined two of the skaters I'd admired most to practice, and tomorrow I would again. I was spending my Sunday off eating a delicious rendition of my favorite comfort food, not quite as good as my old nanny's cooking but close.

The weather was warm but not sweltering. Birds fluttered from one awning to the next along Hobb Creek's main street. Only a handful of cars had puttered up and down the road while I'd been having my lunch.

I couldn't remember ever enjoying this much *peace* in my entire life.

Maybe I was a small-town girl at heart after all.

A middle-aged couple strolled by, the woman shooting a glance at me that she quickly jerked away when she realized I'd caught her. I chewed on my pierogi without taking offense.

Rafael and I *did* kind of stick out here with our darker complexions. Small-town Ontario wasn't exactly a hub of multiculturalism. And on top of that, I was a newcomer.

No one had been outright unfriendly. I could handle a little wariness.

Really, I'd spent most of my life feeling like an outsider even back in Austin. It wasn't as if I could have gotten really chummy with any of the other kids at my schools. And I hadn't wanted to immerse myself in the family business and the people involved in that.

The only place I'd really felt at home was on the ice, and I'd never gotten to enjoy an actual community there, only Coach Balakin's company.

I was glad no one was badgering me about what I was doing in Hobb Creek, sticking to just observing. No doubt more pointed questions would come once the locals realized I was sticking around, not just visiting as a tourist.

Good thing I had my cover story all set for that moment. I smiled to myself before popping the last delicious morsel into my mouth.

As I drained the last of my cappuccino, a woman who didn't look all that different from me—other than being at least thirty years older—ambled up to the café door. Her wavy black hair was strung with silver strands, and her tan skin looked about as weathered as my mom's on the rare occasions I saw her without makeup. But there was a roundness and warmth to her face that I'd never have associated with Mom.

With the chime as she opened the café door, the voice of one of the waitresses rang out. "Oh, Dr. Ribeiro, you made it! Will you have your regular?"

The door closed before I could hear the doctor's answer. I couldn't help peering through the window and caught the waitress's sunny smile as she ushered the woman to a prime spot by the window.

She wasn't seen as an outsider, obviously. Maybe there was hope that I'd be offered similar enthusiasm someday.

I tried to imagine myself still living here in thirty years, and my mind balked at the idea. Mostly because I couldn't picture myself still skating as a forty-nine-year-old.

Well, I wouldn't be pulling off triples anymore, but if I kept myself limber, I didn't have to give it up completely.

My last gulp of the bittersweet coffee was spoiled by a puff of exhaust from a grumbling pickup truck that veered a little too close to the patio for comfort. I narrowed my eyes at it as it roared out of view—and noticed a guy sauntering in my direction on the opposite side of the street.

He didn't fit the typical small-town vibe at all: mid-twenties, sporting a couple of tattoos that poked from beneath his muscle tee, head tipped at a brash angle. About half a block away from where I sat, he turned toward a store and rapped his knuckles against the window.

I knit my brow. The place was a toy shop with the name *Harry's Treasures* painted across the glass in perfect cursive. Above and below the words were illustrations of a teddy bear, a bouncing ball, a jump rope, each rendered with careful precision.

What the hell did this cocky guy want there? And if he *did* want something in there, why had he simply propped himself against the doorframe with his sinewy arms folded over his chest like he was waiting for something?

This guy wasn't a regular customer. What was his deal?

As I watched, my nerves prickling with uneasiness, an elderly man appeared in the doorway. The younger guy pushed himself fully upright, flexing his shoulders in a posture that exuded menace. His laugh carried down the street, but there wasn't much warmth in it.

He jabbed his thumb toward the doorway. The old man raised his hands as if in protest, his own stance humble, but the guy shook his head. Drooping further, the old man—who I was pretty sure owned the toy shop —ducked back inside.

He returned less than a minute later with a letter-sized envelope he handed over with obvious reluctance. The cocky guy checked inside, clapped his target on the shoulder, and started ambling away.

"Sorry, Miss, are you ready for your bill?" a voice said, startling me out of my daze. I realized I'd gone rigid in my chair, and my waitress—Beth—was peering down at me with obvious concern.

"Oh, um, yes, please," I said hastily. My heart kept thudding as I dug my wallet out of my purse to pay for my meal.

I knew what a criminal transaction looked like when I saw it. No way were the contents of that envelope something legit. What the hell was going on in Hobb Creek?

The cocky guy was still in view a couple of blocks down the street. Not walking too fast but like he owned the place.

My teeth gritted. I tossed down a few bills that included a substantial tip and set off after him.

I stayed on the opposite side of the street and at least a block behind him, with regular glances at the store windows I passed as if I were simply taking a stroll. As I trailed the guy off the main street and through a residential section of town, it occurred to me that this might not be the smartest move I could make.

I should be staying as far away as possible from anything criminal. Anything that might tie back to my mother, no matter how tenuous the connections.

But I couldn't shake the memory of the hopelessness

I'd seen in the old man's stance. My sense of peace had been fractured.

I needed to at least know what was going on. That was a reasonable strategy, wasn't it? Even if I decided to avoid getting involved, it'd be easier if I knew exactly *what* to avoid.

Yeah, even I wasn't totally buying that story. But it kept me meandering past the rows of houses to the edge of town. My hands rose, my fingers trailing over the subtly sharp edges on the set of rings I liked to wear when I wasn't skating.

They looked pretty, and they could cut a guy with a swipe of my fist. Both features I appreciated.

When the commercial buildings I'd noticed before on the outskirts came into view, I slowed my pace even more. The cocky guy strode right on across the sprawling parking lot to where the pickup truck I'd seen before, a van, and a sports car were parked close to a boxy white storage building.

I stopped in the shade of a tree at the edge of someone's lawn and pulled out my phone so I could pretend to be focused on it rather than the activity across the lot. If I got any closer, it'd be obvious what I was after.

A couple of other men came out of the storage building. I couldn't make out what they said, but the macho posturing came across just fine. They shouldered each other and barked laughs with an attitude that reminded me way too much of the lower lackeys who hung around Mom's mansion back home.

Even more apprehension gripped me. So when a low,

deep voice spoke up from right behind me, I nearly jumped out of my skin.

"What do you think you're doing?"

My hand had already shot to the knife in my pocket before I recognized Rafael's voice. I spun around and elbowed him as discreetly as humanly possible.

"Are you trying to give me a heart attack?" I hissed under my breath.

I wasn't exactly surprised he was nearby—it was becoming clear that his bodyguard habits weren't dying just because we'd left the dangers of my old life behind. He'd probably been shadowing me from a discreet distance from the moment I'd left the bungalow.

But he didn't normally emerge from those shadows to hassle me with questions.

"I'm trying to figure out why you wandered all the way out here," Rafael said, still keeping his voice quiet.

I motioned vaguely behind me, toward the storage building. "There's something sketchy going on here—I'm sure of it. I saw one of those guys take an envelope from a store owner who really didn't look happy about it, and… just look at them!"

Rafael didn't miss a beat. "I already have."

I stared at him. "What?"

He gazed back at me steadily. "It's not exactly a big town. It didn't take me long to get a full lay of the land. Seems like a bunch of minor thugs decided to form a small-time gang out of that building."

"Here?" I said, still finding it hard to wrap my head around this development even after what I'd seen. "How much criminal business can they even get up to?"

Rafael shrugged. "They hit up Hobb Creek and a few other small towns in the area—collecting protection money, dealing drugs, stashing stuff in that storage building that's probably stolen or illegal. People who want to profit by breaking the law can always find some way of doing it."

I scowled. "And what the hell are the local police doing? Just sitting on their asses?"

"I don't know if they've even noticed what's going on. The regular locals are too intimidated to speak up. From what I've seen, the law enforcement presence in this area is stretched thin and not very competent anyway."

I turned my scowl directly on him. "And you found out all this stuff and didn't tell me?"

Rafael lifted his eyebrows just slightly. "Why would I have? What does it even matter?"

"Well, I—they're making trouble for the town! *My* town."

"Lou, you're supposed to be staying *out* of anything that looks like trouble, remember? Lay low and skate. Wasn't that the plan?"

"It was," I grumbled. "It is. But that doesn't mean I have to like it."

The townspeople I'd met so far didn't deserve this shit. They should get to enjoy their peaceful surroundings without some assholes ruining it.

And *I* didn't deserve this shit. I'd driven across an entire country to escape the criminal side of my life, and somehow I'd driven right into more of that garbage.

What if this gang did make a connection with the

wrong person, and someone recognized me? As unlikely as it was, their very existence was a threat to my freedom.

I set off back toward town, shoving my hands in the pockets of my jeans, but my thoughts kept roiling in my head. No, I didn't like this at all.

But what exactly could I do about it that wouldn't make the threat even worse?

SIX

Luciana

MY LEGS PUMPED as I built up my speed, my dark hair trailing behind me in its ponytail. Bending my knees into a squatting position, I positioned my ankles back until they were beneath my thighs.

An ache spread through my muscles—this was one of the first moves I'd ever learned, but holding it always strained my endurance. I adjusted my weight until I was sure I was steady and then lifted my right foot while sinking even further down, clasping my gloved fingers around the toe of my skates.

One Mississippi. Two Mississippi.

God, this move was torture. I dropped my leg after several more seconds and stood only to speed up again.

All my senses were wired with the awareness of my two fellow skaters at the other end of the rink. This was my third time training alongside Niko Okabe and Jasper St. Pierre, but every time I glanced their way, butterflies fluttered in my stomach.

I still couldn't quite believe I was actually training on the same ice as them.

Not only that, but Niko had even given me a few tips here and there when Jasper was taking a breather or doing something simple like stretching. And always with plenty of praise, as if he really did believe I was somewhere close to the same caliber as the two of them.

That idea felt even more impossible. Could he really just be that nice?

But if he honestly thought I had that level of skill… then had all Coach Balakin's criticisms and discouragements been lies? Or had being in the presence of two greats somehow elevated me too?

I couldn't wrap my head around it, but one thing I knew for sure was that I intended to give a performance worthy of Niko's praise. If I was going to level up to the standards I'd been aspiring to so long, I couldn't settle for anything short of perfection.

Again, I lowered myself back into the move. This time, my bravado carried me through the ache in my legs for little more than thirty seconds.

But I would be damned if I let my weakness faze me. I tried over and over, until I thought my muscles would snap like rubber bands.

Finally breaking out of my position, I lowered my right leg and stood, albeit a little wobbly. I'd held the pose for as long as I could that time, but the pressure on my ankles and thighs was murder.

Leaning against the side of the rink, I stretched one leg and then the other, trying to keep my expression natural. The last thing I wanted was Niko or Jasper noticing my sweaty face and heaving chest.

"Great legwork with that shoot-the-duck," Niko called. "You were really cruising! Nudge that foot just half an inch higher, and it'll be even easier."

"Thanks!" I called back as evenly as I could. "I'll try that next time."

Which wouldn't be until tomorrow—or next week, if my legs got any say in it.

I would have glowed with the praise, but as my gaze slid from Niko to Jasper next to him, I caught the bigger man scowling at me.

The second our eyes met, Jasper jerked his head away, his mouth pressing flat. But I knew what I'd seen. Especially since I'd seen it more than once over our training sessions.

Anytime Niko paid much attention to me, Jasper started looking even grouchier than usual, which was a massive feat. The coolly handsome face he put on during his professional performances had to be as much of a costume as the intricate outfits he wore, because I'd only caught rare glimpses of it as he ran through his routines here.

I'd have thought he was simply annoyed that I was stealing some of his coach's attention… but he didn't seem all that happy when Niko was focused on *him* either.

Like right now, as Niko turned to him and murmured something I couldn't hear. Jasper shook his head sharply, a storminess coming back into his eyes that I could see even from halfway across the rink.

Sometimes they'd joke together, and I'd see a looser side of the hotshot skater. But just as often, an odd tension would come over his brawny frame for reasons I didn't understand.

What was buzzing around in that gorgeous head of his under those tussled auburn waves?

Niko had obviously noticed it too. As Jasper pushed off into a circuit of the rink, building up to a jump, the slimmer man's constant smile briefly faded.

For just a second, he looked almost… *sad*.

It wasn't the first time I'd seen Niko look at Jasper like that, either. I couldn't shake the impression that there was more to his insistence on crossing the ocean to train Jasper than either of them were letting on.

But it wasn't my business. If I got too nosy, I could kiss this once-in-a-lifetime chance good-bye.

Jasper launched himself into a breath-taking double Axel. As he swerved around past me, I offered a thumbs up. "Nice one!"

I'd been trying to make friendly, but Jasper just grimaced. "I was aiming for a triple," he muttered.

I would have said something about how it was impressive to be able to switch intentions and pull off a double so smoothly when you realized you weren't going to land the harder move, but I suspected he wouldn't appreciate my insight.

Gulping a little more water, I rolled my shoulders. My skin was starting to feel muggy under my long-sleeved thermal.

And I couldn't say it was totally due to my work on the ice and not the company I was keeping.

I tugged off the thermal and tossed it onto my bag in the stands. My faded Metallica tee hung to my hips, matching my plaid leggings better than the plain blue shirt had anyway.

Who said you couldn't bring a little style even to practice?

"What's that on your back?"

I glanced over to see Jasper tipping his head toward me, his expression still grim but a hint of curiosity in his voice. My hand moved to the rough-edged neckline of the shirt that dipped to reveal the tops of my shoulder blades.

Oh, he meant my tattoo.

I patted it and offered a tentative smile. "Got this a few years ago."

With a tug downward, I revealed enough of my back that they'd be able to decipher the dark lines as angel wings, swooping from my spine to the tops of my shoulders.

"It's kind of in honor of the skating," I added. "I love feeling like I'm flying."

The second the words came out, my face flushed. I'd never told anyone that before.

Jasper didn't say anything particularly caustic, though. He just grunted, his gaze skimming down over my clothes. "So you're a real punk, then."

As I rolled my eyes at him, Niko shot me one of his brilliant grins. "The tattoo is beautiful. And earned. You move like an angel when you're skating."

My cheeks were outright burning now. I didn't know

what to say to that other than a mumbled, "Thanks," that felt totally inadequate.

"Well, come on," Jasper grumbled at the other man, and Niko swerved around with a flash of what might have been guilt crossing his face.

No, I really didn't understand their dynamic at all.

While I worked on a few of my spins in one corner of the rink, Jasper soared past me in another attempt at his triple Axel, and then another. The first time, he stumbled and swayed when he landed a smidge too soon in his rotation.

The second time, he pitched forward right onto his knees.

As he shoved himself upright, cursing under his breath, Niko skated over. He grasped Jasper's arm to help steady him.

"You're in your head too much. You know you can do this—I've seen you make it. But you need to relax and let yourself get into the flow."

"I need to get out of this fucking slump," Jasper growled. He pulled his arm away from Niko and frowned at the other man. "Are you here to be my coach or my therapist? Because I didn't ask for the former and I'm *definitely* not looking for the latter."

Niko held up his hands, too easygoing to take offense even as I bristled on his behalf. "Frustration will trip you up more than anything—speaking as a coach. Why don't you take ten, grab a drink, and cool off?"

Jasper ducked his head. "Sorry. I—" His jaw tightened, and he skated off to where he'd left his bag in the stands.

Niko turned to me, his smile returning if not quite as sunny as before. "That means *you've* got to deal with me now, Angel. I saw you struggling with that Biellmann spin."

I couldn't hold back a wince. I'd been doing so well for a moment, but then a wobble had crept through my legs.

Niko chuckled. "Oh, don't look like that. You almost had it! Here, let me show you —"

He moved to my side and ushered me towards the center of the ice. I glanced toward Jasper, wondering if this would piss him off even more, but he had his back to us as if he didn't care.

"Like this," Niko said. "Do you mind if I...?"

He gestured a few inches from my body, asking if he could touch me. I nodded, a sharp dip of my chin.

His slender fingers dropped down to my waist, holding me steady, while his other hand rested on the outside of my left leg. Warmth rushed over my skin.

Dear lord, I hoped he couldn't feel that his touch was turning me on.

He patted my leg lightly, which only sent more sparks up it. This close up, his gleaming eyes and warm smile were nothing less than magnetic.

"You'll want to keep this leg as straight as possible. And you might try catching your foot at your side rather than behind you to keep your center of gravity."

How was I supposed to process his advice when my brain was short-circuiting at his touch? Coach Balakin had definitely never had this effect on me.

Focus, Lou. You're supposed to be a professional here.

But as I inhaled Niko's light, oceanic scent, I couldn't

help noticing that his gaze veered to the rise and fall of my breasts, just for an instant before he jerked his attention to my face. The gleam in his eyes now might have been a little heated too.

He kept his tone as breezy as before. "Does that make sense?"

"Yeah," I said, willing my voice to stay steady. "I just always seem to lose my balance a little just before I'm fully in position."

His hand dropped to the small of my back, and my pussy clenched. I leaned into him just slightly and *knew* I wasn't imagining the flash of interest in his expression.

He wet his lips, and then it was gone again, hidden behind his cheerfully casual demeanor. "If you lean back just a bit when you feel the wobble coming on, that might get you right again before it shows. If you're still having trouble, it always helps to practice standing by the boards, getting a solid feel for the position."

Would he ever let me get past the professional front and discover the passion I knew was simmering underneath? Or maybe he wouldn't think it was worth altering whatever odd relationship we had now.

Either way, I didn't think I'd be able to resist taking my shot with him if I got the chance.

Just not on the ice. And definitely not in front of Jasper. Who knew how the grouch would react if I started outright flirting with his coach?

Niko stepped away and set his hands on his hips. "Now let's see another Biellman spin in that signature Lou style. Don't look nervous! You've got this."

At his comments, a different sort of longing welled on

—one that'd gripped me since I was five years old. One that Coach Balakin had never satisfied.

I let myself voice it before I could second-guess the impulse. "Do you *really* think I'm good enough to compete? Like, the real competitions, sectionals and all that?"

Niko's eyes widened. "Are you joking? You should have been out there already. I don't want any injuries this year, because it's a crime that the world hasn't already seen what you can do."

His voice was so emphatic that I felt both immensely relieved and ridiculous for having asked. "Okay. Good. I just—I wanted to be sure."

Something in Niko's expression softened. He squeezed my shoulder, sending another spike of warmth through my chest. "I wouldn't lie about something like that. It'd be cruel to send someone out with expectations they can't meet. But you've got it, Lou. I could see you not just competing but blowing everyone else out of the water."

Jasper's skates clicked against the ice where he was just stepping back onto the rink. He gave me a wary glance. "Whoever was coaching you before must have been an idiot if they never bothered to tell you you're good."

Bitterness tainted his voice, but I could tell he meant it. And if he meant it enough that he'd bothered to say it no matter how much my presence annoyed him...

I guessed I had to believe it too.

Niko glanced between the two of us, and a glint of mischief lit in his eyes. "You know what, I have a better idea than more spins. Lou, come over here."

He motioned me over to stand just a couple of feet

from Jasper. The guy dwarfed me, standing a full foot taller and broader through his whole frame as well.

We both watched Niko, Jasper looking as puzzled as I felt.

"What are you doing?" he grumbled. "Sizing us up for a photoshoot?"

Niko squinted at both of us and rubbed his hands together with one of those eager smiles. "I'm thinking a little more ambitious than that. Let's mix things up a bit and do some basic exercises in synchronization. Jasper, take Lou's hand."

"What?" Jasper protested.

Niko raised his eyebrows. "Maybe you'll have an easier time getting out of your head if you have someone other than yourself to focus on."

Jasper stared at him for a few seconds. My gut knotted.

He really disliked me that much that he wouldn't even give it a try. Not that I was so keen on running through the basics hand-in-hand with the grouch beside me, but I'd still be willing to—

"Fine," Jasper bit out, and snatched my hand without any further warning.

His solid fingers engulfed my much slimmer ones. Something about the feel of them, despite how reluctant he was acting, sent a jolt of electricity up my arm.

Niko waved toward the other end of the rink. "All right, you two. Skate forward, but keep your arms up. Hands together. I want you to match the strokes of your skates. And… go!"

Niko sounded more like a coach than ever before.

There was also a thrum of excitement in his smooth voice that was new.

As Jasper and I pushed off, I stole a glance over my shoulder. Niko looked like he was trying hard not to bounce off the walls with excitement. Something about that expression made my pulse stutter, like I was about to go over the big drop in a roller coaster.

"Hey, eyes forward." Jasper tapped the back of my hand with his thumb. "Whatever he wants us to do, I want to do it right."

Of course he did. If there was anything I knew about this man's career, it was that he was a perfectionist.

It sounded simple enough—just skate to the end of the rink. But Jasper's height meant we had to position ourselves carefully to keep our clasped hands raised without straining my shoulder, and keeping pace between my shorter legs and his longer ones required careful precision.

It took several strokes wildly off and then several more slightly out of sync, but I felt us catching on to each other's rhythm. By the time we reached the far boards, our feet were gliding forward in unison.

It was kind of thrilling, seeing it happen. Was this what Niko had been picturing?

"Spin in sync, a full 360 and then back to face me, and skate on over here a little faster," Niko called.

I glanced at Jasper, as intent on impressing Niko now as he was. We eased into the start of our spin, judging each other's speeds, and managed to curve around to face each other and then Niko at almost the same moment.

It would be easier with a plan and music to time our

movements to, but we were doing pretty damn fantastic anyway.

We'd glided halfway back to Niko when he barked out another instruction. "Swivel and make the rest of the trip backwards!"

I whipped to the side automatically—unfortunately at a clashing angle to what Jasper's instinct had been. Our shoulders collided, and I skidded on the ice.

Jasper's arm shot out. He grasped my bare elbow to steady me, and I had to brace my other hand against his chest just for a second before I had my balance.

It was an incredibly nice chest, all packed with muscle. And when my gaze flicked upward as I drew my hand away, Jasper's gaze caught mine.

I could have caught fire from the heat that had flickered in those gray-green eyes. A giddy quiver rippled through my body.

The glint of hunger disappeared as quickly as it'd arrived. Jasper's face turned stormy again.

"Come on, let's get this done."

Well, it wasn't as if I didn't have plenty of other much more welcoming eye-candy to appreciate on this rink.

We pushed backward and made it to Niko with only a few slips out of sync. He was grinning even wider now, a feat I hadn't known was possible.

"I have a brilliant idea," he announced.

"More brilliant than this one?" Jasper asked in a dry tone.

"You could say it's more of the same idea." Niko cocked his head, his hair swishing across his forehead with a flash of the neon pink streak. "How would you two feel about trying pairs skating?"

"What?" I burst out at the same time as Jasper sputtered, "Are you kidding me?"

Niko wagged a finger at us. "Don't discount it out of hand. It would give you both a fresh perspective. By collaborating, Jasper will have different skills to focus on, and Lou won't have to face her first competitions alone. If you decide to keep at it that long. We'd just be seeing how it goes."

He turned to Jasper. "You should find it pretty easy to do lifts with Lou given your size difference. And the two of you got in sync so easily just now. It's meant to be."

My mind blanked with shock. Of all the things I might have expected him to suggest, this would never have occurred to me. I'd never skated with a partner in my life.

But we had gotten into the groove awfully quickly. It'd been *fun*, as jerky as Jasper could be.

I'd really get to stretch my skills, and embracing the challenge would mean skating literally alongside one of the greats. What did I have to lose?

Other than whatever speck of good will Jasper might have still felt toward me.

His hands had balled at his sides. He looked from Niko to me and back again.

I couldn't tell what he was thinking, but he was giving off the vibe of a volcano on the verge of eruption.

His jaw worked. Then his fingers uncurled from his palms with what looked like Herculean effort.

"Pairs?" he said. "Are you sure?"

Might as well jump in the deep end while I had the

chance. "I'm in. If Niko thinks it's a good idea—it couldn't hurt to see how we handle it, right?"

Jasper aimed a brief glower at me before turning back to his coach. "I was never planning on working with a partner."

Niko laughed. "You never planned on having me coach you either, but look at how well that's working out. Give it a shot, St. Pierre. What's the worst that could happen?"

I guessed he had a point—enough of one that Jasper sighed. "Okay. Sure. Why not?" He glanced at me again. "But the minute I sense that you're slacking off, Punk, I'm out."

I crossed my arms over my chest. "You won't have to worry about that."

And just like that, I'd somehow partnered with the grumpiest guy in Ontario.

SEVEN

Luciana

I TOOK a deep breath and leaned back on my hands. I'd say one thing for Ontario—it sure had beautiful lakes.

The scents of pine and cedar wafted from the trees standing along the hill I was sitting near the base of. A whiff of roasting meat carried from the barbeque pits farther along the shoreline. The water lapped gently at the rocks that gave way to a narrow stretch of sandy beach.

I wasn't the only one from Hobb Creek who'd come out to this spot just north of town on this fine afternoon. The warm early September day had brought some of the local kids right into the water, jumping and splashing.

Their parents watched from the towels they'd spread out on the sand. A little ways further, a group of teens had stretched out to sunbathe.

It all felt so perfectly, blissfully normal.

I'd always found that immersing myself in nature eased my nerves—and oh, did I have a lot of nerves skittering away right now.

Niko had ended today's training session early… because tomorrow, Jasper and I had our first pairs practice.

Tomorrow, we'd find out whether I could match him or end up looking like a total dunce despite Niko's faith in me.

It shouldn't have mattered. A week ago, I'd had no skating prospects at all. So what if I ended up back in the same place?

But I wanted to be the great skater Niko said I was.

And a larger part of me than I wanted to admit wanted to see admiration spark in Jasper's striking eyes too.

I grimaced at myself. Getting the hots for *both* of my new skating companions didn't seem like the best idea. Especially when the second one spent about ninety-nine percent of the time being a total grouch.

But telling that to the butterflies that'd taken permanent residence in my lungs hadn't worked out so far.

I inhaled another gulp of forest air and brushed the dry needles off my plaid leggings. A few of the older beachgoers had glanced my way with looks that weren't completely approving. Maybe they saw me as a "punk" too.

My fashion sense wasn't that out there, but it was definitely different from most of what I saw in Hobb Creek.

Oh well. They'd just have to get used to me as I was,

because I was done squeezing myself into a box for anyone.

But I had picked a perch away from the main beach area where I wouldn't make the locals feel intruded on. That way I didn't have to worry about getting questioned either.

I glanced at my phone. Five-thirty. Rafael and I had made a habit of eating dinner together at seven every night, so I still had plenty of time to exhale my nerves.

God, it was perfect here.

Except maybe it wasn't exactly perfect. A voice reached my ears, faint and carrying from somewhere behind me.

I couldn't make out the words, but the tone was distinctly distressed.

I was way more familiar with that sound than I wanted to be.

With my senses on high alert, I got to my feet and ventured through the trees up the hill. It only stood about twenty feet over the lake with an easy slope my toned legs had no trouble scaling.

As I reached the top, the voices became a little clearer. A cry rang out, still faint but with obvious pain.

My stomach knotted. I crept down the other side of the hill, peering between the tree trunks.

What the hell was going on?

When I got close enough to make out movement up ahead, I froze, keeping behind a broad oak tree for shelter. As I watched, I gradually picked out the figures in this drama.

A couple of guys who looked to be in their twenties were pacing in and out of view in a small clearing beyond the base of the hill. One of them was the cocky guy I'd seen badgering the toy store owner.

They were from that small-time gang Rafael had identified.

That would have been enough to raise my hackles on its own, but a third figure knelt on the ground between them. A teenaged boy, I saw—he couldn't have been more than sixteen from the peek I got at his smooth face, still a tad soft around the edges.

One of the goons lunged at him and smacked him across the head. The kid cowered and gasped in pain.

My body went rigid. This was so many levels of not okay that I wanted to scream.

"So what I'm hearing is that you don't have the money," one of the goons said. "Is that what I'm getting from you?"

The boy cringed. He let out another yelp when the prick behind him cuffed him in the head.

"I—I have some of it," he stammered. "The guys at school, they just wanted to try the stuff! T—they didn't have a lot of money, so —"

"So you let 'em have our product for free?" the first man asked. He tutted to himself. "I'm afraid that's not how we work around here. Tell him how we work around here, Barry."

Barry, the bigger goon by a good twenty or thirty pounds, pulled back his fist and slammed it into the kid's ribs. The highschooler slumped onto his side with a choked noise.

They'd tried to bring the kid on—to peddle drugs for them, probably, based on their conversation and the business endeavors Rafael had mentioned. Stupid to turn to an inexperienced teen for that anyway.

It was their idiotic mistake, and they were making him pay for it.

My gut churned. I hated this, *hated* it.

It was far too easy to picture the faces of my mother's lackeys in these assholes' overconfident and cocky grins. It was like I'd run all the way across the continent for nothing. Nothing at all.

"I have some of the money." The high schooler coughed, choking out a string of phlegm that he hastily wiped away. "I can get the rest, I swear! J—just please give me a little time. Just a few more days!"

I peered from Barry to his fellow thug. They looked momentarily pensive, as though they were considering the kid's offer.

What should I be hoping for? The only thing I could ask from the universe was for two asteroids to come down and squash these two assholes, but of course, I couldn't count on killer space rocks.

I was here… but I really shouldn't draw attention to myself. If I burst into the clearing and gave the two goons a much-deserved ass-kicking, the very next thing I'd have to do was leave town.

The gang would still be here, just even more pissed off than before. And if Mom ever got wind of a petite young Latina woman who'd started handing wannabe gangsters their asses, she'd tear Hobb Creek apart looking for me even if I'd already left.

If I was going to do anything about these pricks, I had to plan it carefully. I had to make sure they were completely done and that they never realized who'd hit them.

"I don't know, Barry," the mouthy guy said. "Do you think we can trust this kid? I mean, he's already screwed us over once before…"

The high school kid's eyes zipped left and right as the thugs stalked around him. I braced my hand against the rough bark of the tree trunk, and conviction hardened in my chest.

I wasn't going to watch these goons kill this kid in front of me. Low profile or no, there were some places I drew the line.

If Rafael was shadowing me from afar like usual, he'd just have to bite his tongue and deal with my decision.

I had my trusty knife in my purse, but it wasn't going to do me any good at a distance. My gaze swept over the ground for something, anything, I could use.

There. I leapt forward a couple of steps and snatched a rock the size of my palm off the ground. Then another, and another, and another.

Tucking the extras under my arm, I eased closer through the trees. The goons were looming over the kid again.

One of them had gotten out a switchblade. Oh, hell no, there was no way I was letting this continue.

Before either of them could make any further threats or use that knife, I hurled the first rock from my hand.

It collided with Barry's flabby cheek, striking him directly below the eye.

"Hey!" The asshole spun away from the kid. "What the fuck was that?"

"What?" the skinny guy asked. "The hell are you going on about, dipweed?"

Barry squinted into the sunlight, staring toward my patch of forest. He was looking about forty degrees in the wrong direction, although even if he had looked my way, I doubted he'd have made me out in the shadows.

I bit down a laugh. If I thought he looked stupid before, the flabby douchebag looked even more like a buffoon now.

"I don't know," Barry sputtered. "Something *hit* me." He touched his cheek.

And it's Lou Cordova with the pitch. She lines up her shot… and there it is! Strike!

I nailed the skinny bastard with the second rock, right in the temple. His hands flew up to his face.

I whipped the last two rocks in quick succession, braining Barry in the side of the head and scraping the skinny guy's chin. With a yelp and an angry shout, they barged toward the trees.

I ducked behind the nearest trunk, but not before I spotted the kid sprinting to safety while they were distracted. Mission accomplished.

"Who the fuck is throwing shit at us?" Barry bellowed.

I didn't stick around to answer him. Hightailing it through the trees, I'd vanished over the top of the hill before I even heard their footsteps crunch into the layer of pine needles on the forest floor.

Emerging on the beach side, I slowed to a casual stroll and made my way to my car in the small parking lot. When I reached it, I glanced over my shoulder.

The two would-be gangsters were just marching out of

the trees, scowling but with no real target to direct their anger at.

I hid a smirk as I slid into the driver's seat of my car. They'd never know who'd interrupted their beatdown.

But as I started the ignition, my good humor faded.

I'd interrupted them for now. Soon enough they'd be hassling that kid—and who knew how many other people in town—all over again.

But my next steps no longer felt like a question. Something was stirring within me, something righteous and full of fury.

I had to get these guys out of here. They were a threat to me and to everyone in this town, and I'd be damned if I was going to stand back and watch them take over the place while I was the only one around remotely prepared to do battle.

I'd made my decision: I was going to *fuck* with them. These guys were clearly brainless, leaderless idiots, nobodies who were just making a buck off the innocent locals.

It hadn't been hard to screw with the two goons here. There shouldn't be any need to resort to much violence. My mind would be enough to do this gang in.

I rolled my shoulders and thought of the tattoo stretched across my back.

Maybe Niko was right—maybe I was *exactly* what he had called me.

An angel. An avenging one.

EIGHT

Niko

MAGIC.

That's what I was watching. There was no other word for it.

My two trainees could create something miraculous on the ice, even if they weren't aware of it yet. My job was to make them see it themselves.

I followed them with my eyes, taking in every dip of their shoulders and every subtle movement of their limbs. They'd only gone through two practices with a focus on pairs, but their synchronization was already impressive.

I wasn't a total stranger to pairs skating. I'd done some as a teen before it'd become clear I was better off carving a path on my own, and after I'd made the suggestion, I'd gotten in touch with an old friend back in Japan who was more experienced in that area and had offered some tips.

So I thought I'd been guiding them reasonably well as they spun and swayed across the rink.

But a lot of it they'd picked up without much help at all. Lou had risen to the challenge with the same fierceness I'd seen her approach every part of her skating, and the occasional snarky remarks she exchanged with Jasper only seemed to add more vigor to her powerfully graceful moves.

As for Jasper… He'd been tense to start, but he was pretty much always at least a little stiff during practice. I'd watched him loosen up more than ever before while he had to concentrate on Lou's timing as well as his own.

He wasn't worrying about how fast or how high he could go on his own, only about matching another skater with at least as much talent as him. He tried to act as if he was still skeptical, but I'd even caught a few brief smiles when they'd nailed a spin.

Which meant it was time to try something a little more complicated.

I leaned over the boards to call out to them. "I think that's enough work on the ice. We're going to move on to lifts next."

Lou skated over to me, looking unusually uncertain. "Lifts? Already?"

Jasper mirrored her expression; his silence was somehow louder than his usual sarcasm.

"You've got it." I waved them back towards the stands. "You can take your skates off over there. You won't need them for this."

The two of them shared a look.

"Come on," I stepped between them to lay my hands

on each of their shoulders. "Don't doubt me. Look at how far you've come already. Here, follow me. Let's get our lift on!"

Jasper snorted. "Niko, no one says that."

"I say that. Now come on, let's —"

"Get our lift on," Lou finished for me. I could hear the smile hiding underneath her words. "Yeah, yeah."

They followed me back to one of the storerooms where I'd set up a little surprise for them earlier that day. Neither one spoke as they passed by the piles of equipment that I'd dragged out to make room for the —

"Foam pads?" Lou said once I'd pushed the door open.

A sea of thick blocks of foam layered the floor from wall to wall. We had to nudge some aside while walking inside, treading on others.

"Foam pads!" I said, grinning back at her. "So you don't bust your head open or break your neck if you fall. You're welcome."

She stared at me a moment before nudging me in the shoulder playfully. "Okay, okay. Thank you. This is... I feel *way* better about this now."

"Of course," Jasper said. "This is how serious figure skaters always practice lifts. Don't tell me you didn't know off-ice practice is a thing."

Oh, Jasper.

I knew he was touchy lately, but every now and again, he'd gone out of his way to prod her. Lou usually shot back in kind or annoyed him even further by giving him some silly, singsong retort, but this time, she just stared down at her sneakers.

"No, I didn't." She twirled a strand of dark hair around

her pinkie. "I've never skated with anyone else before. When I trained, it was just me and my coach. That's all."

"There weren't any other skaters around trying things like this?" I asked.

Lou shook her head. "Nope, I've never seen lifts done except on TV and the live performances I've made it to." She shot a cheeky grin at Jasper that didn't totally reach her eyes. "So, if I suck at first, it's not totally my fault."

Jasper reached up to scratch behind the back of his head. I could see the discomfort scrawled across his face, but I wasn't about to step in and help him out here.

He was the one who'd stuck his foot in his mouth and provoked that slump in Lou's spirits when rarely anything seemed to faze her. Whatever was going on under his prickly exterior, I couldn't sort it out for him.

As much as I wished I could.

"I've never practiced them either," he admitted, staring pointedly at the foam pads I'd laid out on the floor. "So we can both suck together, Punk."

The first hour was full of a lot of awkward positioning and sudden tumbles. But though Lou's hesitation got the better of her at first, she gained confidence as quickly as she always seemed to. There was no denying her enthusiasm for giving the attempts her all.

Still, once she was up in the air, there were times when she would glance down at the ground and wobble in the palms of Jasper's hands. Something about the way she was holding her body didn't seem exactly right, but I couldn't tell what it was.

As Jasper lowered her back down after at least a few dozen trials, annoyance fluttered across her soft features.

She set her hands on her hips, frustration knitting her brow. Her hair had dampened along her forehead with sweat. "What am I doing wrong?"

I cocked my head. "There's definitely something a bit off, but it's hard for me to tell just watching. Here, let's try it you and me so I can feel exactly how you're shifting your weight in the air."

She moved to meet me without hesitation. Jasper stepped back, watching the two of us with hooded but curious eyes.

"Alright, whenever you're ready." I bent my knees, trying to picture us out there on the ice.

Lou didn't waste any time waiting around. She nodded once and squared her shoulders, stepping towards me. "Ready."

My left hand clasped her right one as I used my other palm to push upward on the junction between her hip and leg. With one shift of my shoulders, she was up in the air, her legs at a perfect ninety-degree angle.

Every brain cell in my head was trying to focus on the way Lou felt in my hands as a skater, but the awareness of her as a woman—a very attractive woman—filtered through despite my best efforts. Her limbs weren't just strong but also sleek, and a hint of a tart but warm scent that was all her filled my nose.

A small part of my mind started imagining how it'd feel to run my hands farther over her trim curves. A totally unacceptable thought from a coach.

I'd never been very good at suppressing my natural desires. But I could make sure they didn't affect the work we were doing together.

I raised her to the full height of the lift, noting the shifts in her body and tuning out the rest. Before I could dwell more on how wonderful she felt in my hold, I set her down on the foam pads again.

"What, too heavy for you?" Lou's eyes shined playfully.

"Oh, please." I tsked at her. "I could lift both you and our favorite raincloud here with one arm if I wanted to."

Jasper shot me a baleful look from the sidelines.

"I think I see where your trouble is," I went on. "You're tensing up your core. It needs to be steady but not rigid."

Lou laughed. "So tighten my abs, but also stay relaxed. Why didn't I think of that?"

From the humor in her tone, I could tell she wasn't actually dismissing my advice. I nudged her shoulder with my knuckles teasingly. "You know what I mean. It's all about balance—both in the air and within yourself."

"Hmm, are you sure you're not actually a yoga guru?"

Even as the joke spilled from her lips, her gaze turned more thoughtful. She looked down at herself, setting her palms against her stomach as if she were feeling out the differences in how she could flex the muscles there.

That dedication was what made this woman so compelling, wasn't it? She kept her spirits high through criticism, not letting any of it hit her hard but paying close attention all the same.

I wasn't sure I'd met another skater so determined to improve but also so able to roll with the punches.

Okay, that wasn't the only thing I admired about her. There was the energy she brought to every attempt, bold but not foolhardy beyond her capabilities. Her easygoing confidence that never drifted into arrogance.

She would have been justified in a little arrogance, really, but instead her lapses were in the other direction, into insecurity. Somehow she had no idea how skilled she already was.

She was an undiscovered star, a diamond hidden away here in Hobb Creek. I had made up my mind to change that.

After she and Jasper rose to their highest potential, everyone would know her name — and remember why they knew his. The whole world would be able to appreciate the stunning imagery that they were able to create.

She was the catalyst that would push Jasper out of his rut. I just knew it.

But when she momentarily swept her hair out of its ponytail to run her fingers through it, waking up the urge in me to touch those silky waves myself, I pulled myself backward, away from her. The attraction I felt could never be acted on, or I could ruin everything.

I motioned toward the doorway where the locker rooms awaited. "I think I've tormented you two enough for one day. You've come amazingly far already. Better to let today's lessons sink in so you can meet tomorrow's practice with a positive attitude."

Jasper narrowed his eyes at me. "You're quitting now?"

The edge in his voice sent an uneasy prickle over my skin. "I wouldn't call it quitting. There is such a thing as too much practice."

"I've never noticed that there was with you before," he

muttered, and stalked out of the room before I could say anything else.

My stomach knotted. We'd managed not to talk about anything that'd happened before I'd shown up at his grandparents' house other than past skating performances. He grumbled a lot, but mildly enough that I didn't take it personally.

I thought I'd heard a little anger in his tone just now, though. Was he still angry at me underneath?

I'd tried to touch on that very sensitive subject a couple of times, but Jasper had deflected me before I'd gotten anywhere close. So I'd settled for making up for my screw-up last year as well as I could without bringing it up directly. It obviously hadn't been enough yet.

Lou gave me a little wave and vanished into the hall after Jasper. I stayed in the converted storage room for a few minutes, breathing deeply and clearing my head.

The training. I just had to focus on the training. Everything good I could do for either of my current charges would grow from there.

In my mind, I replayed the key moments from today's training. Lou's joke about me being a yoga guru came back to me with a spark of inspiration.

I had actually practiced yoga on and off at a studio back home. The main teacher had shown me a position that'd flipped a switch in my head when it came to maintaining balance. It might help Lou as well.

With a burst of hopeful enthusiasm, I hurried down the hall to the women's change room. If I caught her before she left, she could give it a shot tonight and it might have leveled up her abilities by tomorrow's session.

I knocked on the locker room door but didn't hear an answer. Had she already left?

Worried that I'd missed her, I pushed inside. "Lou?"

I'd only made it a few steps before I processed the hiss of running water. And the image that went with that sound.

Lou was in the shower area in the corner of the change room, behind the curtain that hung across one of the three stalls. It hid any details, but the silhouette of her lithely curved form showed vaguely against the translucent material.

My dick jumped to attention. The rest of me backpedaled as fast as humanly possible.

But she'd already heard my call. Before I made it to the door, Lou poked her face around the edge of the curtain, her dark hair plastered to her head. "Niko?"

Heat burned my cheeks as I averted my eyes. "I'm sorry. I didn't realize—I was in a hurry to tell you something—it can wait."

"No, no, it's fine. I was almost finished. Just give me a second."

I didn't know whether it would be more rude to stay on her request or insist on leaving anyway. I settled for turning so my back was to her.

But I heard every motion. The click of the water turning off. The rustle as she reached for the towel she'd left on a nearby bench. The soft whispers of it rubbing over her light brown skin.

Stop imagining what that looks like, I ordered my brain.

My brain did not cooperate.

"Are you going to tell me what's up or are you just

going to leave me staring at your back?" Lou asked in an amused tone.

I dared to turn around, assuming she'd gotten dressed faster than I'd expected. But she was standing by the bench with only her towel wrapped around her body.

Well, a little of her body. The thin terrycloth fabric covered the swell of her breasts while leaving plenty of smooth skin and a tempting dip of cleavage on display. It only hung to mid-thigh.

When she shifted her weight from one foot to the other, the ends of the towel slipped a little apart, opening a gap almost to her right hip. I jerked my gaze away, but not before noting the few droplets of water that still clung to her upper legs. My pants had gotten uncomfortably tight.

Could she tell? Oh, kuso!

Lou flipped her damp hair back over her bare shoulder and gave me a look that felt both curious and assessing. If my face had been hot before, now it was totally burning.

And it wasn't the only part of me on fire.

"Don't leave me hanging," she said. Did her voice usually sound that sultry?

Was I just imagining it because of how turned on I was right now?

"Well, I just—" I fumbled with my words and closed my eyes for a second to gather myself. "The training, the lift today. Balance. You mentioned yoga. I had a teacher who showed us a pose that was good for enhancing your sense of equilibrium."

Lou let out a low laugh that was undeniably sexy. "So you really are going yoga guru on us."

"Maybe a little bit."

She sauntered closer with a sway to her hips that brought my gaze sliding down her body before I caught it and yanked it upward again. A sly smile was playing with her lips.

Lou was always pretty, and I loved seeing her face set in its frequent determined expression. But this new seductive persona made her a whole different kind of gorgeous.

I couldn't say I liked it better, but certain parts of me were responding—a lot.

"What's the matter?" Lou said, close enough now to tap me right in the middle of my chest. That smile turned even slyer. "I'm not going to believe you've never seen this much of a woman before. I'm not sure I've ever read an article about you that didn't make a point of mentioning how you swing both ways."

Somehow my cheeks seared even hotter. "I—well—that is true—I just wouldn't normally—"

She eased even closer, the warmth of her presence tingling over my skin, and trailed the finger she'd tapped me with down my sternum all the way to my belly. An ache formed in my stiffening cock.

Lou gazed up at me. "Is there a problem?" She didn't let her fingers slide any farther, which part of me was desperately grateful for and the other part deeply regretting. "I've gotten the impression that there's a spark between us. But if you're already dating someone or I've made a mistake, I won't be offended."

I swallowed hard.

"It's not that," I made myself say. The truth was I hadn't pursued anyone in months—and there were very few people, men or women, who'd ever affected me as much as she did.

"Then it's something else?"

It was, wasn't it? When had she become the flirty one and me the awkward dolt?

The answer came to me like a bolt out of the sky. "I'm your coach. It wouldn't be appropriate—"

Before I could continue, Lou snorted. "Is that what's bothering you? I don't see why it should matter."

I found my composure enough to put a little sternness in my expression, trying to ignore the feel of her fingers against my stomach. "Relationships between someone in an authority position and a student can easily become exploitive."

Lou arched her eyebrows at me. "I promise you I'm not the slightest bit concerned that you might 'exploit' me. Actually, I'd really like you to." Her smile stretched into a grin.

I could practically come in my boxers when she looked at me like that.

"I *am* still your coach," I had to say.

"Are you, though? I mean, it's a totally unofficial position. I'm not paying you. Neither of us has any power over the other. We're both consenting adults, no real authority either way."

I couldn't help acknowledging that she had a point. But was I only thinking that way because I wanted her more with every passing second?

At my continued hesitation, Lou's teasing demeanor faded. She moved her hand over to curl it around my own. My fingers squeezed hers of their own accord.

"Just to be clear," she said, her gaze searching mine, "this isn't just about scratching an itch or something. You know, you're the first person who's ever made me feel like me skating is something *good*. Like I could be bringing something great into the world by doing it. You have no idea how special that is to me. I can't stop myself from wondering if the spark between us means our connection could be incredible in other ways too."

The honesty in her voice sent a pang through me that was more than just desire.

She sounded like a woman who knew what she wanted—and who really did want *me*. Would I really be protecting her by denying her and myself?

Or maybe this was a chance to create a different kind of magic.

A few doubts still niggled at the back of my head, but they'd been quieted enough that the hunger in me overwhelmed them. I tugged her even closer, and my head bowed as if by a magnetic force.

Lou bobbed up to meet my lips halfway. The second her mouth melded with mine, whatever sparks had been forming between us flared into a total bonfire.

She tasted like cinnamon sugar with a hint of bitter coffee, sweet and invigorating in one petite package. With a swift movement of her soft lips, our mouths were parting and her tongue slipping over mine.

My free hand came to rest on her side and froze at the feel of the towel. I'd almost forgotten how little she was wearing.

But Lou leaned into my touch encouragingly, looping

her own arm around the back of my neck. Her whole body pressed flush against mine.

I suppressed a groan and kissed her more deeply. My thumb stroked up and down her side.

My fingers tingled with anticipation, and I couldn't resist stroking them upward. My palm came to rest against the curve of her breast.

If I'd had any doubt about her enthusiasm for this encounter, the encouraging murmur that escaped her lips erased it in a flash. When I swiveled the heel of my hand over the pebbled peak beneath the fabric, I received a needy whimper.

Lou arched her back at the contact and kissed me as if she needed my touch like she needed air.

I *had* hooked up with plenty of partners in the past, but somehow this fiery woman had me as giddy as a teenager making his first confession.

Her hand trailed down my back. She tucked her fingers under the hem of my shirt and brushed her thumb across my bare skin.

I shifted my hips against her, desperate to feel those bare thighs against my own skin. More of the slope of her breasts spilled out from the towel beneath my fingers, the hem dipping almost to her nipples.

A little gasp of pleasure burst from her lips. That sound was heaven.

My dick throbbed as my thoughts ran wild. I envisioned the towel slipping lower, revealing all of the perfect mounds.

Lou's hand stroked higher, her mouth claiming mine in a wilder kiss—

And a buzzing sound emanated from the bench behind us.

Lou pulled away with a muttered curse. She glanced back at her phone, which buzzed again with another alert.

"Crap," she said. "I really have to get going. I hadn't planned for a detour."

Of course she couldn't have planned for me to barge into the change room while she was showering. My face heated all over again, but before I could do anything like apologize, Lou turned back to me and touched my cheek.

The eagerness in her eyes melted me. "I *do* want to plan for it to happen again. To be continued?"

Relief and joy shot through me in tandem despite the ache in my groin. "*Definitely* to be continued."

Lou flashed a smile that promised so much more to come. "Great. Can't wait for the sequel."

I stepped out of the change room to let her get dressed, adjusting my pants as I went and willing my erection to calm down. Once it was no longer obscene, I headed out through the streets to my apartment.

Halfway there, it occurred to me that I had never gotten around to telling Lou the details of that yoga pose. Well, I guessed it wasn't totally my fault that I'd gotten distracted.

I found a video of the pose online and texted her with it. Just as I was about to slide my phone back into my pocket, it chimed with an incoming email.

I glanced at the subject line and paused.

"Ninth Annual Dellville Figure Skating Competition," I read in a murmur. "What do we have here?"

NINE

Luciana

HOBB CREEK LOOKED like a totally different town in the dead of night. I could hardly believe that it was the same little hamlet that had captured my heart.

The continuing trickle of passersby from the early evening had headed home or onward in their tourist journey. Only a couple of lights still shone in windows.

Not a single soul roamed the streets. The only movement that caught my eye was a stray cat jumping from rooftop to rooftop and a brief streak of a shooting star.

I stopped for a second to take that sight in. When was the last time I'd been in a position to simply stop and stargaze?

Beside me, Rafael let out a soft grunt, reminding me

that I wasn't exactly in that position *now*. We had a mission to carry out, one that'd been my idea.

"Everything looks kind of eerie at night, doesn't it?" I murmured, hefting the two large water jugs I had tucked under my arms, which were burning with a familiar ache from today's training session. The straps of a backpack that held a few more jugs dug into my shoulders. "Even in a peaceful town like this. Maybe more here."

Rafael let out the mildest of sighs as we tramped on down the street, dodging the dim pools of lamplight, toward the edge of town. "Well, it is three in the morning."

"Always the voice of reason," I teased, grinning over at him. My legs were sore too, but the thought of the mischief I'd planned kept me light on my feet. "Had to make sure our targets would be asleep."

My bodyguard adjusted the jugs cradled against his bulging arms and shot me a skeptical look. "Are you really sure this is necessary? You're sticking your nose into places it doesn't need to be."

I grimaced at him. "It's my town now. It's totally my business. It helps me and everyone else here—except the jerks who deserve a little hurt."

"If they realize you vandalized their property…"

"They're not going to find out. I know what I'm doing. And it probably isn't *their* property anyway. I bet they stole most of the vehicles they're driving."

"That doesn't make them worth bothering with."

I stopped and spun toward him. "If you don't like the plan, you can go home, and I'll do it all myself."

Rafael's mouth set in a tight line. "Let's go," he said gruffly, like I'd figured he would.

He might argue sometimes, but he never backed down from what he considered his duty. Although I didn't totally understand why he'd decided it was still his duty to protect me when no one was paying him to do that job anymore.

Not that I was complaining.

Sometimes he made good points. But tonight we were doing things my way.

Those goons were going to get a taste of their own medicine, and I was the wicked doctor doling out doses.

As we came up on the last few houses before the final road that separated the town proper from the nearby sprawl of storage buildings and warehouses, Rafael gave it one more try. "I thought you wanted to get away from the criminal side of your old life."

"I will when I have the option," I said. "I can't just ignore these goons. But that doesn't mean I have to use the kind of tactics Mom would either. This is all Lou, all the way."

Mom would have sent her men in with guns blazing and mowed the two-bit gang down. I was simply going to show them that sticking around this town was more hassle than it was worth.

No bloodshed, no scarring the good people of Hobb Creek. Just a little old-fashioned vehicular sabotage.

Even if I wanted to protect my new neighbors, that didn't mean I had to deal out the kind of carnage the Deadly Rose was known for. I wasn't her heir anymore.

I peered across the road and the wide parking lot. A

few security lamps cast a yellow light around the front and sides of the big white building the gang operated out of. In the shadows that blanketed the rest of the lot, I made out the shapes of several cars, a couple of pickup trucks, a van, and a jeep.

As I scanned the scene, the front door to the storage building swung open. A couple of men sauntered out, swaying a little, and got into the nearest car. The thumps of the car doors shutting rang through the night.

After they drove off, the whole area was totally silent.

"No guards," I whispered to Rafael. "Could they be more amateur?"

When he looked at me, I thought I saw a hint of a smile curling his lips despite his previous protests. "They've never had to deal with anyone like you around here before."

I smirked back at him. "And it's about time they did. Masks on."

I figured we could sneak onto and off the lot without getting caught, but it was always wise to cover one's ass just in case. Rafael and I set down our jugs and dug our ski masks—black to coordinate with our long-sleeved tees and sweats—out of our pockets.

The cloth felt uncomfortably warm against my forehead and cheeks, but it was a small price to pay to ensure no one who caught sight of us could ID us.

Jugs held tight, we glanced up and down the road and then loped across. I motioned for Rafael to start on the cars to the left of the lot while I swerved right.

At the closest car, I knelt by the fuel door and took out

the flathead screwdriver I'd brought for this job. I fit the head into the gap between the door and the rest of the car.

All it took was a little pushing and wiggling, and the fuel door popped open. "Bingo," I said under my breath, and quickly unscrewed the fuel cap underneath.

Then I lifted one of the water jugs, held the narrow mouth to the opening, and poured the entire two gallons into the tank.

The sickly smell of the gasoline the water was sloshing around with prickled into my nostrils. Wrinkling my nose, I closed everything up and hurried on to the next vehicle.

The van's fuel door snapped open even more easily than the previous car. Another two gallons of water gurgled into its tank, then I was moving on to a junky-looking sports car, and finally one of the pickup trucks.

Every last one of their vehicles was going to be fucked. If they figured out what the problem was early on, they might be able to avoid most of the damage, but I was betting the bozos weren't quite smart enough for that.

I was just emptying the last dribbles of water into the truck's gas tank when the hinges squeaked on the storage building door—now less than twenty feet away from where I was crouched.

With a hitch of my pulse, I ducked down even farther. A voice called out as if to someone still in the building.

"Yeah, I'll be back in the morning. Can't leave her hanging too long, if you know what I mean."

The leering bravado in the asshole's voice set my teeth on edge. But what if he headed this way?

As quickly as I could, I twisted the fuel cap back on

and eased the fuel door shut over it. Footsteps rasped across the asphalt.

They were heading in my direction. Shit.

I curled my fingers around the handles of the now light-as-air jugs and backed away from the truck toward the sports car, staying low to the ground. The last few steps, I dashed.

Dropping down behind the trunk of the sports car, I sucked in a breath and peeked the way I'd come. The man who'd come out of the storage building looked like he was heading around the hood of the truck rather than stopping to take it.

Fucking hell. I glanced around, judging the distance to the van and then to the road beyond.

The prick started whistling, and I took that as my cue to keep moving.

Setting my sneakers quietly on the pavement, I fled for the shelter of the van. I'd just flung myself around its rear end when the whistling stopped.

"Hey, is someone out here?"

I clamped my lips tight—and nearly choked when a large form emerged from the shadows next to me.

It was only Rafael, frowning with concern. He beckoned to me, and we both took off for the streets of the town now within reach.

We stayed low and kept the van between us and the goon. I didn't look back until we'd hurtled several steps down one of the town's streets past a couple of quaint houses.

I probably should have hustled on back all the way

home. But I couldn't resist peeking back to watch the first results of our handiwork.

It didn't look like the wannabe gangster had worried too much about whatever he'd thought he'd seen or heard. He was whistling again, the sound cut off a second later by the thud of a car door closing.

As he revved the ignition, I braced myself. The engine rumbled.

Then came a sputter. A hacking like the engine was coughing its lungs up.

The guy shut it off and twisted the key again, and you'd have thought that poor car had come down with tuberculosis.

Delight dancing in my chest, I turned to Rafael and nodded that we should go. A grin plastered itself to my face the whole way back to the bungalow.

I'd wreaked my little bit of havoc. Let's see how tough these douchebags would actually be when push came to shove.

TEN

Luciana

"IF YOU COULD AVOID KNEEING me in the nose, that would be appreciated."

I glanced at Jasper as he lowered me, trying to judge the ratio of grumbling to dry humor in his voice. I was pretty sure this time he was leaning more toward the latter.

"As long as you don't gouge my thigh with that deadly thumb of yours," I retorted cheekily.

His mouth gave a twitch that I was pretty sure by now indicated a suppressed smile, because my new partner never seemed to worry much about showing his frowns and grimaces.

Of course, it was hard to tell with him, even with a few practices as a pair under our belts. I couldn't say he'd ever been actually *friendly* with me.

Did he really have a problem with skating with me, or did he simply feel like he had to maintain his reputation as a grump?

Niko clapped his hands together. "You're getting closer every time! Let's see that once more."

I shook the tension out of my limbs and glided around the rink to get back into the starting position for the simple star lift we'd been working on. Jasper synchronized his movements with mine without complaint.

From the corner of my eye, I tracked the rhythm of his blade strokes and the power that emanated from his brawny body. There was no denying that he could make a spectacle on the ice—one it was impossible not to appreciate.

We reversed course and glided backward, me veering in front of him. As I turned toward him, Jasper grasped my hip and one of my hands to sweep me into the air as if I weighed nothing at all.

I caught the start of a wobble with my hand against his broad shoulder. Extending one leg toward the ceiling, I stretched the other straight behind me.

Jasper whirled around and around, and my ponytail streamed out from my head. The exhilaration took my breath away.

Then he eased me down and set me on the ice at just the right pace for me to pull away from him.

No matter how much he grumbled, nothing mattered more to him than creating a beautiful image on the ice. If I hadn't been able to tell that from watching his performances on TV, working with him would have proven it.

I could respect the desire even if I wouldn't mind him getting an attitude readjustment. He had to realize how committed I was and warm up to me eventually, right?

As we skated toward Niko again, our self-appointed coach stretched his arms with a languid grace that reminded me of a cat in the sun. "I think that's enough for one day. Great job, you two. You're really killing it out there."

Jasper snorted and stomped toward the benches to grab his bag. "I guess we look a *little* less like idiots now."

I tried to restrain my wince at the sting of his words. Ouch.

I knew I was learning a hell of a lot from working with him, but maybe I was holding him back. Diverting him from the training that would put him back in the spotlight as a star.

That's what Coach Balakin would have told me, wasn't it?

I moved to retrieve my own duffel bag with my chin high, doing my best not to let my dampened spirits show in my posture. Apparently I didn't do a good enough job at hiding it.

"Hey." Niko planted himself next to me as I hefted my bag over my shoulders. He caught my gaze with a typical twinkle in his bright brown eyes. "Don't mind him. He just doesn't like being outside his comfort zone. The two of you really are making fantastic progress."

I couldn't exactly accuse him of lying. "It feels good," I admitted. "Working with someone, building a routine together instead of being limited to what I can do on my own."

Niko grinned. "Then my plan is succeeding. I can tell Jasper appreciates it too, even if he has a funny way of showing it."

"'Funny' is not the word I'd use," I muttered.

Niko muffled a snicker with his hand. "That's fair."

His gaze slid over me, stirring a sudden heat beneath my skin with the memory of our interlude in the change room a few days ago. "We're finishing a little earlier than usual. Do you feel up to adding a little endurance work to today's practice."

Curiosity sparked in my chest. "Sure. What did you have in mind?"

He motioned to my bag. "Get changed and toss that in your car, and we'll go for a hike."

That actually sounded like exactly what I needed right now to clear the cobwebs of doubt from my brain. I shot him a smile that I hoped didn't look too fawning. "Perfect. I'll meet you out front in ten."

When I found Niko in the parking lot, he didn't actually look like he'd changed much other than pulling off the fleece pullover he'd been wearing against the arena's chill. The black fitted tee showed off his lean muscles to delicious effect.

I was definitely not drooling. Okay, maybe a little.

I tossed my bag in the trunk of the car and glanced down at my cargo pants and sleeveless top with its glittery skull print. Maybe not typical hiking gear, but it'd do.

As I turned toward Niko, I made a subtle gesture with one hand beyond his view. *Stand down*, it said.

Rafael would be watching, as he always was. But I didn't want him following us on this expedition *too* closely, not when I had high hopes about all the sorts of endurance we might explore.

He'd trail behind where he could hear a gunshot or a yell for help, but he'd give me my space. Or at least, if he didn't, he'd have only himself to blame.

Niko motioned for me to follow him. "There's a good trail that starts just a few blocks from the arena."

I raised my eyebrows at him as we set off together. "I wouldn't have taken you for a hiker."

He beamed at me. "There's something about being surrounded by natural beauty… It soothes the soul. I think that's the right way to say it. You Americans don't have the same respect, but you can always start cultivating it now."

"Hey, I have plenty of respect for trees and lakes," I informed him.

He chuckled. "That's why I'll show you my favorite spot around here."

We set off through the streets and then veered into a patch of forest at the edge of town, not far from the road to the beach. When the ground slanted upward, I started to feel the burn in my legs with the exertion, but Niko chattered on about the various routes he'd discovered around town without any sign of flagging.

"First thing I do when I'm settling into a new place," he said. "Find all the best hiking paths and views. That's what helps me feel at home."

"It is beautiful out here," I said, dragging in a breath full of the fresh scent of fir needles.

"Wait until you see where you're going. That's the best part."

The path turned rockier and steeper, and I scrambled up a few stretches accepting Niko's hand for balance. The last time, he kept his fingers curled around mine and tugged me forward with him.

I wiped my brow, glanced up, and stalled in mid-step.

We'd come out to the crest of a hill overlooking a placid lake. I couldn't tell if it was the same one with the town's beach—no sand or people were visible from our vantage point.

The sunlight sparkled across the water as if it were a multi-faceted jewel. The leaves on the trees around the bank rippled with a light breeze, flashing hints of yellow and orange amid the green where the autumn colors were just starting to creep in.

"Wow," I said. "It looks like something out of a fairy tale."

"I told you." Niko shot me one of his grins and sat down cross legged on the wide slab of stone along the edge of the peak.

I sank down next to him, keeping a few inches of distance between us, not sure how bold I should be. The mood didn't feel right for suddenly jumping his bones.

"Are there places like this back in Japan?" I asked him.

"Oh, much prettier than this. But Canada can offer an acceptable temporary substitute." He winked at me. "As long as I find one peaceful spot, I'm good."

Somehow after all the articles and TV spots I'd perused about Niko Okabe, I'd never known he was a nature-lover. I guessed that didn't fit the rebel narrative the reporters liked to play up.

The words tumbled out before I could think better of

them. "It must be nice to get away from the whole media circus. All those people constantly judging you."

Niko's eyes widened, and my gut plummeted. If I'd accidentally put my foot in my mouth—

Then he shook his head with a light laugh, clearly undisturbed. "People can have their opinions. It doesn't affect who I am. I always tell myself that if anyone shows a prejudice, it says more about them than me."

Relief washed over me that I hadn't offended him. "Good. That sounds like a really healthy way to look at it. I should probably work on that kind of mindset too."

Niko's voice took on a lightly teasing tone. "And what sort of pressures have you been dealing with, Angel?"

We were not getting into any details there.

"Nothing like what you've faced," I said. "I can't imagine having reporters shoving microphones in your face and asking such personal questions—like it's their business who you're dating or anything like that."

Niko shrugged, his gaze returning to the lake. His handsome face looked nothing but serene.

"It hasn't always been easy. There are some issues where my home country isn't as… progressive as yours. But that's exactly why it's important to me to always be upfront about it. I've made a reputation where being different from what's considered normal is part of my character. It's my—what's the word for it…?—trademark. So it's expected rather than shocking now. For the most part."

"It mustn't have been fun getting to that point."

"We all have our struggles." He nudged me with his elbow. "Focusing on other people's opinions doesn't do anything but hold you back."

I wished I believed that as fully as he clearly did. How did this man manage to keep such an upbeat attitude regardless of the pressures heaped on him about everything from his sexual orientation to his fashion choices?

The media portrayed him as a playboy and a daredevil, but I saw nothing but an incredibly resilient man who was playing the best game he could with the hand he'd been dealt. The best game he could while still being *himself* rather than conforming to anyone else's expectations.

Wasn't that why I'd come all this way too? I wished I could soak up his confidence until it became my own.

Maybe I couldn't absorb all of his self-assurance, but I could certainly get closer to him than I was right now.

I peered at him sideways, evaluating my next move. My pulse thumped faster, but I'd never been the type to take the coy route.

How much longer would I even get to revel in his company? The future felt so uncertain.

The one thing I knew for sure was that I wanted to enjoy his presence in every possible way while I could.

The swell of emotion in my chest was something I'd never really felt before. My hookups back home had been totally casual, burning off pent-up energy, never putting my heart on the line.

But Niko was different. Niko wasn't looking for anything from me or trying to prove a point. He *saw* me like no one else ever had—not even Rafael, as loyal as my bodyguard was.

How could I not want even more?

I scooted closer to him and slipped my hand back around his. "In the interests of not holding back... what do you think about picking up that 'to be continued' now?"

Niko met my gaze, both mischief and hunger flaring in his. "I think that's the best idea I've heard all day."

I pushed onto my knees and around to meet him as he dipped his head. Our lips collided with a giddy rush that swept through me from head to toe—and had my panties dampening in an instant.

His tongue twined around mine, his lips soft but steady. I groaned, wanting him more with each passing second.

My fingers found their way into his hair, tracing those black and pink strands as if I could permanently commit the feeling to memory. Niko let out a faint groan and wrapped his arm around me to pull me even tighter against his toned frame.

I couldn't resist sliding my hands down his body to the hem of his shirt. The dip of his abs was screaming to be touched, and there was nothing I could do but oblige it.

I knew I was right when he arched beneath me, a perfect cue to keep going. My fingertips trailed upward over his chest.

At the thudding of his pulse against my palm, a spike of excitement surged through me. I raked my nails softly against his shoulders and the slender curve of his neck.

He didn't protest when I tugged the tee right off him. I tossed it into a crumpled ball on the forest floor and took in his exquisitely sculpted torso with a sharper pang between my legs.

I only had a few seconds to appreciate the new view before Niko drew me into another kiss. He slipped his hand beneath my shirt and locked the peak of my breast between two of his lithe fingers.

I gasped at the jolt of pleasure, and he smiled against my mouth. Then his tongue swept between my lips again, stoking the flames already blazing inside me even higher.

Niko cupped my breasts, thumbing over my peaks. He teased me gently, bringing me to the brink of pleasure with only his deft hands.

It wasn't enough. I wanted more.

Taking the initiative, I tossed my shirt and sports bra after Niko's tee.

Niko murmured something in Japanese that sounded awed before switching back to English. "You're stunning." He dropped a kiss to my shoulder and then the crook of my neck before his fingers traced the top of my feathery tattoo. "An angel in every way."

I snorted. "Maybe not *every* way."

A grin that was downright devilish crossed Niko's face. "I happen to think angels should be allowed to have a good time too."

He nibbled the sensitive spot just below my earlobe, and a breath stuttered out of me.

"Hallelujah," I mumbled, and he chuckled with a wash of warm breath down my skin.

He massaged my breasts with little tweaks of my nipples until I was whimpering, then eased one hand down to trace along the waistline of my cargo pants. If my panties had been damp before, his touch so close to the place where I was aching most had me soaking them.

But he didn't delve farther, only stroked my belly and my breast while his lips worked their sweet magic on my neck. I squirmed, shifting my hips in a plea for his touch, and he simply nipped my jaw.

I gasped and decided that enough was enough. *I* wasn't going to be shy about what I wanted.

I slid my hand down his chest and pressed it against the bulge at the crotch of his sweatpants. The already rigid erection there twitched against my touch, and Niko groaned.

"A very impatient angel," Niko murmured. "I can take care of you."

In an instant, his deft fingers had the fly of my cargos open. He curled his hand right over my panties, his breath stuttering as he encountered the proof of my incredible arousal.

A burst of bliss radiated from my core at the contact. Niko's fingertips worked my pussy in gentle, slow circles through the thin layer of fabric. My head swayed back, my eyes closing.

I wanted to block out everything except Niko, close myself off to any sensation that wasn't purely him. I was barely aware of the soft coos of need that were making their way between my lips, joining the birdsong in the forest's quiet chorus.

The way he was able to read my body was unreal. He flicked his thumb over my clit and set a pulsing pace with his fingers until I thought I'd explode just like that.

But he kept my climax just out of reach. Every time my pleasure raced higher, he'd slow down his ministrations, until I was moaning in desperation.

Just when I thought Niko would tease me forever, he

tipped me back on the rough stone. With a careful yank, he peeled my cargo pants off me.

The next thing I knew, he was pulling my panties to the side and opening his lips against my pussy.

At the first lap of his tongue, I cried out. My fingers clutched at his smooth hair, the only thing I could hold on to through the rush of startled ecstasy.

Sighing, I spread my hips slightly to allow him further access. At his groan of approval, the vibration of his voice sent a shiver up my spine.

His tongue was like magic against my clit. I shuddered at every deft touch, every slick swipe between my legs.

He shifted lower still, traveling further down towards my slit. When his tongue delved right inside of me, my vision hazed.

I had to have him right fucking now.

I got enough of a handle on myself to tilt his chin up with one finger. His eyes flicked to mine, amusement dancing in his bright brown irises.

His lips gleamed with my arousal. My pussy throbbed at the sight.

"Condom?" I rasped.

His smile turned wicked. He fished a foil packet from his pocket.

The next few moments were a blur. My hands were on Niko, peeling away the few remaining layers of clothing that he had left. He was gloriously hard, his dick searing against my palm.

I took a second to appreciate the straining length of him before my hands went to work, stroking and pumping him, toying with him in the same way as he'd done to me minutes before. I only released him so that he could handle the condom situation, and even that took too long for me.

He rolled it over his shaft, his eyes meeting mine. The glow of desire I caught in those two dark orbs left me breathless.

With no patience left at all, I pushed him down on the ground and straddled him. As I rocked against his rigid cock, he gripped my ass checks and squeezed.

"Fuck," I muttered, and lined myself up.

The tip of his cock pressed against my entrance. I sank down, biting my lip at the sensation of him filling me. When he pushed upward, my world transformed into blissful static.

I blipped back to reality in time to savor his first few thrusts. Even as he bucked his hips upward, he still managed to keep one hand massaging my breast to send extra quivers of delight through my body.

I set my hands on his shoulders and found my own rhythm soon enough. Locking eyes with Niko, I matched the motion of his hips.

His mouth dropped open as he expelled a soft groan. I ground my body against his, desperate to be closer to him even now.

I raked my nails lightly down his chest, urging him on, and he sped up his pace. The smacking of our bodies together tossed me upward—I felt like I was soaring above the tree line, my head high up in the clouds.

The only thing I could hear was our soft cries echoing through the forest and the sounds of our merging flesh.

"You're so hot," he managed to say. "So wet. So *perfect.*"

"Jesus, Niko." I arched my back as he thrust deeper. "Keep going, just like that."

My nails dug in further, my heart fluttering as he whispered an endless slew of praises. His name floated from my lips in a breathy sigh.

Niko pumped harder, his strong arms wrapping around my waist. I could tell that his climax was nearing, threatening to spill over at any moment.

I wasn't far behind him, if I was behind him at all. My mind reeled with every stroke of his shaft inside me.

His breaths transformed into heavy panting that twined with my heightened cries like a symphony. If I opened my eyes and looked at him, I would come immediately and I knew it.

"Lou…" His hand rose to my cheek, calling my gaze to him. It was almost as if he could read my mind, knowing exactly what I needed.

I couldn't hold back any longer. I gazed down at him, taking in the flush of his cheeks and the fervor shining in his eyes.

My thoughts went completely blank. The only thing I could focus on was the pulsing waves of pleasure that swept through me with each passing second.

My breathing became harsher, my pitch higher.

Heaven. Euphoria.

Pure fucking bliss.

"Niko, I'm—"

My moan of completion cut off my words. I shuddered against him with the power of my orgasm.

He cut me off with his own cry. I felt his grip tighten, and his cock twitched madly inside of me.

He gasped out my name, stiffening against me as he surrendered to the same rapture that I was spiraling through. We rocked to a halt against each other.

My head dropped down. Our lips touched again in a kiss that was strangely innocent, as light as a butterfly's landing.

For a moment, the only thing that either of us could do was catch our breath in each other's arms.

Niko gathered me against his chest and kissed my forehead. "That was incredible. You can be my hiking partner any day."

A giggle tumbled out of me. I snuggled against him, soaking up his warmth as the breeze brushed over my skin. "Worthy of a few encores?"

His tone turned sly. "I'd definitely enjoy collaborating with you like that again."

We couldn't cuddle there forever, though, as much as I longed to extend the moment. Evening was falling, and Rafael would be getting restless.

The last thing I needed was him barging in and making a mess of this. There'd be no encores then.

I peeled myself off Niko, and we reassembled our clothes. The walk back toward town passed in companionable silence, hand-in-hand.

Niko veered in a slightly different route than the one we'd taken to get on the path. I only realized when I saw the gang's storage building coming into view up ahead.

My stomach clenched.

An SUV had parked on the shoulder a couple of

blocks closer to us. A frazzled looking woman got out, retrieved a toddler from the backseat, and lay her down beneath the open hatch.

Emergency diaper change, I guessed.

Rafael and I clearly hadn't outright destroyed the gang's entire fleet of vehicles, because at the same moment, a red truck peeled out of the lot, its tires screeching against the asphalt. As it sped toward the SUV, a guy leaned out the passenger side window.

"Stupid whore!" he shouted at the woman. "Get the hell outta here before we *make* you."

The young woman, clearly shaken, snatched up her son as the truck roared by. She clutched him against her and then hustled to return him to his seat as if terrified.

My chest had totally constricted, all the joy I'd been holding on to vanished. When I glanced at Niko, a cloud of worry had settled over his face.

My first effort hadn't been enough. The goons were still racing around being menaces, and they were threatening Niko's sense of peace as well as everything else.

I couldn't let them ruin even more.

ELEVEN

Rafael

POUR a dollop of olive oil in the pan.

Toss in the pepper, onion, and garlic.

Follow with the tomato puree and wine.

And let it simmer.

I inhaled, breathing in one of my favorite childhood scents, my mouth watering at my own handiwork.

This was it, the dish that was going to blow Lou out of the water. If I couldn't fix her broken taste buds with enchilada de camarones, then I didn't know what would do it.

"That actually smells really awesome, Rafael," she called from the living room.

"What do you mean, 'actually'?" I asked, stirring the marinated shrimps in. "Por supuesto! As a Latina woman, you should be drowning in drool already just from the aroma alone."

"Drowning in drool?" She flashed me a teasing smirk from over the back of the sofa where she was sitting flipping through TV channels. "Well, you'll have to excuse me if I don't need the water wings yet. It does smell awesome, but what matters is how it tastes."

"It tastes amazing. If you weren't so busy shoving pierogies and cabbage rolls in your mouth, you'd have discovered that by now."

She leaned her arm over the sofa back to better face me with a flash of her silver rings, the cheeky grin that I'd come to adore years ago lighting up her dark brown eyes as well. "Hey, now. You're *really* missing out by passing on the golumpki. My nanny could make some that would knock your socks off."

I shook my head, breathing out a heavy, mock sigh.

It was hard to get all that invested in the argument when we'd been having variations on it ever since I'd found out she preferred Polish food over anything close to the cuisine of her heritage. So what if she was three generations removed from the ancestors who'd arrived from Mexico? She had no idea what she was missing out on.

But on the other hand, I couldn't really blame her if she associated comfort more with the Polish nanny who'd raised her through most of her early childhood rather than that mother of hers. The Deadly Rose was about as maternal as a machine gun.

I'd resigned myself to her odd food preferences, and these days our well-rehearsed banter wasn't much more than an inside joke. But that didn't mean I was going to stop demonstrating the fantastic flavors she'd been missing out on. The Cuban recipes I'd grown up with might not be the exact same as what her great grandparents might have made, but they were a hell of a lot closer than her usual comfort food.

I glanced at the shrimps. Perfect.

"Well, hold on to your socks." I grabbed the ladle. "Because I'm about to rock your world."

Lou stuck both bare feet up in the air and wiggled her toes at me. The nails were painted in an alternating pattern of neon green and black. "Already one step ahead of you."

She broke into peals of laughter, her smile lighting up the room so brightly that it could have been sunrise instead of eight o'clock at night. Something tightened in the pits of my stomach even as my heart jumped up into my throat at the sight.

How had the scrawny, scrappy ten-year-old I'd been assigned to nine years ago grown into a woman this beautiful? How in all the levels of Hell was that acceptable?

I *had* known her since she was ten. The year she'd officially become an adult, I'd had my thirtieth fucking birthday.

I should not have been entertaining thoughts that would have gotten me consigned to Hell just for having them pass through my head.

Swallowing hard, I jerked my gaze toward the TV instead. A man in a suit stood in front of a bunch of colorful boxes while a nervous contestant sweated it out beside him.

I'd never liked game shows, but pretending to be interested in it was better than letting the slightest hint show of the heat that'd flared under my skin. I'd stare straight at the sun if it somehow drowned out the attraction that sparked when I least wanted it to.

Which was basically always.

Of course, it got even harder to ignore Lou when she peeled herself off the sofa and sauntered over to where I was doling out our dinner. She'd developed a slight sway to her hips that I wasn't sure was even purposeful.

And when she leaned her elbows onto the counter, the neckline of her tee dipping to reveal a deeper shadow of cleavage between her breasts…

"Here, eat up." I shoved the plate toward her a little harder than I'd meant to. "I don't see how you're eating enough after spending so much time skating. You're going to end up working your muscles to death if you keep this up."

"What are you, my nutritionist?" she asked, already popping a forkful into her mouth.

Her eyelids dropped in a swoon that both gratified the cook in me—and made my traitor cock twitch. "Mmm, this really is good. I'm not usually that into the peppers. Obviously Mom should have hired you as chef instead of that fancy pants we had at home."

I raised my eyebrows at her as we moved to the table. "But then who would have made sure your rebellious ass didn't get hung out to dry?"

It was the wrong comment, because it encouraged Lou to shake that undeniably pert ass before she settled it into her seat. Cue another cock twitch.

"I'm sure I'd have survived somehow," she said breezily.

I sank down across from her, grateful that the lower half of my body was now out of view. "Well, I'm glad you like it. It's one of my favorites. My abuela's old recipe that she brought with her from Cuba."

Lou shoved another forkful into her mouth. "I wonder if my great-grandparents didn't care about recipes or if Mom chucked all those out before I came into the picture."

She chewed thoughtfully for a moment and then waved her fork at me. "I was thinking. I saw a truckful of those douchebags outside their hideout yesterday. They're still going around being massive assholes. Obviously I didn't hit them hard enough for them to decide to get out of town."

"I'm not surprised," I said, watching her warily. "Idiots have a tendency to also be stubborn."

"Too bad for them that I am too. There are plenty of other ways we can pick away at them until they realize they're better off finding a new stomping ground."

I suppressed a groan. "I assume you're going to tell me about these other ways."

"Of course!" She shot me a mischievous grin that tugged at both my heart and my groin. "I thought about mocking them with graffiti, but I don't think that'd have enough impact. I've got to make things difficult for them, not just annoy them."

"Naturally," I said dryly, putting on an impassive expression to hide the worry spinning up through my stomach.

"I could smash some windows—on their cars or the building itself—but after just one, the noise would probably be enough to bring them running outside. A single window wouldn't really be big enough."

"You settled on something difficult and big, then. I'm thrilled."

Lou laughed at my deadpan remark. "Oh, don't worry, it's nothing *risky*. I came up with the perfect strategy: tire spikes. All you need is some scrap metal to play with. Set them down at night near the cars, the pricks drive over them the next day, and poof! No one's roaring through town terrorizing people."

She dug into her meal, radiating confidence in her plan. And I couldn't even fault her that assurance, as nerve-wracking as I found it.

How had the gang princess adapted to small-town life so quickly—while also championing the town in her own way? Lou had always been a bold spirit, but now that she'd had a taste of freedom, she was like a wild bird finally released from its cage.

I just had to make sure she didn't fly too far too fast.

"Remember, we're supposed to be keeping our heads down. If you're caught messing with these guys—"

Lou let out a dismissive huff of breath. "I won't be caught. Laying down a few strips of tire spikes will be a hell of a lot faster than pouring all that water into the tanks. It's not like I want those goons taking up more of my time than they have to when I have so many more interesting things to devote it to."

Something about the sly shift in her tone had me

bracing myself. "You mean your skating," I said casually, knowing it was something more than that.

"I mean, there's always *that*." She tugged a strand of her dark hair free from its habitual ponytail and curled it around her finger. "But now I'm also hooking up with my sort-of coach, which makes the whole thing even more fun."

Even though I'd had some suspicious thoughts when she'd signaled for me to hang back the other afternoon, jealousy roared to the surface beneath my well-practiced cool. I tucked my hands under the table as they clenched, my jaw echoing the motion for a split-second before I caught my reaction.

Lou could sleep with whoever the fuck she wanted. I'd made it awfully clear that *I* wasn't game, hadn't I?

I could hardly expect her to become a nun.

But I couldn't stop the images from playing out in the back of my mind, sending an infuriated ruddy haze over my vision. That guy's slim hands running over her body, his lips pressed against hers…

Did he have any idea how to treat her the way she deserved? What kind of asshole got it on with a girl he was supposed to be coaching anyway?

"That seems a little hasty," I said, straining to keep my voice steady. "You haven't known him very long. Are you sure you can trust him?"

Lou snorted. "Trust him for what—not to be an undercover spy for my mother? Or a gang lackey? I think a couple of weeks of skating with him for hours nearly every day is plenty of time to be totally sure of that. Oh, and the *years* before that when I followed his competitions on TV."

"There are other ways he could hurt you."

She rolled her eyes. "I was the one who seduced *him*, FYI. You should be rejoicing. He's a huge step up from the kinds of guys I was stuck hanging around with back home."

Okay, she might have had a slight point there. But the guys in the gangs I understood. I knew how to read them.

I knew fuck-all about how some figure skating star operated.

"Just doing my job," I said with forced calm. "That's why I'm here."

Lou leaned back in her chair, narrowing her eyes at me. "Then I'll remind you that it was your idea to come along. You know, my skating partner is all kinds of hot too, even if he's a jerk half the time. Maybe I'll see if I can get him to loosen up in all the right ways too."

I obviously hadn't hidden my disapproving reaction quite well enough, and now she was pissed off at me—and trying to rile me up on purpose. At least, I sure as hell hoped that comment about the other rink-jock was throwaway provocation, not her real feelings.

I opened my mouth and ended up shoving the last few bites of my dinner into it rather than saying anything. The heat of the meal churned in my gut alongside the flares of temper I rarely struggled this hard to contain.

She wasn't a child anymore. I knew that. She was a grown woman, and it wasn't my place to boss her around, especially now.

But when she made jabs like that, fuck, did I want to bend her over the table and—

No, that was definitely not the direction my mind should be going in right now.

I pushed my chair back from the table, tossed my plate in the sink, and strode down to my room in the basement without another word.

Never had I been more grateful for the punching bag I'd been able to pick up at a sporting goods store in the larger town several miles outside of Hobb Creek. I went right at it, slamming one fist and then the other into the thick material.

The bag's chain squeaked. It swung away from me and back into another vicious punch.

I poured my tension out into the blows, letting the padded instrument absorb all of it. I hadn't bothered to wrap my hands, and in a matter of minutes, my knuckles were raw. But I kept going, letting the sting ground me.

I'd followed Lou all the way up here to keep her safe. She might be grown up and a woman who knew what she wanted, but anyone, no matter how tough, was vulnerable on their own.

Especially anyone with a mom like Mireya Cordova, who wasn't likely to take her heir's disappearance sitting down.

So I was going to do my fucking best to protect Lou from the things she actually needed protection from—and that included shielding her from all those urges I never should have felt to begin with.

TWELVE

Luciana

JASPER and I finished the final rotation and glided to a stop as our extended legs lowered to the ice in tandem. Our blades hit the ice perfectly in sync, and I couldn't restrain a broad grin.

Niko let out a whistle from where he was watching by the boards and gave an enthusiastic round of applause before skating over to join us. "You two are really killing it. That last spin was breathtaking. You've come a long way, you know—both of you."

The warmth of his smile sparked with my own joy, sending a deeper flood of triumph through my chest. But when I glanced at Jasper, he simply shrugged, his mouth slanted in a direction that had more in common with a frown.

Geez, was there *anything* that would perk this guy up?

Or was he still peeved that he had to put up with my constant presence?

The thorn of insecurity didn't have time to dig deep before Niko's eyes lit with a sly glint I was coming to recognize. "Considering how much you two have evolved since we first gave pairs a try, I think it's time you got the chance to show off for a wider audience."

My gaze shot to the stands. "You want to invite people from town to watch us practice?"

Jasper sighed. "He's talking about some kind of competition. He wants us to perform someplace else— right, Niko?" He didn't sound happy about it.

The shorter man chuckled without any sign of noticing Jasper's lack of enthusiasm. "That's exactly what I'm getting at. Now before you say anything, it's just a small local competition. An event in Dellville—a city a couple of hours from here. No official criteria for competing, so it's fine that Lou is a newcomer and not registered anywhere yet. It'd give you the chance to get used to having more spectators and to get some objective feedback from judges without too much pressure."

"Judges," I murmured. The memory of Coach Balakin's disappointed tone when he pointed out my flaws echoed up from my memory.

I squared my shoulders against the recollection. The guy coaching me *now*, who absolutely knew what good skating looked like, thought I could handle this.

Luciana Cordova didn't let anyone else decide what chances she took a shot at.

Niko nodded, studying my reaction with a slight softening of his expression. "I can tell you how good you are all day long, but I know Jasper here will never believe me. This will give you objective proof of how far you've come."

He nudged Jasper teasingly with his elbow, but his gaze stayed on me. He could probably tell my confidence wasn't on the most stable ground either.

"I've never competed before," I said. "So starting with something small sounds just right to me. What's the point of doing any of this if I'm not going to put myself out there properly?"

I paused, taking in Jasper's uncertain expression. "Unless you think it's too small to be worth bothering with for *you.*" Which was a stance I could totally understand after he'd made it as far as the Olympics in the past.

Before Jasper could reply, another thought struck me with a jolt of panic. I turned back to Niko.

"How much publicity would a little local competition like this even get? It's not, like, broadcast outside the city or anything?"

Jasper snorted. "If you're looking to get on TV, I don't think a backwoods competition like that's going to do it for you."

I exhaled silently, not wanting him to realize I was incredibly relieved rather than disheartened by the fact. Thank the Lord.

I was supposed to be in hiding. I couldn't risk blowing my cover with any competition where someone who recognized me might spot me. But if it was only a small one in a city I'd never even heard of before—so no doubt Mom hadn't either—that should be safe.

A giddy shiver passed through me. I could finally get out there and make a spectacle on the ice like I'd always dreamed.

But Jasper still didn't look convinced.

"We just show up and skate?" he asked Niko.

"There's a qualifying round," Niko said. "But I have no doubt you'll be in the top ten pairs who're approved for the official competition day. I wouldn't be surprised if they don't even have more than ten pairs and it's just a formality."

Jasper rolled his eyes. "Such a vote of confidence."

Why did he always have to have such a stick up his ass? Couldn't he give this a chance?

I might have voiced those snarky questions, but Niko stepped in with a much more diplomatic attitude than came naturally to me. "I'm only putting the idea out there. You don't have to answer now. Just think about it."

Jasper hummed to himself noncommittally, his gaze veering back to the ice. I waited for the word *no* to roll off his tongue, but instead, he tilted his chin back upward, a steely expression on his face.

"I'll think about it—alone."

With one graceful push of his powerful legs, he was gone, soaring all the way to the other side of the rink. I eyed him, watching him mentally prepare himself before flying off into a series of jumps.

His form was impressive, stunning even. I didn't

understand how Jasper could have any doubts about his abilities.

What was it in that handsome head of his that tripped him up when push came to shove?

Was he afraid that even the minor pressure of this "backwoods" competition would throw him off his game and he'd embarrass himself?

Before my eyes, he kicked off into a flawless triple Axel. My jaw dropped so fast it nearly hit the ice.

Here was a glimpse of the skater I'd seen on television, the man whose career I'd followed. Even with no music, Jasper swept across the ice as if he were moving along to a symphony, one only he could hear.

With his broad shoulders and brawny chest, he looked regal, princely even. I couldn't help but stare.

And possibly my fingers were tingling with the impulse to find out what those shoulders and that chest would feel like if I got to handle them for more than just fleeting lifts.

Niko's hand came to rest on the small of my back as he joined me in watching the other man. A headier tingle rushed through me at the ease of that casual intimacy— along with a little pang of guilt.

I probably shouldn't be checking out another guy while the one I'd been hooking up with was right next to me, should I?

Niko dipped his head so his warm breath ruffled my hair as he spoke. "He's pretty amazing, isn't he?"

"I can see why you'd cross an ocean for the chance to coach him."

"Mmhm. And is his skating the only thing you're admiring?"

A blush flared in my cheeks. Was I really that obvious?

I groped for an appropriate answer. "I—I mean, he is something to look at. Objectively speaking. If you can get past the infuriating personality."

Niko laughed. "That wasn't an accusation. I'm not going to be offended if you're interested in him too."

I guessed I might as well admit it now. "I might have a bit of a thing for hot, grouchy men, it turns out. But I also like the cheerful, sexy ones." I prodded Niko in the chest with my thumb. "So you don't need to worry."

Niko's smile didn't waver. "Not worried at all. If you can crack that man's shell, I'd be *happy* to see you do it. I didn't get the impression that you're the kind of woman who's looking to be tied down, Lou. I don't mind you playing the field as long as you stay honest with me."

I swallowed the rock that had somehow found its way into my throat and found it dissolved on its way into my stomach. He sounded like he was honestly okay with the idea of me pursuing Jasper too.

Not that I had any illusions about *Jasper* being okay with it. I wasn't sure it'd be worth the hassle of taking a hammer to that guy's shell in the first place.

I shot a glance over my shoulder, an unexpected wobble passing through my stomach. "Does that mean you're playing the field too?"

Niko gave my temple a quick peck. "Between training the two of you and enjoying your company in other ways, my days are pretty full as it is. I didn't expect even you to sweep me off my feet."

He said the last bit with a teasing note that I couldn't help giggling at. "So I'm your Prince Charming now?"

Niko flashed one of his brilliant grins. "Princess Charming-ko."

We both dissolved into laugher. When I got control of myself, I noticed Jasper had glided over to the boards where he'd left his water bottle.

He jerked his gaze away just as I looked at him. He was probably wondering what the hell was wrong with the two of us.

Niko's approval gave me a little boost of courage. I pushed off and skated over to join my partner.

Oh, fuck me. Did he have to toss his head back like that while he swallowed, his Adam's apple bobbing on full display?

Did some part of me have to want to lick the sweat right off it?

His dark blue tee clung to his well-muscled form. I yanked my attention back to his face.

I was coming over here to talk, not to ogle him.

Okay, maybe a little bit to ogle.

I tried to plan something clever and suave to say, but the words just tumbled out as I stopped next to him. "You looked amazing out there."

Jasper raised a skeptical eyebrow at me. "It was just a random string of moves."

"What, and I'm not allowed to appreciate the skill it took to pull them off?" I resisted the urge to stick my tongue out at him, which would make him *so* much more impressed with my maturity. "If you're fishing for compliments, sure, you're even more amazing when you're performing one of your routines. I always loved seeing you in the televised competitions—you manage to make even the most athletic moves flow together into such a gorgeous picture."

Jasper lowered the water bottle. He stared at me with such a startled expression that I had to fight the urge to look down at myself and make sure my faded concert tee hadn't caught fire.

"Really?" he said without a hint of his usual snark. Something in his gray-green eyes had shifted; the storm looked a little less tumultuous.

Did he really have to ask that?

I set my hands on my hips. "Yes, really. I wouldn't go around giving you compliments I don't mean just to thank you for being such a kind and considerate guy. Because you're not particularly kind and considerate so far."

Jasper let out a sudden sputtering sound as if he'd managed to choke on the air. "Got it. No false compliments around here."

I couldn't resist punching him—fairly lightly—in the shoulder. Or as close to his shoulder as I could easily reach when standing more than a foot shorter than him.

"The point is, I meant it. I always knew I'd get lost in the world you'd create on the ice. Never saw anyone else who could put on a show the same way."

Jasper scratched the back of his head, appearing lost for words. His awkwardness melted a little of my irritation with him.

As unbelievable as it seemed that a guy who'd once been seen as such a prodigy that his avid fans had dubbed him "Saint Jasper" might lack in confidence, he was clearly affected by my words.

"Well… thank you," he said finally, peering at the ice for a beat before meeting my eyes again. He hesitated and then offered a wary but genuine-looking smile. "That's always been my goal. Bringing the vision in my head to life so I can take the audience there with me. I'm glad to know it's worked."

"Of course it's worked. I bet it'd still work just fine if you let go of whatever's eating at you like Niko keeps saying."

I leaned back against the boards, thinking back over the routines of his I'd watched. A sigh twinged with longing slipped over my lips. "Like that Chopin piece you performed for your short program the first year you were at Nationals. I watched that so many times…"

Maybe I shouldn't have said that. Jasper's eyes narrowed—but then a flicker of wonder passed through it.

"That's the music you were skating to when we caught you in here during our practice time that first day."

I gave him a crooked smile. "Because I've been trying to recreate the same vibes." A longing wiggled up inside me, and I decided to risk the question. "I'd love to see your routine live. If you wanted to get in a little more solo practice today."

Jasper's lips parted, his stance tensing. For a second, I was sure that he was going to say no, to tell me to piss off.

He closed his mouth again, and his jaw worked. "It wouldn't be the same without the costume."

His voice was softer than I'd ever heard it before. It woke up a hunger in me to see him even more unguarded.

"I can imagine that part," I said coaxingly. "I've seen it enough times. But to have you right in front of me…"

He wet his lips, and I realized his face had flushed just a little. Had my interest affected him that much?

"All right," he said abruptly. "Why not? It'd be good to run through that program again anyway."

I managed not to clap my hands in joy like a total fangirl. "I'll cue up the music for you!"

He looked a little tense as he swept off toward the center of the rink. How long had it been since he'd performed this routine from years back?

Well, he'd agreed. He could always change his mind if he was that worried about it.

But when the first strains of the song reached him in his opening position, all the tension fell away from his posture. I hooked my arms over the top of the boards and leaned back to enjoy the moment to its fullest.

Symphony and skater became one. The music built to its familiar crescendo, one that I'd committed completely to memory.

Jasper's powerful body breezed across the ice, never missing a form, never skidding, never faltering. All the confidence I'd seen in past performances rose to the surface as if it'd never left.

He landed every jump with total grace. Whirled through his spins like the music had him in its grasp. Tears pricked my lashes, my emotions surging in time with the melody and the beautiful image that Jasper had created for me and me alone.

By the time he'd finished the routine, he'd totally

stolen my breath away. My hands burned with the force of my clapping.

Jasper skated back to me, his chest heaving with the exertion and an odd mix of pride and puzzlement etched on his face. "I made it through the whole thing with no errors."

"It's not the first time."

"Well, no, I just—" He looked back toward the rink and then shook his head.

"Whatever you're thinking, stop," I had to order him. "You looked absolutely spectacular out there. Like, it's a miracle that I haven't dissolved into a puddle of awe just from seeing it firsthand."

I pressed my hands to my face in giddy embarrassment. "Holy crap."

Jasper blinked at me, but his face had brightened. "What?"

My voice came out in a whisper. "It just hit me again. Somehow I'm skating pairs with Jasper St. Pierre. How the fuck did that happen?"

I pinched myself just to make sure it really *was* happening. Jasper watched and then broke into the first real laugh I could remember hearing from him.

I started giggling too. "I'm sorry. You have no idea how crazy this seems to me. A month ago, I didn't think anyone was ever going to see me skate other than my long-suffering coach, and now somehow this is my life."

The memory of the very real suffering Coach Balakin must have gone through in the end cut through my good mood, but I kept the pang of loss off my face.

"And here I thought you were trying to avoid feeding

my ego," Jasper said in an unusually relaxed tone. He paused. "I like watching you skate too, you know. You get across some pretty impressive visuals yourself. It's not like it's a hardship skating with you."

I caught my jaw before it dropped right out of my head. "Sometimes you sure make it sound like it is."

Jasper ducked his head. "That's not—that's not really about you. And I wasn't sure at first. But you've definitely got some moves, Punk."

The compliment set me aglow. "You don't know how much it means to me to hear you say that. Telling some kind of story on the ice with the picture I'm creating— that's what I'm always striving for. It might sound cheesy, but there's so much awfulness in the world. I want to be someone who's bringing more joy and beauty to people."

"Yeah," Jasper said, his attention completely focused on me again. He cocked his head. "Can I ask you a question?"

"Can I stop you?" I retorted with a smile to show I was teasing.

Jasper drummed his fingers on the boards. "Did you really not know you were good enough to compete—to tell those stories on the ice—any of it? How could you *not* know?"

How could I not have?

The question expanded in my mind, repeating over and over. Ever since Niko's first assurances of my skill, I'd asked myself that same thing until I could barely think about it anymore.

I could say it was Coach Balakin's fault—that he'd

claimed I was falling short of even the most basic professional standards. But was it really?

He'd been an experienced figure skater. He'd competed for Ukraine decades ago.

Could he really have gotten it so wrong? Or had there been another hand at work, directing his coaching just as it'd orchestrated his murder?

Had he truly seen me as a failure… or had Mom paid him off to lie to me in the hopes of killing the dream she'd always seen as pointless?

I couldn't explain even a fraction of those possibilities in detail, so I settled for a vague approximation.

"I think it's mostly about my mother. She didn't really support my interest in skating—talked like it was a waste of time, like I wasn't good enough to bother. It's hard to have a clear idea of what you're capable of when you've got a voice from someone that close to you in your head all the time."

For the second time in this conversation, Jasper stared at me, momentarily speechless. He swiped his hand across his mouth.

His voice came out a bit hoarse. "Yeah, I can see how that could happen, especially if you never got the chance to get much outside feedback. My dad actually wasn't at all supportive either. If he'd had his way, I'd have quit before I was even competing in Juniors."

"What?" I burst out, shocked and horrified by the thought of a world without Jasper St. Pierre ever showing off his talent. "That's ridiculous."

The news stories about him had never even hinted at any conflict in his family. But then, the figure skating world usually shied away from drama when it could. The community preferred to give the impression of being as elegant in their lives as they were on the ice.

Jasper shrugged. "I'd say it's just as ridiculous that your mom tore you down. I hate to think how much we've missed seeing because you stayed out of the competitive circuit so long."

An unexpected sense of closeness settled over me. I reached out and rested my hand against his bare forearm.

A jolt of electricity shot through my nerves. Jasper's gaze darted to meet mine, and I thought I caught a flicker of answering heat there.

"I think things have worked out pretty well in the end," I said quietly. "Here I am, training with you—and Niko. I can't imagine what I'd trade to have instead of this."

A little of the flush I'd seen before colored Jasper's cheeks again. "I think it's pretty fantastic that you're finally out here pursuing your dream. And even if I act like an ass about it sometimes, I'm glad I can be a part of that."

I couldn't resist leaning a little closer and arching my eyebrows at him. My pulse thumped double-time, but even though an ache was forming between my legs, I had other things on my mind than getting busy.

At least, not that kind of busy.

"Does that mean you'll give this Dellville competition thing a try?"

Jasper's gaze slid down my body, trailing heat in its wake. I was going to melt into a very different sort of puddle if he kept looking at me like that.

He swallowed audibly but managed to stay on topic. "You really want to, huh?"

"I'd like to find out what I can do when I've got more than a couple of people watching."

His expression set into a more familiar expression of determination. He squeezed my hand—just for a second, but emphatically enough to spark another wave of heat through my body—and then pushed off toward Niko.

"Hey, Okabe! Sign us up. Those other Dellville skaters aren't going to know what hit them."

THIRTEEN

Jasper

GETTING HUNG up on some woman I hardly knew wasn't a good idea. I was supposed to be focusing on my art, not dreaming up erotic scenarios.

But as many times as I told myself that, as many pops of excitement as I squashed in my chest before heading into practice, here I was at nine o'clock at night sitting in my Mustang outside the bungalow Lou was renting, my heart thumping around like I was a preteen about to call his crush on the phone for the first time.

It was ridiculous. I was here to drop off the weights I'd said I'd lend her, nothing else.

I spent hours nearly every day around this woman. It wasn't as if seeing her for a few minutes right now was ever so thrilling.

Sure, so maybe I was a little curious to see our

unexpected punk prodigy in her home environment, but it wasn't *that* big a deal.

Apparently I'd sat around too long convincing myself of that. As I pushed open the car door, Lou came bounding out of the bungalow.

"Hey! Thanks for bringing them by. Let me help you carry them in."

The next thing I knew, she'd loped across the weedy lawn in her bare feet, her slim curves teasingly visible through her rough-hemmed tee and distressed jean shorts. She leaned through the passenger side window I'd left open to let in the cooling evening air and snatched the set of ankle weights off the seat.

I grumbled something not particularly articulate about personal space and grabbed the two pairs of dumbbells, but the truth was her audacity left me more giddy than irritated.

She always kept me on my toes, wondering what she'd do next. I should have hated it.

Instead, way too often, I found myself waiting in awed anticipation. I hated *that*.

"It's no problem," I made myself say as I hefted the jumble of weights over to her house. "I didn't realize you had so little equipment with you for training off the rink. These are extras I had lying around."

"Still, I appreciate it. Come in, come in. The place isn't much, but it's home for now."

I hadn't meant to come inside, but here I was, stepping into the warm glow from a bowl-like light fixture that looked like it'd probably been installed in the seventies.

The furniture was kind of shabby compared to my

apartment, but there was something appealing about the lived-in feel to it. I'd been inhabiting my Ikea-furnished space for three months, and it still barely looked like I'd moved in.

A hint of spice hung in the air, something rich and savory. Had she been cooking?

Was there anything she *couldn't* do?

I held up the weights awkwardly. "Where do you want these?"

"Um… I guess over in the corner next to the TV is fine. I like to get caught up on my talk shows while I'm working out."

I shot Lou a look, trying to judge if she was joking, but her hint of a smile gave nothing away.

I set the pairs of dumbbells down next to the maple TV stand and glanced around. A couple of doors stood at the far end of the living space beyond the kitchen area, presumably a bedroom and bathroom. Just past them, a shadowed flight of stairs let down to a basement.

Not a bad setup, really. It was bigger than my apartment, and a hell of a lot more private, with her own big yard and everything.

I rubbed the back of my neck, feeling twice as awkward now that I had nothing to hold on to. "Nice place you've got here."

"Oh, whatever." Her hands rested squarely upon those grabbable hips. "Leave my poor house alone. It's the best place I could find on short notice."

Did she really think I was being sarcastic?

I'd have protested, but I wasn't sure I wanted to

encourage a friendlier vibe… and her last couple of words had caught my attention more.

"Short notice? You just out of the blue decided to crash into Hobb Creek?"

Something flickered in Lou's gaze, the trace of a smile vanishing before she plastered one that looked a little stiffer on her face. "That's about the size of it. Obviously I made the right choice, huh?"

"Seems like it," I had to admit. "You really came all the way up from the States just because you saw a few positive comments about the rink?"

She shrugged. "It just sounded like a nice place. And I wanted somewhere as different as possible from big city life."

There had to be more to it than that for her to have rushed here with so little preparation. Her answers were awfully vague.

I caught another question before the itch of curiosity propelled it from my throat. I wasn't here to badger her for her life story. Even if I *was* awfully curious now.

I couldn't really blame her for being hesitant to open up to me, could I? I'd spent more time grumbling at her than having a real conversation.

Could anyone blame me for having my doubts? She *had* crashed into town—and into my life. How the hell was I supposed to just accept that?

But the last couple of practices, it was like we'd found a common wavelength. I'd found myself not just fending off sparks of excitement when I reached the rink each day, but craving her company after she left at the end.

It felt… dangerous, how much I was starting to enjoy our partnership. I'd never imagined skating pairs before.

How could it work this well?

"Well," I started, figuring she probably wanted me out of her hair, but Lou chucked the ankle weights next to the dumbbells and made a beeline for the kitchen.

"You want something to drink? I shouldn't make you come all the way out here and forget how to be a good hostess."

My lips twitched into a crooked grin. "It was only a three-minute drive."

She shook her head. "I always forget how small this place is. But hey, the offer still stands. I think we deserve at least a beer after all the work we've been putting in."

Obviously she'd spent all of her time in the bigger city she'd mentioned. Where exactly had she come from?

I swallowed that question too and shrugged. "Yeah, okay. A beer would be great."

It'd have been pretty rude for me to totally shut down her offer, right? Accepting had nothing to do with not actually wanting to leave her presence.

I sank down onto the sofa, stretching my legs out on a diagonal so I could get more comfortable on the narrow cushions.

Lou appeared at the other end a moment later, clutching a bottle in each hand. "I changed my mind. Or, well, I forgot I don't have any beer. How's hard cider instead?"

How was she so charming even looking embarrassed over the slip?

I reached out. "Cider's even better."

She passed mine over and plopped down on the other end of the sofa without any hint of self-consciousness. From what I'd gathered, she'd only been living here for a few weeks, but she'd gotten comfortable fast.

A set of silver rings, a little thicker than I saw most women wearing, decorated the fingers of her right hand. I nodded to them. "Gotta ramp up the punk style when you're off the rink?"

Lou wiggled her slim fingers. "I don't think you'd appreciate it if I had these on while we *are* on the rink. I just like them. They make me feel tough."

She let out a laugh and fit her lips around the neck of the cider to throw back a gulp with an enthusiasm that made my dick twitch. I jerked my gaze away and took a sip of my own cider.

She had good taste. It was tart and crisp but still with a faint sweetness.

"Where'd you get these?" I asked.

Lou waved toward the front door. "Oh, there's a local brewery about a half hour outside of town that I stumbled on when I was cruising around on one of our days off. Couldn't help going in for a little taste test."

I raised my eyebrows. "Going totally local, huh?"

She laughed. "Might as well while I'm here. Especially when the locals have good stuff."

"Yeah. It's not a bad town at all, tiny as it is. I guess wherever you're from had a pretty different vibe."

I was kind of fishing for more information about her past, but Lou didn't take the bait. She leaned back against the sofa, a soft smile playing with her lips that made her look even prettier than usual, which was saying something.

"It really is a great town. A lot of people have been welcoming, and the people who aren't have kept it to themselves. Well—no, that doesn't count."

I studied her. "What doesn't?"

She waggled her bottle at me. "Nothing important. I thought I might get bored someplace this small, but I haven't really at all."

"Same," I admitted. "But then, Niko keeps us so busy there isn't a whole lot of time to get bored."

Another laugh tumbled from Lou's mouth. "That's the truth. So he was just as much of a slave-driver before I showed up?"

"Oh, yeah." I paused, feeling I owed the guy who'd flown halfway around the world to drag me out of my slump better than that. "A very nice slave-driver, though."

"The most cheerful slave-driver ever."

I couldn't restrain a chuckle. "Yep, that's him."

"He does know what he's talking about," Lou said. "I never would have thought of trying pairs if he hadn't brought it up."

"He's really very good at the whole coaching thing. I can't believe he's never done it professionally before." I paused, abruptly embarrassed both to have said that out loud and that I'd never given Niko the compliment to his face.

"He obviously thought you were pretty special, coming all the way over here to train you."

"Yeah."

The chaotic emotions her comment stirred up might have shown on my face. As I took another swig of my cider, Lou clapped her hands together and changed the subject.

"So, we're going to be competing. When do we get to pick out costumes?"

Her enthusiasm brought back my smile. "Normally I don't think about costumes until at least the basics of the routine are sorted out. So I can make sure it all fits together. But, ah, I wouldn't generally be picking them out."

The second the words had left my mouth, I kicked myself. I never talked about this part of my approach.

But Lou was eyeing me with nothing but eager curiosity. "What do you mean?"

I'd put it out there now. She was going to find out soon enough anyway, wasn't she?

I drained the last of the cider and set the bottle on the coffee table, nearly falling off the narrow cushion as I did. This sofa was not made for someone my size.

"I sew them myself. The costumes. I could never find anything that fit my vision perfectly off the rack, so I just… taught myself."

Lou's eyes widened. "Holy shit. No kidding? That's amazing. I never would have guessed—you obviously taught yourself well."

"I'm glad you think so."

"Why don't the reporters ever talk about that? It's such a cool part of your story."

I ducked my head. "I don't usually bring it up. Always assumed people would think it was more weird than cool, I guess. It's just something that kind of happened."

Lou snorted. "I could almost say that about skating in

general for me. Went to see one of those stars on ice shows when I was five years old, begged my mom for a pair of skates and lessons, and the dream just kept getting bigger all on its own."

A momentary melancholy crossed her face, and my stomach clenched at the memory of her comments about her unsupportive mom. Not all of her associations with her skating career were happy ones.

"You want to talk about uncool," she added, springing up. "You should see—"

She darted over to where her equipment bag was resting by the wall and dug into one of the side pockets. Then she sank down onto the sofa—closer this time, just a few inches away from where I was leaning my arm across the back.

My awareness of her nearness tingled over my skin, but I pulled my attention to the scrap of fabric clutched in her hands.

"One of the laces from my very first pair of skates," she said, stroking her thumb over the fraying strip of woven material. "I like to have it with me to remind me of how far I've come, even when it didn't seem like I'd come anywhere near far enough. My good luck charm."

She grinned at me, but I hadn't missed the dash of pain in her statement. As hard as it was for me to wrap my head around it, this woman hadn't believed she was good enough for an awfully long time.

My voice dropped lower of its own accord. Somehow my hand ended up coming to rest on her shoulder with a tentative graze of my fingertips.

"Having seen you skate, I find it hard to imagine there's any limit on how far you'll take it."

Lou met my gaze, her dark eyes shimmering with enough emotion to flood me with heat. "And here I thought that to you I was just a punk who barged in on your practice time."

The heat rose to my face at that remark. God, I really had been a prick to her, hadn't I?

"That's just… me," I muttered. "I don't do people very well."

The light dancing in Lou's eyes turned sly. She teased her fingers over my own shoulder, watching my reaction. "Hmm. I'd like to believe you just haven't had enough experience with the right people. But we can keep working on that."

My throat had gotten abruptly rough. "On the ice?"

"Or maybe…"

She set the old lace down on the coffee table and rose up onto her knees on the sofa. Just the right height to touch my cheek and lower her mouth to mine.

The press of her lips sent a shock of total bliss straight through my body. I'd wanted this so much, but I'd tried to ignore that desire so determinedly that having it made real left my mind reeling.

My hands rose of their own accord, delving into her silky waves. Lou tussled my hair in turn, drawing sparks over my scalp with her fingertips.

She deepened the kiss with a flick of her tongue across my lips, and I parted them to welcome her in. My tongue swept over hers, tangling them together in a very different sort of partnership than we'd attempted before.

One kiss flowed into another. My cock rose behind my jeans, which were becoming uncomfortably tight as it hardened.

Our breaths mingled, and I claimed her mouth even more avidly than before. What was it about this woman that I wanted to meld her right into me?

One of my hands slid down her side to her hip. Lou took that as a cue to scoot closer, her knees coming to rest against my thigh.

My cock stiffened even more, and my fingers curled against the frayed fabric of her jeans. I adjusted them as if to tug her right onto my lap, but something about the impulse made me hesitate.

Desire clanged through me. My pulse was racing, my skin burning up. She was driving me crazy, and we hadn't done anything more than kiss yet.

This was dangerous.

Before I could catch my reaction, I jerked away from her. My hip banged into the arm of the sofa.

Lou stared at me, her own face flushed, her lips deliciously swollen. Fucking hell, how could I be throwing away this moment?

The same question seemed to be running through her mind. "Is something wrong?"

I fumbled for an answer. "I—I'm just not sure this is a good idea."

She cocked her head, knitting her brow. When she sucked her lower lip under her teeth to worry on it, I just about short-circuited and yanked her back into my arms after all.

"Do you think getting together like this would be bad for our skating partnership?" she ventured.

There—that was an excuse that made sense. A hell of a lot more sense than *I like you too fucking much.*

But I found I couldn't outright lie. My mouth opened and closed and opened again.

"I guess having that kind of physical connection might actually help us work better together. But the emotions that could come with it—that can get messy."

The glint of mischief came back into Lou's eyes. "Oh, then there's an easy solution to that. We'll just have to avoid falling in love, and it'll be no big deal."

"Right," I said, my throat suddenly hoarse. "I should have thought of that. No big deal."

Other than the fact that I had the sneaking suspicion I was already falling for her, hard.

Lou stroked her fingers along my jaw with a heady shiver of sensation that made it really difficult for me to care about my reservations.

I could keep myself detached, right? I'd managed to navigate training with Niko all this time.

And God, did I want this woman.

But Lou hesitated, gazing at me. All at once, she looked oddly shy.

"I should probably tell you before anything else happens between us—Niko and I have been getting pretty close too. He knows I wasn't planning on being exclusive. I don't want you to get the wrong idea about what I *can* offer."

Even as a jolt of jealousy hit me, I found I wasn't

actually surprised. Not after seeing the two of them interacting at the rink.

All the shared laughter and the little touches came back to me. My gut twisted.

He'd gone after her—or she'd turned to him first—

What was I even bothered about? It wasn't as if I'd even been making overtures of friendship with either of them.

And I didn't really want to look too closely at the convoluted threads that jealousy split into.

Being with Lou like this felt good. Better than I'd felt off the ice in ages.

Why shouldn't I enjoy it while it lasted? For once in my life, surely I deserved a moment when I wasn't taking everything so damned seriously?

"That's totally fine," I said, with only a tiny strain I smoothed out of my voice. "No commitments. Just having fun."

Lou beamed at me. "I can do that."

I shifted forward, setting my hand on her waist. I'd been the one to pull away, so I'd better make it one hundred percent clear how much I wanted her after all.

"What are we waiting for, then?"

I tugged her onto my lap, and she straddled me as if there was no place she'd rather be. As my hands dove back into her hair, her mouth slammed down on mine.

My eyes closed. I wanted to relish this moment as much as I could, soak up as much as she allowed me. A shudder ran down the length of my spine, jolting me forward into her embrace.

Her hands splayed across my chest, running over my

pecs and then down to my abs. Heat flared everywhere they touched.

I kissed her harder, and her teeth grazed my lower lip to electrifying effect. She slid her fingers right down to the hem of my shirt and then up underneath, tracing the planes of my muscles over my bare skin now.

Fuck, she was sex incarnate. I tore one hand out of her hair to match her explorations, dying to feel all of her beneath my fingers.

When I cupped her breast through her shirt, an encouraging gasp passed from her mouth into mine. It egged me on.

I stroked my palm back and forth over that delectable mound, and the gasp transformed into a series of short whimpers.

Lou started to rock on my lap. At the brush of her groin against mine, it was a wonder my erection didn't explode right out of my jeans.

I grabbed her hip and yanked her flush against me. A groan reverberated from my chest at the torturous contact.

While she ground against me as fervently as her mouth seared into mine, I tucked my hand under her shirt and traced the soft skin of her torso up to her bra. With a tug, I dislodged the cup from the swell of her breast, giving me full access.

Lou let loose a breathy moan as I tweaked her pert nipple. She leaned in, her position urging me to twist sideways on the sofa. My head bumped against the hard arm, but I didn't give a fuck about the minor pain when I had this woman writhing on top of me.

Our mouths crashed together again and again. I hiked

her shirt higher and massaged both her breasts at the same time.

Lou rode me with little bucks of her hips, turning my cock hard as steel. I needed to feel *all* of her. I needed her riding me for real.

I drew my hand down to the fly of her shorts, adjusting my position to get the right angle—and realized a second too late that I'd misjudged the narrow sofa. My broad shoulder veered right over the edge of the cushion, and gravity took over.

The next thing I knew, we were tumbling onto the floor with a bone-jarring thud. We'd rolled as we fell, and I caught myself before I crushed Lou under my full weight.

Lou blinked up at me now braced over her, and her mouth twitched with the start of a giggle. We'd both have burst out laughing a moment later if footsteps hadn't thundered up from the basement at the same moment.

A huge man burst into the living room, his dark face hardened with rage. "Get the fuck off her, *now!*"

FOURTEEN

Luciana

THIS WAS a complete and total nightmare.

As Rafael charged at Jasper, looking like he planned to hurl him off me and straight through a wall, Jasper scrambled to the side. I leapt up, my body still flushed from the *very* enjoyable interlude my bodyguard had just interrupted.

Rafael raised his fist as if to slam it straight into my skating partner's gorgeous face, and I jumped between them with my arms spread wide.

"Stop it!"

Thank all that was holy for Rafael's swift protective reflexes. He didn't want to pummel *me*.

He jerked himself backward, dropping his fist. But his temper hadn't totally flamed out.

"That fucking asshole tried to—"

"It's fine," I broke in with the mafia princess tone I only brought out for special occasions. "We were messing around on the sofa, and we slipped off by accident. I'm totally okay. I *told* you I was having Jasper come over."

The furor in Rafael's dark eyes simmered down. He looked from me to Jasper, who was standing there tensed like he wasn't sure if he should be running for his life, and back again.

"I didn't know I'd find him tackling you to the floor," he growled.

I set my hands on my hips. "It. Was. An. Accident." One we could have recovered from to go on to much more fun if Mr. Overprotective here hadn't stormed into the room like a maniac. "And it was at least as much my fault as Jasper's. So calm the fuck down and go back to whatever you were doing before you started your volcano impression."

Rafael took a step to the side, not exactly retreating. His eyes narrowed as he studied Jasper, and the bulging muscles along his shoulders flexed with subtle menace.

Oh, for fuck's sake.

I spun toward Jasper, groping for a way to salvage this mess. "I'm sorry. Just a misunderstanding. Rafael's a friend of the family—he came along to watch out for me—he's just doing it *very badly* at the moment."

Rafael let out a grunt just shy of a growl.

Jasper's stance went even more rigid. He was nearly as tall as the other man, and brawny enough to have made me drool on more than one occasion I'd never admit to, but even to him, Rafael's massive frame and obvious hostility would have been intimidating. It wasn't as if the figure skater would ever have found himself in a gang brawl.

I turned back to my bodyguard. "Would you go back downstairs? We're both okay, and we were kind of in the middle of something."

I made those words as pointed as I could, and Rafael finally eased backward. But it was too little, too late.

Jasper was backing up too, edging toward the door. His wary gaze darted between me and Rafael. "Obviously you have a lot going on. I'd better head home. Gotta rest up before practice and all."

I wasn't going to argue with him to stay. Things had gotten way too awkward already.

"I'm really sorry," I said. "Stupid sofa."

I gave it a playful kick for good measure, trying to lighten the moment, but it didn't work. Maybe because Rafael hadn't quite reined in his glower.

Jasper rubbed his neck like he often seemed to do when he was uneasy and bobbed his head in acknowledgment. "No big deal. I'll see you at the arena tomorrow."

Then he was ducking out the doorway like he couldn't get to his car fast enough.

The door thudded shut in his wake. Rafael paused by the top of the basement stairs like he was waiting to make sure the guy wasn't going to sneak back in the second he lowered his guard.

Like there was any chance of Jasper *wanting* to return after the scare he'd just had.

Ugh. Was there any chance he'd forget all this in a day

or two, and we could pick up where we'd left off without it being an issue?

Somehow I found that hard to believe.

The car's engine rumbled and faded as Jasper drove away. Rafael's shoulders came the rest of the way down, and he moved to head back downstairs like he hadn't just completely ruined my night.

A fresh wave of frustration crackled through me. "Where do you think you're going?"

He glanced back at me without a trace of remorse in his expression. His tone was back to its usual even deadpan.

"You told me to go downstairs. Just following orders."

Oh, he was going to play it that way, was he? I marched a couple of steps closer, glaring at him.

"I asked you to get going *before* the guy I was hoping to hook up with took off. You terrorized him. What the hell were you thinking?"

Rafael's mouth tightened into a frown. "I was thinking that I heard a bang and rushed upstairs to find you pinned to the floor under some guy twice your size who I'd never seen before. How could I have known he wasn't attacking you?"

I rolled my eyes. "I wasn't *pinned*, and you could have waited two seconds to see if I was actually in any danger. I have a mouth—I'd have yelled for help if I needed it. Hell, I'd have been kneeing him in the balls if I'd objected to what was going on."

"Two seconds could make the difference between life and death. That's not a chance I'm willing to take."

"Maybe with a fucking assassin. He's a figure skater, not a professional criminal. Christ, Rafael."

Rafael's frown deepened. "You trust these guys too much. Just because they're skaters and you watched them on TV or whatever doesn't mean they couldn't have bad intentions."

I threw my hands in the air. "You sound more like a mom than my actual mom ever did. I'm a big girl. Fully grown, officially an adult. And I've been training with them for weeks now, so yeah, I do know them enough to trust them not to rape me. But even if I didn't, *you* know I can look after myself better than any woman these guys have ever been with. You expect me to believe you honestly couldn't tell I wasn't fighting for my life?"

"I didn't have a whole lot of time to analyze the situation."

"Don't give me that bullshit," I snapped. "Even after I told you it was fine, you kept staring him down like you were trying to punch him with your goddamn eyes."

A flicker of discomfort crossed Rafael's face. He knew I was right—he knew he'd gone too far.

Seeing it only fueled my anger. "You got all grouchy when I told you he was coming by, just like you did when I mentioned I slept with Niko. You never wanted him here to begin with."

"I'm trying to protect you—"

"You're trying to stop me from having any kind of private life at all!"

Rafael shut his mouth and turned that glower of his on me. It wasn't fair that it could heat me up inside all over again even while I was so pissed off at him.

But that had always been the problem. He could get me hot and bothered, but he'd never let me act on the desire.

The words kept tumbling out, propelled by not just tonight's annoyance but years of pent-up frustration.

"You've decided you don't want me even though I pulled out all the stops to show you I was interested, and that's fine. I backed off. I'm not standing around mooning over you. But you don't get to turn me down and then block me from having fun with every other guy in the world too. You made it clear that it's none of your fucking business."

Rafael blinked at me, his stance stiffening. His frown had twisted into something vaguely sickly looking.

"Lou—"

I flicked my hand toward him. "I don't want to hear it. You won tonight—I didn't get to fuck a very hot guy who's actually interested in me. But if you're going to have a problem with me hooking up with whoever I damn well want, you can go back to Austin."

"Don't be ridiculous. You can't—"

"I can get by on my own just fine. *You* insisted on coming with me—I didn't ask you to. I left home so that I didn't have to live my life under someone else's thumb, and I'm not going to let you bully me into doing things your way now."

Rafael winced. He lowered his head, his expression still grim.

"I'm sorry," he said. "I shouldn't have interfered. I'd never try to take away your freedom. Of course you know what you're doing. I won't barge in like that again unless I'm sure you need me."

They were all the right words, but I couldn't hear much actual remorse in his voice. He sounded like he was speaking by rote, going through the motions of an apology when he didn't actually regret what he'd done one bit.

I gritted my teeth, because there wasn't anything specific I could call him on—and then he'd already spun on his heel and started trudging down to his basement room, ending the conversation completely.

For a minute or two, I stood there, my breath rushing in and out of me as I gathered my composure. When my nerves felt a little steadier, I sat down on the sofa hard, trying not to think about the delight Jasper had sparked in my body there less than half an hour ago.

Thoughts of the man downstairs loomed too much at the forefront of my mind.

Rafael and I had argued before, of course. I couldn't count how many spats we'd had when I'd chafed against his protective nature through my teens.

But since I'd passed my eighteenth birthday, he'd eased off on the domineering attitude, and we hadn't *really* clashed that whole time.

Until now. And this felt different from any argument we'd ever had before.

It didn't matter that he didn't want to jump in the sack with me. Rafael was the one constant presence in my life, the one person I'd always been able to count on. When he'd thrown in his lot with me over my mom, I'd thought that meant the trust between us ran as deep as could be.

But after the way he'd acted tonight, the way he'd

defied me for no reason other than whatever petty grievances had provoked his hostility… I wasn't so sure after all.

Was he my rock, or a stone I'd have to stumble over on my way to claiming my freedom?

I didn't want to ask those questions. I wanted to believe this was just a temporary tiff.

But as I flicked on the TV to try to distract myself, I couldn't shake the sinking sensation creeping through my gut.

FIFTEEN

Luciana

SOMETIME BETWEEN LAST night's encounter and this afternoon's practice, Jasper had reverted back to the same prickly grouch that I'd started to know so well.

"Let's try that new lift again," Niko called from the sidelines. "I think you almost had it this time!"

Jasper grumbled something about not having it the last thousand times but got back into position anyway. My heart raced as his hand settled on my hip, the other grasping my hand. Then I was soaring up into the air.

For a moment, we were perfectly balanced.

But only for a moment.

As we whirled around, Jasper's arms wobbled. And over his head, so did I.

"Shit," I said, trying my best to right myself, and added an extra *Shitshitshit!* in my head for good measure.

His arms had shifted, throwing off my fragile balance. There wasn't much I could do from above.

He let out a few curses of his own as he attempted to adjust himself, but it was too late. The damage was done. I was teetering over.

I braced myself to fall in the least painful way, instincts honed by years of collisions with the ice, but Jasper managed to catch me against his chest before I hit the ground. He quickly set me on my feet, his face flushed and his eyes dark with frustration.

"That was my fault," he admitted with a grimace. "I fucked up. I'm sorry."

"It's okay. These things happen." I straightened up and smoothed my tee shirt. "You made sure I didn't eat ice too badly. No harm done."

The truth was that we both knew what was eating *him*. Obviously his visit to my house last night had thrown our dynamic out of kilter—whether because we'd made out or because of Rafael barging in or both, I couldn't tell.

I'd tried to bring it up at the start of practice and again during our snack break, but he'd brushed off my attempts both times. The second occasion, he'd taken off to the other end of the rink rather than talk to me.

So yeah. Things were definitely *not* okay, but I had no idea how to fix them.

When we skated back around toward Niko, he was watching us with a thoughtful expression. Had he guessed that something had gone down between us outside of practice?

Lord help me, had Jasper told him about it?

No, I was pretty sure I was safe from that

embarrassment. When Jasper clammed up, you'd need a jackhammer to force him open.

But our coach had clearly caught on that something wasn't quite clicking between us. He motioned toward the stands.

"It's time to wrap it up for the day. You guys have been really putting your all in. Don't skimp on your cool-down stretches now!"

Jasper didn't argue that we should keep at it a little longer, but then, maybe he was just grateful not to have to be around me much longer today.

My heart sank. Was he really that pissed off with me for whatever reason, or was something else behind his renewed shitty mood?

We skated off in separate directions to loosen our muscles. I could feel Niko's gaze from the center of the rink, shifting between Jasper and me.

Maybe we needed some more time off the ice and away from each other. If Jasper and I were going to get the hang of the short routine Niko was choreographing for us even well enough to pass the qualifying round, then we had to get our heads straight.

And it seemed like being around me was having the opposite effect on my partner.

I stretched out my aching muscles, doing my best not to steal peeks at Jasper's muscles rippling beneath his own tee. Getting caught ogling him would only make this whole situation twice as embarrassing.

As I cooled down with slow glides across the rink, the chill of the arena's air seeped into my skin. Rubbing my arms, I cruised over to my bag in the stands to grab my hoodie.

I was just stepping off the ice, my gaze meandering across the stands, when a splotch of blood red caught my attention up near the top of the rows of seats.

My heart lurched, a colder sweat breaking over my skin. An image of Coach Balakin's bloody body flashed behind my eyes.

I grasped the boards, drawing in a shaky breath against the rush of horror.

It was fine. Just something red attached to the door— hanging there by the handle.

I had to get a grip on myself before I started freaking out all over the place every time I saw a freaking *color* at a rink.

Still, I couldn't help approaching the door cautiously, swaying a little on the skates I'd hastily hooked the guards onto. I didn't remember seeing anything dangling off the door before.

When I got close enough to squint through the shadows, I stopped in my tracks, my pulse hiccupping all over again.

Okay, I definitely would have remembered seeing that.

A gauzy red scarf was tied around the door handle— that was what had caught my attention. But one end of it wrapped around the neck of a fashion doll who hung there as if from a noose.

The doll's dark brown hair was wrapped in a ponytail. She'd been decked out in black leggings and a muscle tee —workout clothes.

Was that... supposed to represent *me*?

My stomach plummeted to the floor.

I yanked the scarf off the handle and examined the doll from front to back. Her perfect plastic smile glimmered, but her eyes had been Xed out.

As if to indicate she was dead.

Goosebumps quivered up and down my arms. I spun around, scanning the stands.

Who the hell had left this here? I hadn't noticed anyone coming in or out.

They must have slipped it on so stealthily even Rafael hadn't caught on, wherever he was lurking in the dark alcoves, because there was no way my bodyguard would have left this sick display for me to find on my own.

Niko had gone over to talk to Jasper in a low voice I couldn't make out. Neither of them was paying any attention to me.

My hand tightened around the doll. This incident had happened because of me—I didn't want to drag them into the mess if I didn't have to.

Balling the plastic figure in the fabric of the scarf, I shoved open the door and marched out into the hall. The space was empty, only a single voice carrying from the reception area up front.

"Yeah, we'll have that all set up for you on the sixteenth."

I hustled over in the hopes that I might catch the culprit, but all I found was the arena manager, Olive, leaning over the reception desk with her back to the entryway. She was scrawling something on a scrap of paper in the jumble of objects there that she'd somehow pull into a cohesive schedule.

"Perfect," she said, in that same saccharine sweet customer service voice. "We'll see you then. Uh-huh. Okay, g'bye."

She set the reception phone down, tapping her pen with her veiny hand, and startled a bit when she glanced up and noticed me.

"Oh, Lou," she said, relaxing immediately. Her gaze skimmed over me, taking in the skates I was still wearing and my lack of equipment bag. "Can I do anything for you?"

I didn't really want to wave the doll in front of her either. What would some small-town local make of ominous threats?

She'd either freak out or think I was crazy. Or maybe both.

"Oh, I just wondered if you've seen anyone come in while we were training. I thought I spotted someone by the door a little while ago, but I was so focused on the routine I couldn't pay attention, and then they were gone."

Olive frowned. "I'm sorry, dear. I only got in about fifteen minutes ago. I haven't seen anyone since then, but maybe they were already gone. Did they disturb you?"

Yeah, disturbing was definitely the word for it. But I plastered a smile on my face, since there was nothing the manager could do for me anyway.

"Oh, no, I was just curious. Thanks all the same!"

I hustled back to the rink and hurried down the stairs, watching Niko and Jasper from the corner of my vision. If I didn't want any strange looks and uneasy questions, I had to get my finding out of sight before the men came this way.

My heart didn't stop thudding double-speed until I'd tucked the bundle of gauzy fabric into the bottom of my equipment bag. My nerves were still twitching with apprehension as I leaned over to finish my cool down with a few sitting stretches.

Niko joined me a minute later, his head cocked. "You went out for a minute. What's up?"

I shrugged like it was no big deal, willing away the sour taste in my mouth. "Nothing, just thought I saw someone I knew by the door. My mistake."

His face relaxed, so I must have lied well enough. "If Jasper's attitude today has been getting to you—I know he can be kind of—"

"It's fine," I broke in. "Really. I know what he's like, and we all have off days." I stretched my arms over my head and forced another smile. "I for one am looking forward to chilling out and a big dinner."

Niko chuckled and went to grab his own bag. My gut twisted with the lies.

What could I tell them? That I might have brought down the wrath of a bunch of criminals not just on me but on my skating colleagues too?

Who else could have left this childish threat, after all? It would be just like those asshole wannabe gangsters.

I had no idea how they might have figured out that I was the one who'd messed with their cars on two occasions now. No one had spotted me so far, and I'd been wearing my ski mask both times.

Maybe they had no idea I was connected to their vehicular troubles. Maybe they'd just noticed there was a new chica in town and decided to haze me in their own sick way.

Jasper and Niko weren't equipped to deal with that kind of problem. But me—I could take them all down without breaking a sweat if I let myself go full Deadly Rose.

Rage replaced the queasy feeling in my stomach.

If these asshats thought they could scare me out of this town — *my new home* — then they had another thing coming. They were small fry, barely even a legitimate gang.

I'd ordered around squads larger than them as a fucking teenager. Mom's empire stretched around the globe.

They had no fucking idea who they'd just pissed off.

Niko headed up the stairs with a cheery wave. Jasper trudged by with significantly less enthusiasm. I chucked off my skates and gave the blades a brisk wipe before shoving my feet into my sneakers, hopped up on a combination of nervous and furious adrenaline.

My equipment bag weighed heavy on my shoulders, but I'd gotten used to making the walk to the bungalow rather than driving. All part of my endurance training.

And today it gave me a chance to burn off a little of my jangling unease while my gaze roved over the streets and my mind spun through the possibilities.

Buoyant music drifted through the door to the hair salon. The staff at my favorite café were busy stringing the patio railing with a garland of autumn leaves that the local trees were only just starting to match.

It wasn't right that a place this peaceful and happy had such a dark cloud looming over it.

And now that cloud was coming for me.

I picked up my pace as I headed into the quieter residential streets. The back of my neck prickled as the memory of finding the doll floated up through my mind.

But no one said a word to me until Rafael's brisk footsteps caught up with me just as the bungalow came into sight up ahead. Like usual, he preferred not to show himself until it was inevitable.

"Everything okay?" he asked in his usual low, even tone. "You seem a little more tense than usual."

He really hadn't noticed the gross gift that'd been left for me, then—or enough about my discovery of it to realize what had happened. Wherever he'd been watching from, it mustn't have given him a view of the door. His main priority was keeping an eye on me and the area around the ice, after all.

I opened my mouth automatically, ready to tell him the whole story… and then closed it again.

Did I really want to admit that my crusade against the shithead gangsters might have come back to haunt me? That one way or another, they'd managed to get under my skin, however slightly?

After the way he'd reacted to Jasper last night, I suddenly wasn't convinced I could expect him to handle this new threat with a cool head.

What if he demanded that we leave town immediately? What if he decided this whole running away thing had been a stupid idea and dragged me home?

I knew how to fight, but I wasn't kidding myself to think that I could overpower Rafael if he got it in his head that he knew what was best for me.

"We're having a little trouble with the routine Niko's choreographing for us," I said instead. "I don't like that we're struggling."

If Rafael made any connection between our possible difficulties and his intrusion last night, he didn't show it. He just nodded.

"Go easy on yourself for once. You work your ass off constantly."

He pushed a little ahead of me to open the bungalow door and hold it open, like I really was some kind of princess.

I strode inside, resolve hardening in my chest. Whatever was going on with those dipshits, I was going to handle it. My way, on my terms.

They wanted to play games? They'd poked the wrong tiger.

And now they were about to see just how vindictive this little ice princess could get.

SIXTEEN

Luciana

THE MOMENT that my phone alarm started quietly vibrating next to my ear, my eyes snapped open and I got to work.

Earlier in the day, I'd shoved some goodies I'd bought into a black backpack. Now, I slung it over my shoulder and took one look at myself in the mirror.

With my long-sleeved black shirt and matching pants, I looked like I was about to go burglarize half the neighborhood. Not quite what I had in mind tonight, but the less I was noticed, the better.

I patted the bag, making sure that everything was there.

One, two, three bottles of engine oil.

One bag of steel wool.

One pack of 9-volt batteries.

One extra-long screwdriver.

One black ski mask.

That was all I needed to fuck up a few cars in a particularly terrifying way.

Before I'd only been trying to make the wannabe gangsters annoyed. Now I wanted them to know that if I wanted to, I could blow them to bits.

They'd threatened me. Turnabout was fair play.

That thought didn't loosen the knot in my stomach as I slunk out of the house. I shut the door with the faintest click and paused with my ears pricked.

No sound from inside. Rafael was still fast asleep.

Good.

I darted across the lawn and into the streets of Hobb Creek. Years of training let my feet fall softly on the concrete sidewalks.

But it wasn't getting caught that I was most twisted up about. It was the mission *I* was planning on carrying out.

I'd told myself I was done with the mafia princess life. I wasn't going to let myself become what Mom had tried to mold me into.

What was I going to do if this threat wasn't enough to run these assholes out of town? If they were too stubborn or too stupid to realize they were outclassed?

I didn't want to *kill* anyone. That much I was sure of. Lou, semi-professional figure skater, was not a fucking murderer. At least, not when I had a choice in the matter.

Lord, how would Niko or Jasper look at me if they had any idea what I'd already had to do under my mother's orders?

That wasn't me. I hadn't wanted to do any of it then, and I wasn't going to sink to the same depths now.

There had to be a way to get the pricks out of here without resorting to full out war, and I was smart enough to figure it out.

If I was lucky, my current gambit might even do the trick all on its own.

The whole town was silent and dark except for the pools of light cast by the periodic streetlamps. I avoided those, making a quick dash whenever I had to cross a street.

The last thing I needed was for any of the locals to notice me skulking around and think I was the real problem here. Not that it seemed like them calling the police about a suspicious character would accomplish anything, good or bad, regardless.

When I came up on the end of the last street before the sprawl of the warehouses and their parking lots, I pulled out my ski mask and tugged it over my head. Thankfully it was cool enough at night these days that the layer of cloth actually brought a welcome warmth.

I scanned the parking lot outside the gang's storage building in the hazy glow of the security lamps. The windows on the hideout were dark, but a couple of figures were standing near the main entrance, passing a cigarette or a joint back and forth while they played a grating rock song from a Bluetooth speaker propped on a window ledge.

The idiots had finally figured out a little security was in order. Well, I'd expected as much.

It made my job harder, but not impossible. Too bad

for them the bozos hadn't also figured out that blasting music to keep themselves entertained also meant it'd be that much harder to hear an intruder.

I glanced up and down the cross-street to make sure no headlights were anywhere inside and then hunkered down into an army crawl position. Gritting my teeth at the discomfort of the awkward stance, I slithered across the road and over to the nearest ideal target.

A pickup truck, its hood facing away from the would-be guards. Perfect.

I fished out my screwdriver and wiggled it along the edge of the hood, feeling for the latch. The screeching music drowned out the faint scraping sounds of the tool.

There it was. Slide, click, and nudge that sucker up.

Just a few inches, since I didn't want my project to be noticeable if the guards happened to glance this way. Now, the motor oil.

I unscrewed the cap and extended my arm under the hood to slosh the viscous liquid all across the engine area.

Next I balanced one of the batteries in the perfect nook and tucked a thin but wide swath of steel wool right under it. Then I yanked the bottle of oil back and eased the hood into place.

My heart was thumping hard, but a grin stretched across my face. Perfect.

I'd learned this trick from one of the guys who worked under my mom. He'd been incredibly proud of the revenge trick he'd played on a guy who'd hit on his girlfriend, and he'd shown me all the steps, "Just in case you ever need to teach a guy a lesson yourself, little Rose."

The moment one of these goons turned the ignition,

the vibration would send the battery tumbling into the steel wool for an instant spark, and the front of the car would go up in the prettiest bonfire in all of Ontario. The engine wouldn't outright explode, because this wasn't a movie, but I'd bet the dipshits would throw themselves across the parking lot in terror, afraid that it would.

And they'd be left wondering just how much worse it could get if they insisted on continuing to do "business" around here.

A few more cars were parked close enough together that I could scurry from one to another without coming into the guards' line of sight. I set up my trap another three times and then paused to scan my surroundings, the cloying smell of the motor oil itching in my nose.

My gaze snagged on a massive white shape near the far end of the lot, close to the building's loading area. My pulse skipped a beat.

A delivery truck. That would be the perfect finishing touch for my don't-fuck-with-me demonstration. I wouldn't just be freaking them out but screwing up their plans for whatever they'd meant to transport in it.

But there were a few open stretches between my current position, the two cars at that end of the parking lot, and my ultimate goal. I worried at my lower lip, debating the risk.

If the guards spotted me, I could just run for it, but they might check the vehicles and find my traps before they could go off properly.

On the other hand, I *really* wanted to go for maximum impact here. The sooner the jerks decided it wasn't worth sticking around Hobb Creek, the better.

As I considered the odds, the guards pretty much made my decision for me. One of them started tapping at his phone, trying to find whatever song he wanted to bring up next and swearing at the device, and the other guy lowered his head to peer at the screen too.

They were both distracted. How could I not take this chance?

Sucking in a breath, I dashed for the first of the two cars, keeping low to the ground and softening my footsteps as much as I could. I froze there, listening.

The idiot was still muttering curse words while the current song blared on. I'd made it.

The distance to the second car was a little longer. I didn't let myself second-guess my choices but just ran for it.

I dropped down behind the car just as the song changed.

"There!" the guy said with a sharp laugh. "Fucking piece of junk."

They fell back into their mumbled conversation. I peeked around the car and saw them vaguely eyeing the lot around them again.

Shit.

Well, I'd come this far. It was only maybe ten feet to the truck now, and this side of the lot was particularly dark.

I waited several thumps of my heart until the guards' attention appeared to be pointed away from my area, and then I threw myself into one last sprint.

As I hurtled around the side of the truck, the toe of

my sneaker caught in a dip I hadn't seen in the asphalt. With a lurch of my gut, I careened forward.

Wincing preemptively, I twisted into a roll rather than catching myself on my hands and knees like I wanted to. The pavement jarred my shoulder and ribs, but continuing the momentum of the fall dulled the sound of the impact.

I pushed myself out of the roll into a crouch, every muscle tensed.

"Did you hear something rustling around?" one guard asked the other, and my body went even more rigid.

The second guy let out a huff. "Probably another fucking raccoon. Gimme the light."

The beam of a flashlight streaked across the parking lot, rippling over the truck I was hiding behind without revealing me. The guards didn't bother leaving their post.

"No one there. Like anyone would try to mess with us when we're right here."

They guffawed, and my grin came back. That's what they thought.

I went through the steps of my trick one last time, moving even more carefully than before. This time, I sprinkled the entire last bottle of motor oil across the truck's innards before setting up the steel wool and the battery.

No one was going to drive this baby very far for a good long time. Ha.

I slunk away from the truck into the scruffy stretch of woodland between this parking lot and the warehouse farther north. When I'd put enough distance between me and the guards that my nerves started to settle and the trees completely hid me from view, I headed back into town the long way around.

As I loped through the streets, my good mood faded. My first two tricks hadn't scared the assholes off. What were the chances this one would, even if I had upped the ante?

It doesn't matter, I told myself. *As long as I keep at it, eventually I'll make their lives here so miserable they'll leave.*

As long as I did it *my* way, not my mom's, I could see this through.

When the bungalow came into view up ahead, I slowed my pace, watching for any sign that Rafael was up and patrolling after noticing my disappearance. The house looked perfectly still.

I circled around back and stashed my bag with the empty motor oil bottles in the dusty tool shed it looked like no one had used in years. Then I squirmed in my shirt to turn it right-side out again, so the faded neon graphic on the chest showed.

Just a perfectly normal set of lounge clothes. Definitely not stealth gear.

I edged open the door inch by inch and crept inside. No Rafael waited for me in the living room.

I exhaled with a rush of relief. Maybe I was going to pull this whole thing off without him having the slightest clue.

Then, as I turned toward my bedroom, the same traitorous toe that'd tripped me in the parking lot bumped into a beer bottle Rafael must have set down near the door to go out for recycling.

It tipped over and hit the floor with a thunk. And

there was no blaring music in the house to cover the sound.

Hell, Rafael would probably have woken up even through a blast of alternative rock.

I'd swear it took all of two seconds for his door to creak open. Knowing there was no way I could scramble into my room without him realizing I'd been up to something, I instead spun toward the kitchen, only a few steps away.

When he reached the top of the stairs, I was standing by the fridge with my hand on the door. I glanced over my shoulder at him.

"Oh, hey," I mumbled as if half asleep. "Sorry I woke you up. You've got to stick those bottles someplace else."

My bodyguard squinted through the darkness, looking like he was suppressing a yawn. "Lou? Is something wrong?"

I cocked my head in what I thought was a pretty amazing performance considering my heart was jackhammering at my ribs. "What? No, I was just grabbing a midnight snack."

He frowned. "You got hungry at two in the morning?"

I raised my hands in the air. "It's hard to get back to sleep when your stomach is grumbling away, you know. It's got to be all those calories I'm burning in practice."

Rafael studied me for a moment longer. My skin prickled under his gaze.

I was pretty sure he was suspicious, but my explanation didn't offer any holes for him to poke at. He sighed and turned back toward the stairs.

"Better eat up then. Try to do it more quietly."

"Yeah, yeah," I shot back in typical snarky fashion, and managed not to topple over in relief when he tramped down the stairs.

To completely sell the story, in case he was listening from below, I opened the fridge and grabbed the tin with the last slice of the cherry pie we'd gotten for dessert a couple of days ago. I carried it to my bedroom and set it on the dresser.

I wasn't actually hungry. My stomach had clenched tight.

Well, I could have it for breakfast without Rafael knowing the difference.

As I climbed into my bed, the clenching sensation spread through my entire abdomen.

I didn't like lying to Rafael. He'd been my partner in crime—often literally—for so long.

But he'd proven that I couldn't trust him. What he didn't know wasn't going to hurt him.

And when I got rid of that bungling gang for good, I wouldn't have to sneak around anymore anyway.

SEVENTEEN

Luciana

THE NEXT DAY, the reality of the previous night sat heavy on my shoulders. I couldn't seem to get my bearings in training.

Jasper had been short with me before we began and barely deigned to look me in the eye after my first slip-up. When I fumbled the landing of one of my double jumps, which normally would have been child's play, I thought he'd *really* freak out.

Instead, he remained silent, his eyes trained on the stands over my shoulder, deliberately not looking at me. We were back to square one, all our progress and connection dashed against the ice.

Explaining why my head was in the clouds was out of the question, so I just kept quiet and hoped I was keeping in sync. My mind kept racing back to the stunt

I'd pulled at the gang hangout last night, replaying every detail.

I'd felt good about what I'd accomplished right before I fell asleep, but the second I'd woken up, the full anxiety had hit me like a freight train. Here I was, back in the place where one of those assholes had threatened me with that stupid doll.

What if they came back? What if they did something worse next time as payback?

What if one of them somehow realized who I actually was or brought in allies who would? It seemed impossible that these bozos could have any connection to my mom all the way back in Austin, but the Deadly Rose had people all over the place.

And even that tiny chance niggled at me, eating away at my focus.

Had I terrorized the gang enough for them to decide it was better just to leave town? If they didn't, how in the hell could I come down on them harder without stooping to my mother's level of violence?

Even if I was prepared to slaughter the bunch of them, it'd be quite the challenge to take them all down with only Rafael for backup. Not to mention I'd totally traumatize the entire normal population of Hobb Creek in the process.

I'd end up tainting this peaceful place even more than the wannabe gangsters already had.

I tapped my hand against my thigh, my gaze fixed on the wall without really seeing it. If I could just —

"You in there, Lou?" Niko asked, his tone gentle. "You seem a little distracted today."

I waited for Jasper to chime in with his usual sarcasm. Somehow, his silence was louder than his snarky words could have been.

"Yeah," I replied. "Yeah, I'm paying attention. Sorry, I just didn't sleep so well."

"Okay," Niko said. "Not a problem. If you need a break or anything else, you just let me know, all right?"

God, I did need a break—from the problems that'd somehow chased me all the way up here to what was meant to be my escape.

But Niko couldn't give me that. I wished I could spill at least a little of the worries dogging me with him and soak up the reassurance and affection I knew he'd offer in return, but I had the feeling that if I got at all affectionate with *him* in front of Jasper, that might sour things with the other man I'd started falling for even more than I already had.

"Definitely." I reached up to scratch between the wings tattooed on my shoulder blades. "I'm doing my best to work through it. I'll be fine."

"Maybe we should avoid any lifts practice for the time being," Jasper muttered. "It's no good for either of us if your head isn't in the game."

Even though the words weren't outright hostile—and he had a point, especially when I was the one who'd be hurt worse if I took a bad tumble—I winced inwardly.

How was he going to take me seriously ever again when I kept screwing up practice, I had a strange man living with me who acted like he was going to pummel him, and I—?

I hesitated over that thought. Maybe there was one

thing I could get out in the open with both of my fellow skaters, to clear the air and lift a little of the weight off me.

Jasper hadn't wanted to talk about the altercation with Rafael, but I could force the issue. Make him see that I hadn't been betraying anyone or shacking up with a total maniac who had no reason to act protective.

"Actually," I said, pitching my voice to carry, "before we keep going, I think there's someone I should introduce the two of you to. Since he's going to be around a lot, and I don't want you to be startled if you notice him, as good as he is at keeping a low profile."

Niko gave me a quizzical look, and Jasper tensed. I glided in a semi-circle to face the stands, scanning the shadowy alcoves that I knew my bodyguard would have favored.

I'd made my first comment loud enough that I was sure Rafael would have heard it, so he'd be ready, but now I lifted my voice even more. "Hey, Rafael! Could you come out so the guys can meet you properly?"

For a second, I thought Rafael might refuse, pretend to not even be there. *Not* actually being there at all simply wasn't a possibility.

Then he peeled himself out of one patch of shadows and moved toward the aisle with his typical brawny athleticism. He strode about halfway down the stands toward us, his expression impassive as he assessed the situation.

He didn't say anything, waiting for me to take the lead. Which made sense. He didn't know where I was going with this.

As pissed off as I'd been with him, I couldn't help being a little grateful that he was playing along this far.

I swung back toward my partner and my coach. "Jasper, you two met under not the best circumstances the other night. And I figure Niko should probably hear this story too. Guys, this is Rafael. He's... basically my bodyguard."

That was straightforward enough. Why lie about the parts I didn't have to?

Jasper's gaze jerked to me. "Why would you need a bodyguard?"

He sounded wary but not incredulous. I guessed that was a decent start.

I took a deep breath. "I mean, not officially. I haven't hired him or anything." It was Mom who'd done that, and he was off her payroll now. "You've probably wondered at least a little about exactly what I'm doing all the way out in Hobb Creek."

Niko cocked his head, glancing from Rafael to me. "That question had crossed my mind," he said with a reassuring smile. So certain this couldn't be anything too crazy.

Hopefully he'd never have to find out just how messed up my circumstances were.

I lowered my gaze, scraping the blade of one of my skates against the ice. "The thing is, my home life was... not great. My family was pretty messed up—I couldn't count on any of them—and it got to the point where I didn't even feel safe staying in the house. So I took off. Rafael's been a friend of the family for years. He's looked out for me since I was a kid. He realized what I was planning and insisted on helping me get out."

To my relief, understanding dawned on Jasper's face as he studied the larger man staring down at us. I could practically see him reevaluating their previous altercation in light of this new information.

"He's been kind of watching over me while I get settled into my new life," I added. "So he'll be around a lot of the time. But he knows that he doesn't have to worry about you two."

I said the last bit with particular emphasis for Rafael's benefit.

Jasper's eyebrows arched. "You left behind *your* life just to chase this punk across the continent and keep her out of trouble?" he asked Rafael with a small but audible teasing note in his voice.

Rafael's mouth curved into an equally small smile. His deep baritone echoed across the rink. "Since she is quite the punk, she needed it. I wasn't happy with my situation back in the city either. It was a good excuse to set down roots somewhere else."

Niko beamed at him, taking all the new information in stride—and trusting that I was telling him the truth. "That makes sense. I'm just glad that Lou has had someone looking out for her. Anyone she considers a friend is good with me."

His gaze slid to me again. "Are you okay now—with the home situation, and everything?"

I nodded, my stomach tightening. Technically, that was the biggest lie I'd just told, without speaking a single word.

Jasper rubbed the back of his neck like he often did when he was feeling awkward. "I guess I can see why you came on so strong the other night, considering how it must have looked when you came into the room."

Rafael tipped his head to the other guy in a mildly friendly gesture. "I'm sorry for the misunderstanding. I'm used to people playing not so nice back where we're from. Instincts honed by years of experience. But I was out of line."

Jasper's eyes widened. "Hey, don't worry about it now. No harm done in the end."

To my surprise, my normally taciturn bodyguard kept going. "Really, I don't see any reason for concern. You two have been good to Lou since we got here. I don't think I've ever seen her as happy as she is when she's skating with you. Thank you for that."

Niko chuckled. "She makes us pretty happy too, so it works out well for all of us. Right, Jasper?"

My skating partner cleared his throat. "Right."

A funny wobble passed through my stomach as I smiled up at Rafael. The fondness in his voice had been unmistakable.

It'd sounded like… like it really mattered to him that I *was* happy.

I guessed that shouldn't have been a surprise, but somehow, even now, it was hard to tell how much he actually cared and how much he was just fulfilling a duty he believed was owed.

Niko rubbed his hands together and motioned to Rafael with a playful gesture. "I don't suppose you're planning on getting into skating too? Do we have another prodigy on our hands?"

Rafael let out a snort. "No, my only interest in skating is seeing that Lou gets to keep doing it. It's not like there are a whole lot of guys who look like me getting out on the ice anyway."

I bit back a grimace. There weren't a whole lot of women figure skaters who shared my looks either.

My coach's expression turned more serious. "I suppose that's true. The average complexion does tend to be pretty… pale." He glanced at Jasper. "There is that medalist from Germany who was competing until a couple of years back… Colin! And I've crossed paths with a couple of others."

His attention slid back to Rafael, his tone lightening again. "I'm sure we could make room for you if you ever discovered a secret love for the ice."

A little amusement colored my bodyguard's voice. "I don't think there's much chance of that. I'll stick to watching the three of you defy gravity."

He gave me a short nod and loped back up to the alcove, where he melded back into the shadows. I turned to the rink, my spirits a little more at ease with that one secret off my chest.

Even though my biggest problem was still hanging over me, with my renewed sense of purpose, I managed to ignore worries about the gang well enough to get through the rest of practice without a hitch. Jasper and I flowed through the moves in sync and even landed all three of the lifts in the routine Niko had choreographed with only a little wobble on one.

When it was finally time to head out, I felt much better than I had coming in. I said my goodbyes to the guys, had a quick shower and change, and set off through the late afternoon sunlight across town.

The fresh breeze filled my lungs with crisp early autumn scents. How was it a single conversation could make the whole world seem brighter?

A few of the locals I passed shot me—and my bulging equipment bag—odd looks. I found myself remembering the middle-aged woman who'd badgered me at the grocery store a few days ago about what I was doing in their town.

But while that hadn't been a fun encounter, it wasn't the norm either. At least twice as many of the faces I passed offered friendly smiles.

One older man wiping down his store window even called out, "Good practice, I hope, Miss Lou?"

"Always is," I replied cheerfully.

I walked right down the main street because I'd already been planning on making a quick stop on my way home. The doctor's office was open for ten more minutes when I reached the front door.

I went past the now-empty chairs toward the reception desk. To my surprise, Dr. Ribeiro, the woman I'd seen at the café a few times now, was standing behind it. Her receptionist must have already gone home.

"Oh!" she said when she saw me, and motioned me the rest of the way over. "You're our new skater in town. I've already heard all about you. Small town gossip, you know."

She gave a soft laugh that had the same inflection as her mild accent. Portuguese, I was going to guess based on the little Brazilian flag tacked to her bulletin board alongside various informational papers.

"I guess you probably were the subject of a lot of that when you first moved in too, huh?" I had to say.

Dr. Ribeiro laughed again. "Some, I'm sure. Most are too polite to gossip about me to my own face. But the doctor who was just retiring when I showed up was a curmudgeon, from what they gossiped to me about *him*, so people were happy to have a new face around pretty quickly. What can I do for you?"

I could see how Hobb Creek's citizens would have warmed up to her in a flash with her easygoing, welcoming attitude.

I flicked my hand toward my body. "Because of all the bumps and tumbles I take in a typical day, I figured it'd be good to schedule regular checkups. And I haven't had a proper physical in ages."

Back home, I'd never seen a regular doctor. Mom had always had a guy with medical training in the crew, and he'd looked after any pressing health issues.

"I can write you in. I believe we have some openings next week. What time works for you?"

I ended up with a mid-morning appointment the following Thursday and headed out with a spring in my step with another mission accomplished.

Dr. Ribeiro's voice followed me out the door. "And if you ever need a hand getting your footing here in town, don't hesitate to get in touch."

This had to be small-town life at its best. Friendly neighbors, simple schedules—everything perfectly *normal*.

My satisfaction with how the day had turned out after

all buoyed me the rest of the way back to the bungalow. I walked straight to my bedroom to set down my equipment bag—and stalled two steps inside.

The evening breeze was wafting in with even greater force than usual, through a neat rectangular hole that'd been cut into the window screen.

And on the floor beneath my bedroom window, like someone had pushed it in through that hole, lay the limp carcass of a dead, blood-smeared squirrel.

EIGHTEEN

Luciana

I WAS STARTING to get used to seeing Hobb Creek at three in the morning, but that didn't mean that I had to like it. All I wanted in life was a little peace, and I was *going* to get it.

If that meant I had to crouch on the roof of a building three stories high down the street from the gang's shitty hideout, then so be it.

I sighed and adjusted the binoculars I'd purchased specifically because they were supposed to be enhanced for dark conditions. Finally, when I'd gotten the settings just right, the shapes around the storage building came into focus.

A few lights were on in the building. I noticed that the gang members had taken to parking their cars close to the entrance, where they could be more easily monitored, rather than scattered across the lot.

I smirked. That showed that they were at least a little bit scared of me.

They thought torturing forest animals was going to make *me* run scared? They had no idea who they were dealing with. I could do worse, much worse, if I wanted to.

They were lucky I didn't.

Mass murder was still off the table, even if that was what Mom would have said they deserved. There had to be another way I could make life so difficult for them that they'd move somewhere else.

Somewhere with a competent police force, somewhere that would eat small, poorly run gangs like theirs alive. I wouldn't have to bloody my hands, and Hobb Creek would finally be free.

Headlights appeared from the far end of the road. I ducked beneath the low wall that ran around the edge of the flat-roofed building to keep out of sight and peeked cautiously over the edge.

The lights were attached to a delivery truck similar to the one I'd tampered with a few nights ago. That one was still sitting hood-up right where I left it, but this new vehicle seemed to be in fine working order.

At least, for now.

When the truck stopped in front of the building, the garage-style door to the shipping area whirred upward. A few scruffy young men emerged from inside and heaved open the back of the truck.

One of them hopped up inside and began to hand

boxes down to the others, who hauled the cargo into the shadows inside. I couldn't make out any details on the sides that revealed what the boxes might contain.

I'd messed with the goons' vehicles. Maybe next time I'd need to target their merch.

If I could figure out a way to get to it without getting myself caught in the process.

I lowered the binoculars with a frown, debating my next steps. Then a hand dropped onto my shoulder so unexpectedly that a squeak burst from my lips as I jerked away.

As I spun around in a defensive stance, I found Rafael glowering at me, his arms crossed over his chest.

"What are you doing out here?" he demanded, pitching his voice low.

Shit. I could have sworn he'd been fast asleep when I'd snuck out. How had he found me?

I knew better than to ask. He wouldn't want to give away his secrets and make it easier for me to sneak off on him again.

Instead, I glowered right back at him, rubbing the rings I'd been tempted to drive into his face before I'd seen who he was. My voice came out hushed but harsh with irritation.

"What the fuck are *you* doing, other than trying to give me a heart attack? You're lucky I didn't brain you with the binoculars. If I'd wanted you to come along, I'd have invited you."

"You'd have to try awfully hard to get in a decent blow with those things," Rafael said without a hint of concern or amusement. "And in case you've forgotten, my *job* is being wherever you are, making sure you don't get yourself into even more trouble than necessary."

"And here I thought I got to make the decisions about what's necessary in my own life, not you."

Rafael's jaw tightened. "You know what I mean. Why the hell are you taking off on your own in the middle of the night—without even telling me?"

"Why should I have to tell you?" I retorted, my temper rising at his insistent tone. "I'm the most dangerous thing in this town other than you. If I want to go out for a late-night stroll *on my own*, you have nothing to worry about."

Rafael snorted. "You're obviously not out here just to stroll."

"How's it your business either way? Is it so horrible that I want to do one or two things without you hovering over me?"

His voice took on a growling note. "It is when those things involve messing with a gang of idiots you can't be sure won't shoot you by accident if not purposefully."

I rolled my eyes. "I've dealt with plenty of men with guns before."

"But you don't need to be dealing with these ones. Come on, let's go home. You need to get some sleep."

He turned toward the ladder that had given us access to the roof, like he assumed I'd just go along with him.

My pent-up frustration boiled over. I planted my feet firmly on the concrete surface. "Don't tell me what I need to be doing, Rafael."

My bodyguard's head jerked around, his eyes flaring for just an instant before settling into a darker smolder.

"*Someone* needs to tell you, because you're not doing the best job of taking care of yourself."

My teeth set on edge. "You're not my mother, thank the Lord, so you sure as hell don't need to start acting like you are."

Rafael grimaced. "That's not—just tell me what you're up to. What's so important about these pricks that now you're spying on them at three in the morning?"

I balked automatically at admitting the full truth. Imagine how much more overprotective the man in front of me would get if he found out how the gangsters had started harassing me directly.

"All you need to know is that it's important to me," I said. "And I've been handling it just fine on my own, or it wouldn't have taken you this long to notice."

Rafael's eyes narrowed. "This long? What *else* have you been up to that you haven't told me about?"

Okay, I probably shouldn't have said that part.

I set my hands on my hips. "It doesn't matter. They're my problems, not yours, so I'm handling them—my way."

Something in Rafael's expression deflated. Worry replaced the frustration in his eyes.

"What problems? Lou, if something else has happened —you know why I came here with you. We can do things your way, but I've got to have some idea what's going on if I'm going to have your back."

"Is that really it?" I couldn't stop myself from asking. "You want to have my back—or you want to decide that where I go and what I do meet your standards?"

Rafael was silent for a long moment. He shifted his

weight as if he'd considered stepping closer to me and then decided against it.

"I'm sorry," he said finally, his voice gone a little rough. "I've obviously made you feel like you can't trust me to not just protect you but respect you as well. I know you're not a kid anymore—I know how well you can look after yourself. I realize I was out of line with Jasper the other night, and if I've been crossing the line in other ways, I'm sorry for that too."

My own temper simmered down. "Are you sure you mean that and you're not just saying it because you think it's what I want to hear? Because it sounded like you didn't actually think you should have to apologize right after it happened."

Rafael ducked his head. "Maybe I was still kind of pissed at the time. But I can admit I was wrong. Lou… I just hope you can understand that even if I don't plan on changing our relationship, I do care about you. A lot. I want to see you reach for those dreams of yours—I want to help you get there."

All the rest of my rancor seeped out of me. My arms sagged at my sides.

This was the man who'd been by my side for almost a decade. The one who'd heard all my rants and excitements over the years.

The one who'd thrown away his career in an instant to make sure I had the chance to pursue my own.

"Okay," I said quietly. "I guess it's just hard to accept the whole protect-Lou attitude when everything else about my situation is different. But—I mean, I do appreciate everything you've done for me."

Rafael lifted his eyebrows. "Does that mean you're going to tell me about the problems that brought you out to a rooftop in the middle of the night?"

I blew out a breath, my stomach twisting. But the truth was, I wouldn't mind a little guidance, if Rafael was committed to letting me figure out my own path in the end.

"A few practices ago, I found a doll hanging from the door to the rink—done up to look like me, and tied like it'd been hung from a noose."

Rafael's eyes flashed. "And you didn't tell me?"

"It was right after you freaked out about Jasper! I had no idea how you'd react, and I didn't want to get into another argument about whether I was actually safe at the arena."

His mouth settled into a grim line. "What else?"

Now that I'd come this far, I might as well admit the rest. "This evening when I got home, I found a dead squirrel on the floor in my bedroom. Someone had cut open the screen and shoved it in."

"What?" Rafael sucked a breath through his teeth. All I could think looking at him was that it was a good thing for the culprit that Rafael hadn't caught them, or they'd have been lucky if their next of kin could identify their body when he was through.

"Stupid, gross pranks," I said. "It's obviously the guys from the gang harassing me."

"Have you done anything else to provoke them?"

I grimaced. "After the doll thing, I pulled that trick Frasco taught me with the steel wool in a few of their car engines. No one saw me, but they'd have been pretty pissed after the engines went up in flames. I was hoping it'd finally scare them off, but obviously not."

"Hard to scare pendejos who're too stupid to realize they're outmatched," Rafael muttered.

I glanced back toward the storage building, knitting my brow. "I don't totally get why they're sticking to little tricks instead of blustering right at me. That seems more their style. I have been careful—maybe they don't actually know it's me, and they're just intimidating a bunch of people in town to see how we react?"

"Could be." Rafael rubbed his chin in thought. "All it'd take is one really unhinged prick in the bunch. Or maybe it's got nothing to do with the stunts you've been pulling on their territory, and they're just hostile to any newcomer in town."

"Jasper and Niko didn't mention anything like that."

"They're famous. Bigger consequences. And you're a woman and, well, you stick out a little compared to the typical Hobb Creek inhabitant."

I tugged at a strand of my dark hair, knowing what he meant. Other than Dr. Ribeiro, I was the only Latina I'd seen in town.

All the wannabe gangsters were pale as anything, so that could totally be a factor.

I sucked my lower lip under my teeth. "Well, it doesn't really matter why they're doing it. I'm going to run them out of town either way, prove I'm no one they should have been messing with. And without stooping to the kind of brutality my mother would have expected me to."

Rafael gave me a long, pensive look before beckoning me toward the ladder. This time I came.

"I'm not sure if that'll be possible," he said. "Guys like this…"

"It *has* to be," I insisted. "Maybe we have to get more creative, maybe we've got to find the right pressure point —but I'm not going on a killing spree. I'm not a mafia princess anymore. I never wanted to be in the first place. I'm leaving all that *behind.*"

Rafael rested his hand on my shoulder, warmth washing through my body from his touch.

"Lo sé, Lou. I know you're not that kind of woman. We'll figure it out."

I clambered down the ladder after him, wishing I could believe he knew that for sure.

NINETEEN

Luciana

"FORGET THE DINNER," Jasper said with a satisfied groan that did funny things to my internal temperature. "I'd eat here every night just for dessert."

As he popped the last bite of his maple peach crumble into his mouth, Niko waggled his fork at the other guy from across the restaurant table. "You want maple on everything. I'm lucky you didn't pull out that bottle you carry around and cover the whole plate with extra."

Jasper shot him a baleful look. "Do you know how hard it was to track down anything with real maple syrup where my family was living in the US? I've got to make the most of it while I'm here."

Niko chuckled. "I suppose it's a good thing you're indulging at dinner rather than breakfast, or you'd be lumbering around the skating rink tomorrow with all that in your belly."

A different sort of twinge passed through my body, and the bite of apple pie I was chewing soured in my mouth.

We hadn't exactly been lumbering today, but Jasper and I still hadn't quite found our rhythm. How were we going to impress an audience and a bunch of judges if we couldn't even pull the routine off smoothly in practice?

I had the niggling worry that we were going to make total fools of ourselves. And whose fault was that more likely to be—the renowned professional skater's or mine?

Jasper hadn't commented on our difficulties, but he was clearly still in a prickly mood, even after I'd cleared the air about Rafael.

"I have amazing digestion," he informed Niko, continuing to glower at him, and then pushed back his chair. "Syrup does make a bit of a mess, though. I'd better wash my hands before I hand over my card."

"You do that," Niko said cheerfully. But the moment the other guy had disappeared into the restroom, he pulled out his own wallet. He set down enough money to cover all three of our bills and a generous tip.

I nudged my plate aside. "You don't need to cover me, Niko. I've got plenty of cash."

"It's my treat today. You can give me the gift of accepting it without arguing."

He winked at me and brushed his fingers back through his smooth hair, where the pink strip I could tell he'd freshly touched up seemed to wink too.

I grumbled under my breath but resisted protesting

further as he motioned for me to get up. I did have a good nest egg squirreled away, but it wasn't infinite. And skating necessities added up quickly.

As we headed over to the door of the cozy restaurant to wait for Jasper there, Niko rested his hand on the small of my back in a familiar, warm gesture that made my heart skip a beat. I still wasn't used to having a guy act so sweet with me.

It hadn't ever occurred to me that I'd *want* sweet, but now that I had it, I could admit it was pretty addictive. At least in the gorgeous form of Niko Okabe.

By the door, he turned to me and lowered his voice. "I wanted to ask you about what you told us the other day— about your family. You don't need to give me any details, but are you sure you're safe now? Is there anything I can do that would help?"

My heart swelled with more emotion—gratitude and affection mixed with a little pang of pain that I couldn't be as open with him as he'd been with me. "Everything's good now. You don't need to worry. I just had to get away— there's no reason anyone would come looking for me here."

At least, I sure as hell hoped that was true.

"I'm glad to hear that. It was obviously the right thing for you, seeing how you've bloomed on the rink without anyone downplaying your talent." His dark eyes twinkled. "And maybe I'm a little selfish, to be thankful that leaving them behind meant you ended up where I am."

He teased his fingers along my jaw to tilt my head up and claimed a quick but tender kiss. A giddy shiver ran through my chest as I kissed him back.

Niko's arm tightened around me just for a moment, and I could feel him force himself to ease away. He laughed lightly and gave my temple a peck too.

"But as much as I enjoy your company, I don't want to distract you from what's most important." He glanced across the restaurant to where Jasper was just emerging from the restroom. "I feel that right now it's your skating partner you should be focused on."

"Yeah," I said with a lopsided smile. "I'm still working on that whole partner thing."

"You paid?" Jasper demanded, striding over to us with a frown at Niko.

Niko held up his hands. "What is it you say—guilty as charged?"

Jasper let out a huff but seemed to already realize he wasn't going to get very far trying to change Niko's mind.

After we'd stepped out onto the sidewalk, Niko offered us a cheerful wave, turning toward his apartment, which lay in the opposite direction from where both Jasper and I would be heading. "Well, I'm off. Good work, you two. We'll keep at it tomorrow."

I waved back and glanced at Jasper, catching a flicker of a deeper frown that crossed his face as he watched Niko vanish around the corner.

Was he beating himself up about how our training was going, just like I was? Fretting that we were disappointing our coach, who'd come so far specifically to drag him out of his slump?

Maybe Niko had made a good point just now. We could stand to focus more on each other—possibly without anyone at all looking on.

I wet my lips, a little nervous about Jasper's possible response. "Hey, do you want to head back to the arena for a bit right now? We could get in a little extra practice off the ice—see if we can at least nail the position for that one lift. Niko left the storage room set up with the foam padding."

Jasper looked at me, shoving his hands in his pockets. I got the impression he was evaluating me, and with a certain amount of wariness. "You want to go back?"

I offered a cautious grin. "What better things do I have to do? Maybe we'll surprise Niko tomorrow with our newly perfect form."

My partner wavered for a few seconds longer and then tipped his head, although I still got a reluctant vibe from him. "Fine. Couldn't hurt."

Gosh, what an enthusiastic endorsement. I restrained myself from rolling my eyes, which definitely wouldn't help smooth things over.

We walked back to the arena, the awkward silence making me twice as glad for Hobb Creek's small size. It was only five minutes before we reached the darkened doors—but Jasper had his own key.

No breaking and entering necessary!

I refrained from making that comment out loud and glanced behind me while he unlocked the door. Rafael would be shadowing me from somewhere nearby.

Slipping one hand behind my back, I made a quick gesture with a flick of my fingers, giving him the signal that I needed some privacy.

He'd do a quick sweep of the arena just to be sure no dangers were lurking, and then he'd hang back near the reception area rather than keeping me in view. That way I really could focus completely on Jasper without worrying another tumble—of whatever kind—might bring out Rafael's protective impulses again.

My partner and I tramped over to the storage room Niko had converted for our off-ice training. The foam rectangles still littered the floor.

I brushed my hands down my tartan pants and decided they and the long-sleeved band tee I had on would work just fine for a brief stint of training. I'd already dropped my sweaty athletic clothes back at the bungalow, if I'd even have wanted to get back into them.

"So," Jasper said with a hint of doubt in his expression as he looked around the room. "You wanted to practice that last lift."

I squared my shoulders. "Yeah. It seems like the one we're having the most trouble getting in sync for."

He nodded, not disputing my assessment, and motioned me over to him. His expression stayed grim, all business, but I thought I caught a flicker of heat in his gray-green eyes when he lowered one hand to settle on my hip.

An answering heat coursed through me, having his brawny frame so close. I could smell his woodsy, musky scent, even more delicious than the dinner I'd just eaten.

"Ready?" he asked, with the slightest husky note in his voice.

I lifted my hands into the best starting position. On cue, Jasper grasped my fingers and hefted me up and over his broad shoulders.

I arched in his hold, noting every place my weight

needed to balance, tightening my muscles to make the position as easy as possible for him. Getting into the pose from standing rather than skating into each other wasn't the same—no momentum, no flow of movement. When he set me down again, without the benefit of a glide to carry us through the motion, his hand slipped against my leg and I teetered too far to the left.

"Whoa!" Jasper caught me around my back before I hit the pads and helped me straighten up. He grimaced. "Sorry."

I waved off his apology, hoping my cheeks hadn't flushed too much from the momentary embrace. "It's a little different from what we're used to. At least we were steady while I was up in the air."

"While I was standing still," Jasper muttered.

I managed to laugh. "We'll work on that too."

As we went through the motions of several more standing lifts, I felt the tension radiating off Jasper gradually loosen. When I suggested that we'd proven ourselves enough that he should try carrying me around the room in the pose, he even let out a laugh of his own, if a short one.

"Sure, Punk. If you trust me to swing you around on the ice, I guess this is actually safer."

I prodded him in the bicep. "You can carry me anywhere you like."

I'd spoken without thinking, tossing out the generic flirting remark, but the definite flash of interest in Jasper's gaze got me heated up all over again. As he stepped up to me, my pussy clenched.

Down, girl. This is work time, not play time.

Some part of me didn't see why it couldn't be both, though.

Jasper's solid hands gripped me firmly and hoisted me into the air with new confidence. I caught a wobble before it became a problem and lifted my arm and upper leg into the right configuration.

He stepped forward tentatively and then with a little more speed, rotating in a circuit of the room similar to the loop he'd skate on the rink. He'd almost made it all the way around when his body swayed a little to the right, and I started to slide in his hold.

"Shit!" he mumbled as he tried to steady both of us, but gravity took over. In his hasty attempt to catch me, he ended up tripping over one of the pads.

We both fell in their midst, me landing partly on top of Jasper with an *oomph* of breath from his lungs.

Jasper tipped his head back against the foam chunks. "Great. So we can handle lifts as long as we're staying perfectly still. That'll work out well."

I snorted. "It was only our first attempt. And walking is pretty different from skating."

I eased myself a little upward, and the feel of my body shifting against his muscular frame sent a spike of arousal shooting through me.

Jasper's gaze jerked to mine, his face flushing as if he'd felt it too, and suddenly I couldn't help saying, "Maybe we should take a little break to make sure we're at our best."

Jasper studied me with an inscrutable expression. "A break, huh? Trying to get out of the hard parts?"

But there was no animosity in his tone, and he didn't make the slightest move to nudge me off him.

Taking a gamble, I sat up over him and pressed my hands against his sculpted chest as if to pin him down. I gazed down at him through my eyelashes, tamping down the rush of need rising up from between my legs.

"We had fun the other night, didn't we? It seemed like we were getting in sync in other ways. You know the whole thing with Rafael was a misunderstanding. Is there some other reason you've been keeping your distance?"

Jasper's voice turned rough. "Lou, I— I figured maybe it would be better to keep things professional after all."

I cocked my head. "Because that's what you want or that's what you think you're supposed to do? We don't *have* to go there again. But I'm totally on board, and I don't think it'll be a problem professionally either."

His eyes smoldered as he took me in. I'd swear I could feel his skin growing hotter through his shirt.

But he still hesitated. "The thing is... it already has gotten kind of messy even though we decided we'd avoid that. I'm not really the type to go for a quick lay and then forget about it. I don't want to just screw around like it doesn't mean anything."

I blinked at him with a flutter in my chest. This wasn't where I'd expected this conversation to go.

"Is that your way of saying it *would* mean something to you?"

His gaze darted away from me for a second as if he were embarrassed. "Maybe I wasn't the friendliest ever when we met—"

I couldn't hold back a guffaw at that understatement.

Jasper made a face at me before continuing. "I wasn't sure what to make of you. But you're obviously... a lot of things that I really respect. And admire. Along with being one of the hottest women I've ever seen." His smile turned a bit sly despite his awkwardness.

My throat constricted for a moment before I managed to speak. "Oh. I didn't—I guess I've been around too many guys who only think with their dicks. I wasn't going to push for anything like a commitment, especially when I've been seeing Niko too. But that doesn't mean— It'd be more than just screwing around to me too. Even when you're being a jerk, you're really something, you know."

"Something?" he repeated, definitely teasing now.

I mock-glared at him. "Incredibly frustrating. But also passionate and determined and with that artistic mind I wish I could even halfway match."

Jasper raised his hand to trail his fingers down my arm, sparking giddy quivers even through the layer of thin cotton. "So what are *you* saying?"

I leaned forward until my face was just a few inches from his. "I'm saying somehow I've ended up caring quite a bit about both Niko and you, Mr. Not-the-Friendliest. And who knows? Maybe we'll be better partners on the ice if we embrace all the other ways we'd like to, ah, 'work together' instead of fighting our feelings."

"Well, when you put it like that..." Jasper pushed himself up those last few inches to press his mouth against mine.

Oh, he tasted delicious too—like the sweet maple and tart peaches from his dessert. I kissed him back hard, running my hands down his chest to the hem of his shirt and reveling in the groan that reverberated over his lips.

I didn't have any patience left in me after going

unsatisfied the other night at my house, and the same sense of urgency seemed to have gripped Jasper. He claimed my mouth again and again with a swipe of his tongue between my lips. We devoured each other as if we'd been starving for this.

He sat all the way up, sliding his arms around me to pull me even closer, and I gasped when my pussy collided with the bulge behind his track pants. Jasper groaned at the contact. He ran his fingers up and down my thighs before massaging my ass in a way that just begged for me to grind against him.

As I whimpered with need, I edged my hands up under his shirt over the jackpot that was all his heated, muscled torso. I felt like I'd won another reward with his eager hitch of breath when I gently raked my nails over his washboard abs.

Jasper tangled his fingers in my hair, heedless of my loosening ponytail, and kissed me so deeply stars spun behind my eyes. Then he pulled back just enough to chart a scorching trail along my jaw to nip my earlobe.

"Fuck, I want you so bad," he growled. "I've wanted this since the first moment I saw you on the ice."

My own longing flared hotter at his declaration. Who would have thought—behind all the grumbling and glowering, Jasper St. Pierre had been hungry for me all along.

I rewarded him for the confession by swiveling my hips against his even more enthusiastically. The press of his groin had us both gasping in unison, pleasure flooding my core.

Jasper yanked my tee right off me, and I reached for

the waistband of his pants. When my fingers grazed the bulge of his erection, he arched toward me with a hiss.

"God, Lou."

Our mouths collided again. I stroked his rigid cock through the fabric of his pants until he let out a desperate sound and practically tore them off with my help.

As he yanked off my bra, I tucked my hand right into his boxers. He groaned at the squeeze of my fingers and then bowed his head to suck the peak of my breast into his mouth.

Bliss raced through my chest. I groped at the waves of his auburn hair and rocked against him with my own growing desperation.

"Fuck, that's good."

Jasper hummed against my nipple, drawing it to an even sharper peak. One of his hands slipped between us.

When his thumb flicked across my clit, I bucked into his touch, seeking more. *Needing* more.

At my encouraging moan, Jasper stroked my entire pussy through my pants. Then he shoved his hand under to finger me skin to skin.

His breath came out shaky. "You're so fucking wet, Lou."

"Your fucking fault," I replied with a stuttered laugh, and tipped my head back with another moan.

Intent on paying him back in kind, I gripped his cock and ran my thumb over the head already slick with pre-cum. Jasper only allowed me a few pumps before he captured my attention by slipping one finger inside me.

My grasp wavered as my concentration did too. His

movements were slow and deliberate, and he watched every reaction with growing satisfaction.

His cock twitched in my hand as I breathed out his name. With a ferocity that would have soaked my panties if I'd still had them on, he dragged the rest of my clothes off me and threw them aside.

"Condom," I mumbled, snatching at my purse. I dug out one of the few I kept in there for just in case—thank you, Past Lou!

Jasper kicked off his boxers and tore open the foil packet without a second's hesitation. As he rolled the contents over his shaft, which was as impressively built as the rest of him, I took a moment to admire the view.

All those chiseled muscles on display, honed by years of pushing himself to the limit on the ice. Broader and bulkier than Niko's lean form, but equally delectable.

A girl could appreciate a little variety.

He tipped me back on the pads with another kiss, both determined and lingering. I'd almost melted beneath him when he lined himself up.

I was so slick and ready that he plunged all the way in one go, the heady friction making my head spin. He pulled back and then thrust even deeper, propelling a moan from my lungs.

I closed my eyes, unable to process anything else other than the sensation of him taking me, filling me, stroking me from the inside out. He kissed my lips and my neck almost savagely while running his fingers over my hair with clashing tenderness. My heart swelled at the impression that I was being both claimed and cherished.

Every guy I'd been with back in Austin, every hasty

hookup, had felt like something only about bodily urges. Scratching an itch, relieving tension, nothing all that personal beyond finding the guy hot enough and unobjectionable enough that I didn't mind the momentary physical vulnerability.

With both Niko and Jasper, the experience was totally different. The act reached beyond our physical collision and tugged at my heart.

I didn't think I could give this kind of intimacy up. I *had* to be the woman they saw me as; I had to keep all the darkness of my past as far away from them as possible.

With a surge of deeper desire, I lifted my legs to urge Jasper closer, and he followed me without breaking his rhythm. His cock hit the spot inside that made my whole torso pulse with pleasure, and I caught his mouth in another wild kiss.

My breath had broken into pants. I arched to meet him, welcoming him in every way I could, soaring on the pleasure rushing through my body.

He thrust harder, faster, our skin sliding together with the sheen of sweat that'd broken over it. He squeezed my ass, driving all the way to the hilt at just the right angle, and I blazed over the finish line with an explosion of sparks behind my eyes.

As I clenched around him, shuddering with my ecstatic release, Jasper's hands wrapped around my leg. He hoisted it up almost as if this were a new pairs lift, pounding into me.

I dug my fingernails into his bare back, and he slammed into me with a groan that told me he'd reached his own climax.

We stayed melded together like that for a long moment, coming down from the high. I smiled a little deliriously, my happiness only heightened by Jasper's returning grin and the playful kiss he pressed to the corner of my jaw.

"I don't know about you, but I think that's all the practice I can handle for today," he said lightly as he pulled back to clean up. "You've worn me out, Punk."

I laughed and tapped his side with my foot. "Maybe we should add this to our workout regimen."

The gleam in Jasper's eyes suggested he didn't totally object to the idea. He stole one more kiss, and we scrambled back into our clothes.

As Jasper turned toward the door, though, a pensive shadow crossed his face. His stance was so much more relaxed than when we'd come in, but I couldn't shake the sense that something was still bothering him.

I bumped my shoulder against his arm on the way out. "We got in some good work on the lift too. I bet we'll nail it tomorrow."

"We should definitely be closer," Jasper said easily enough, but his expression didn't totally lighten.

However much I'd gotten through to him, he was still keeping me at a distance. But I didn't know what to do about that other than wait and see if he'd eventually let me all the way in.

And maybe he was right not to, considering how many secrets I was keeping from *him*.

TWENTY

Luciana

I'D BECOME QUITE the regular at the Blueberry Café.

Not only did they have fantastically authentic pierogies, the coffee was ten times better than what I could make with the cheap machine that'd come with the bungalow. The place had become my comfort spot and a regular stop before practice. Sometimes after too.

And on Sundays, I could hang out at my leisure. I'd dropped in today earlier than usual to dig into a stack of the café's trademark blueberry pancakes, drenched in so much maple syrup that I probably should have invited Jasper along too.

Scratch that. He'd have tried to eat my pancakes.

It seemed that some of the locals had noticed my regular appearances there. As I polished off the last pancake, an elderly woman I'd seen in the place a few times before shuffled over to my table. She clutched her purse in her wrinkled hands like it weighed a hundred pounds.

When I looked up, she aimed a bright smile at me, her mouse-like eyes crinkling. "You're our newest resident, aren't you? How are you liking our town, hon?"

I had to smile back. "Loving it. It's a wonderful little place."

"Oh, that's lovely to hear." The old woman's expression got even sunnier. "We don't get many young folks moving into Hobb Creek—mostly they're off searching for their big adventures. Do you expect to stay very long?"

I caught a prying vibe in her comments but simply ignored it. I didn't mind small-town nosiness as long as people weren't pushy about it.

"I'll have to see, but right now I feel like I'd be happy staying here forever," I told her.

"Oh, perfect, perfect. You aren't at all concerned, a young lady living on your own?"

Rafael had done such a good job of keeping a low profile she obviously hadn't even noticed his presence.

My lips twitched with amusement at the thought of Hobb Creek being any kind of a danger to young ladies. "Yes, I like it that way."

"Well, that's good to hear. If you need anything, you ask around for Laurel, and I'll see what I can do."

"Thank you, Laurel," I said, restraining a laugh. She might have been both nosy and a little clueless, but she obviously meant well.

This was what a home was supposed to feel like:

acceptance and support. Two things I'd never felt even within my own house back in Austin.

As my new friend ambled off, I paid my bill and headed out into the crisp but warm early autumn sunlight. I'd parked the Grand Marquis down the street so that I could swing by the grocery store and carry my haul back to the bungalow without straining my already sore arms.

My glow of happiness faded the second I set eyes on the car. It was parked exactly *where* I'd left it, but not *how* I'd left it.

Something was lying at the base of the windshield. Something that'd left ruddy smears on the glass.

With a hitch of my pulse, I hustled over and then stopped when I made out what the things were.

Three dead pigeons lay on the hood of the car, their feathered bodies limp. Well, *most* of them was lying there.

Their heads had been cut right off.

Nausea surged up from my stomach. I clamped my mouth shut against it and the string of curses I wanted to let out.

What the fuck did those assholes in the gang think they were playing at now?

With brisk steps, my heart thumping hard and fast, I yanked open the trunk, grabbed a plastic bag that'd been abandoned there, and used it to scoop the dead birds off the car. With a silent apology to the garbage man, I chucked the bag in the nearest public trash can.

The feathered corpses hadn't been lying there long. A few squirts of the wiper fluid were enough to rinse off the blood. But I sat there in the driver's seat for a few minutes after that, my thoughts and my stomach churning.

This latest threat wasn't aimed just at me. There'd been *three* birds.

They were telling me that they figured Jasper and Niko would be dead meat too.

My teeth set on edge. Those fuckers couldn't get away with menacing my men as well as me.

I didn't know what I was going to do, but I had to do something. Now.

They'd been bold enough to leave their sick little gift in broad daylight. Well, I could be plenty bold too.

I yanked the ski mask I'd used on past expeditions out of the glove compartment and shoved it into the back pocket of my jeans. Then I pushed myself out of the car.

Groceries could wait.

I stalked through the streets, my hands curled into fists, possible plans unfurling in my mind. I didn't have to worry about Rafael interrupting my retaliation, because for once he'd decided I would be safe enough simply going to the café and the grocery store and agreed to take a break from bodyguard duties, but that also meant I was on my own again.

When I reached the last few houses before the edge of town, I veered into the shadows. From there, I studied the parking lot and storage building across the street.

Two men were standing out front drinking beers near the garage-style door. In the several minutes I took stock, no one came in or out of the main door.

And there was another entrance around back. I'd seen it when scoping out the place in the past. I could make it over there without the goons seeing me, right?

All the things they wouldn't want fucked with the most lay inside.

I walked a short distance up the street, past the stretch of trees to the lot around the neighboring warehouse. Then I crossed the road at a jog and circled around through the trees.

When I'd come up on the back of the gang's hideout, I tugged the ski mask over my head. It might not help me hide, but it would at least stop them from getting a good look at my face if I ran into any of my enemies.

A span of scruffy field lay between the yard around the other warehouse I was now standing near and the back of the storage building that was my target. I watched for a couple more minutes, my pulse racing through my veins, and then darted across the uneven ground.

I slowed as I reached the asphalt around the building. Muscles tensed, I walked right up to the back door and pressed my ear to the gap.

Nothing. No music, no laughter, no loud conversations.

Something inside of me jumped for joy. A tug of the doorknob proved it was locked, but I knew just how to deal with that.

In a matter of seconds, I'd applied my pins to the minor security issue as quickly as I had the door to the arena my first day in town. Yanking on the knob again, I whisked myself inside the hideout in one fluid motion.

The douchebags were *so* going to regret messing with me.

My eyes darted around the dim hallway I'd come into, searching for an ideal objective.

Farther ahead, the hall split like the head of a T. Muffled voices carried from around the bend to my ears, but there didn't appear to be any activity in the rooms closest to me.

Setting my feet quietly, I tried the doors in my stretch of hall.

The first opened into what looked like a workout room with exercise mats, weights, a ratty punching bag, and a rowing machine. The second revealed stacks of boxes and plastic crates.

Bingo.

I slipped inside, letting the door shut behind me, and pried open one of the crates. A smirk stretched across my face.

Oh, this was just perfect.

I whipped out several of the bags of white powder tucked inside. When I dug into the plastic with my fingernail, the sharp scent confirmed what I'd suspected.

These guys were holding a whole bunch of cocaine. Too bad for them it soon wouldn't be in any condition to sell.

I ripped the hole wide and poured the powder all over the floor like a deluge of fine snow. Then another and another, until the dirty cement surface was coated with it.

As I tore apart another bag, I did a little dance across the room, the powder hissing under my sneakers. Grinding it into the cracks and grime for good measure. I had the urge to fit in a little jumps practice too, mashing the stuff with Axels and Lutzes, but there wasn't quite enough room.

How many tens of thousands of dollars was I losing

for these guys in a few short minutes? I pictured the cash going up in flames as I continued my stomping dance.

Maybe that would piss off whoever they were supplying or storing the stuff for enough that *those* assholes would run these ones out of town for me. Extra bonus.

I was just grabbing another bag close to the bottom of the now nearly empty crate when a shout filtered through the wall.

"Hey, Delroy, that you messing with the merch?"

A jolt of panic raced through my nerves. I'd gotten so caught up in my revenge that I hadn't been cautious enough—someone must have heard me.

Without risking a second to think, I dashed out into the hall. Footsteps sounded around the corner as I hurtled past the back door.

I sprinted toward the patch of woodland—I could vanish in there like I had the other night. Running on into the woods, I winced at the yells I heard in the distance. But none of them sounded at all close to me.

The gangsters sounded pissed off, but also like they had no clue where the perpetrator of the vandalism had gone.

A tiny smile tugged at my lips. Keeping my head down, I wove between the trees, determined to put more distance between me and the storage building before I let down my guard.

I veered around a steep section of earth jutting up from the ground—and found myself face to face with the flabby guy named Barry who I'd watched berate the high school kid by the lake.

He jerked to a halt, one hand clutching the strap of the bag he had slung over his back. He must have been returning from some illicit business of his own. Shit.

"Who the fuck are you, and what are you—?" he spat out.

I didn't wait around to hear the rest of his question. I just flung myself in the opposite direction.

My feet pounded across the fallen autumn leaves and crackling twigs. I swerved left and then right, until I found myself coming up on the road on the edge of town.

I paused, my chest heaving for breath, my ears pricked. No sounds of pursuit reached my ears.

Was it possible he hadn't bothered to run after me? I was probably in better shape than most of those pricks anyway. Or maybe I'd simply lost him in the woods, and he'd given up.

With a sigh of relief, I tugged off my ski mask and looked down at myself. My stomach lurched.

My star-dappled Henley and distressed jeans were dusted with a fine layer of cocaine. There was no missing it against the black fabric of my shirt especially.

Hell, it was dappled all across the front of the mask too.

Barry might not have been able to identify me specifically with the mask covering my face, but with one glance at my figure in the fitted clothes, he wouldn't have had any doubt that I was a woman. Or that I was the one who'd created the mess he'd find when he returned to his base of operations.

I hadn't been sure whether the gang was targeting me because they knew I'd been making their lives harder or because I was new in town and different. Now they'd definitely be able to narrow down their list of suspects when it came to the assaults on their property.

I swiped the evidence of my crime off my clothes as well as I could with the help of some strips of moss and then trudged across the street, apprehension settling over me like a cloud.

Now that the goons would be that much surer who'd been targeting *them*, how would the assholes come down on me next after I'd screwed up their business so thoroughly?

And how the hell was I going to make sure that confrontation went in my favor—without ruining not just my life but those of the two men who'd lifted that life into something out of a dream?

TWENTY-ONE

Luciana

I KNEW BETTER by now than to assume any of my problems had been solved even when it felt like I'd made progress, off or on the rink. No matter how well things appeared to be going, it seemed like a monkey wrench would inevitably lodge itself directly into the turning gears of my good day.

Today, that monkey wrench was tall, broad, and Jasper-shaped.

My partner had been relatively chill with me—you know, as chill as Mr. Grouchy ever got. He actually smiled when I showed up at the rink and managed to laugh rather than grumble after our first collective stumble during a lift.

Maybe because the subsequent fall in which he'd

cushioned me had reminded us both of how enjoyably we'd ended our last training session together.

But as we moved into the sections of the routine that were more about synchronization than directly working together, a different sort of tension seeped in. And not between him and me.

"I think if you just loosen up your stance a little more, you'll land that much better," Niko said to Jasper after his fourth shaky finish in a row. "Why don't you try this form again a little slower to see if you can feel where you're going wrong?"

Jasper scowled. "A little slower. Right. Like that's going to fix all my problems."

A new storm cloud seemed to have descended over him since Niko had started focusing on his most difficult individual spin, and it was only getting darker. I paused, my stomach knotting as I watched the two of them together.

I'd seen prickly moments between the two men before —well, prickly on Jasper's side—but I'd thought that was just Jasper being himself. It didn't make sense for him to get all snarky with our coach when he was in a good enough mood to brighten up with me.

Unless there'd been more than prickliness underlying their dynamic all along, and I hadn't noticed because our own tensions had overshadowed the trouble until now.

Niko shook his head with a twinkle in his eyes, but I thought I could make out a strain in his attempt at a typically lighthearted tone. "I'm not saying it'll fix *everything*. We've got to start somewhere, right? I know you can hit the mark perfectly if you just get your head in the right place."

"Oh, so now I'm only just starting?" Jasper rolled his eyes. "Aren't you supposed to be building off what I could already do, not sending me back to square one?"

Niko's mouth twisted. He was normally so relaxed, but there was no mistaking the tension in his stance now as he tried to talk Jasper down.

"You know that's not what I meant. Of course you're drawing on all your talent. But you've got to let people fully see it. You're so close to mastering this spin. Come on, from the top, let's keep at it."

Jasper's expression hardened, but he cast off to attempt the move on his own, not even waiting to see if I'd join him. He whirled himself around with a kick of his legs, but even I could see that his temper was getting the better of him.

This time, his whole torso swayed too close to the ice. He broke out of the spin a rotation early with a string of curses.

Niko held up his hands. "All right. Take a breather, skate a few laps around the rink to cool down, and then we'll come back to it. We're not giving up until—"

"Oh, come off it," Jasper interrupted in a snap as sharp as the blades of my skates. "You can quit coddling me. Maybe the problem is you're not half as good a coach as you thought you'd be, and you don't actually know how to solve any of this. You can stop treating me like a pity case and go skate your own fucking routine if you want to see it so badly."

He shot off toward the stands and was stomping up the aisle the second he'd wrenched his skates off.

Okay, then. I had no idea what that fit of anger was all about, but apparently we were finishing practice early today.

I glanced toward Niko, expecting the easygoing man to crack a joke to ease up the mood, but his shoulders had slumped. Defeat was written across his delicately chiseled features.

My stomach sank. I pushed off to glide right over to his side.

"Hey. Are you okay? I don't know what his deal is today, but you didn't do anything wrong."

Niko swiped his hand over his face. "I might not have this afternoon, but that isn't the real issue. I thought I could shake him out of his slump—I thought I could fix the problem… But maybe that was ridiculous when it's my fault in the end."

I frowned. "What do you mean it's your fault? You've been *helping* Jasper—it sounds like he'd still be holed up at his grandparents' house not even skating if you hadn't dragged him out here."

"He might not have ended up there in the first place if I wasn't so thoughtless."

Thoughtless? That didn't sound anything like the Niko I knew. I wasn't sure if he'd just picked the wrong English word for what he meant or something beyond my comprehension was going on here, but I wasn't leaving without getting to the bottom of this.

I nudged him toward the boards, and he meandered

over with me. When he rested his arm against one, I set my hands on my hips.

"All right, I think you'd better tell me what's the matter. What do you think you did? How could you have had anything to do with Jasper dropping out of the competitive circuit?"

Niko sighed and seemed to shake himself. "I've probably already said more than I should. Jasper wasn't in the right headspace, and it seems I'm not either."

"Oh no, you don't. You're my coach too—he's my partner. If there's something more going on, you've already gotten me mixed up in the middle of it. I have a right to know."

His despondent expression wrenched at my heart, but he squared his shoulders as my comments got through to him. He raised his bright brown eyes to meet my gaze.

"It was just a quick moment. But sometimes something small can totally throw things off."

"Something small like what?"

Niko ran his hand back through his streaked hair. "After one of the international competitions early last year, a bunch of us headed out to get some drinks. A little friendly celebration after the rivalries had been settled. I was a little… tipsy, that's the word. And I think Jasper was too. We started chatting in a corner, and it seemed like there were… sparks. So I leaned in and kissed him."

My eyes widened. "You and Jasper hooked up?"

A blush colored Niko's cheeks.

"No," he said quickly. "It was just the one kiss. A *good* kiss, but—"

He cut himself off with even more obvious

embarrassment. "That's not important. I don't know if Jasper had ever done even that much with another man before. He kissed me back as if he was happy to, but then he acted awkward and left. And the rest of the international circuit, he kept floundering with his performance…"

The pieces clicked together in my head. So much made sense that I'd never have figured out without this crucial detail.

All the odd looks I'd seen pass between the two men. Niko's determination to get Jasper back on his feet.

I stared at him. "Hold on. You think you kissing him sent him into his slump?"

Niko made a face. "He was doing so well before. And getting confused about your personal life, attractions and all that, can really throw someone off. I didn't know where his head was—I shouldn't have assumed I could make an advance—"

I shook my head vehemently to interrupt him. "No way. That's the hugest of huge leaps, Niko. I'm sure he had other stuff going on."

"It still could have factored in." Niko hesitated. "It wouldn't be the first time I've messed things up, badly, that way."

I still wasn't buying this whole taking-full-responsibility stance. "So you came all the way around the world to coach him out of his slump because you felt guilty about it?"

"It seemed like the least I could do. And I did want to see him back on the ice. I believe everything I've told him. The world should see his talent."

I eased closer to Niko and looped my arms around his neck in a loose embrace. "Have you talked to him about all this stuff?"

Niko exhaled roughly. "I tried to bring up what happened between us before, but he was obvious about changing the subject when I even hinted at it. I thought it might be better to let him pretend it never happened—write over it as if it doesn't matter. The last thing I want to do is reopen old wounds. *He's* never mentioned it."

These incredible, hopeless men I'd found myself involved with. I blew out my breath with fond exasperation and peered up at him.

"You know how he is. So proud it might as well be bulletproof armor. He probably just needs a little more time to get over whatever's actually eating at him."

Which I suspected was not quite what Niko thought it was.

Niko lowered his head so his forehead rested against mine, his stance relaxing just a little. "I really hope so. I've been trying my best."

I shifted one of my hands to stroke his cheek, his closeness sparking heat all through my body. "I've been able to see that from the first moment I showed up."

My mind tripped back to the things Jasper had said about Niko when he'd dropped by my house—how impressed he was by the other man's coaching. It wasn't my place to share our private conversation, but I felt it was fair to add, "I'm one hundred percent sure that Jasper knows it too. It was just a bad day. The two of you will sort it out."

Niko hummed to himself. "Thank you for listening."

He teased his fingers along my jaw. "You really are an angel, aren't you?"

I couldn't help grinning at him. "Only the most devilish kind."

I bobbed up on my skates to press a kiss to his mouth. My coach let out a rougher sound and kissed me back eagerly.

More heat flooded me as Niko's lean body pressed me against the boards. I breathed in, taking in the rush of adrenaline that came with his familiar cool scent.

When his tongue traced a sensual line across mine, I had to stop myself from stripping his clothes off him right there. He knew just how much to tease me and how to do it in all the right ways.

As our mouths collided again, I let him take the lead, following wherever he wanted to take me. But I couldn't resist stroking my hands over his chest and then his back.

I wanted to feel all of him. It'd been too long since our delicious encounter by the lake.

Niko's hands roamed down my body to my ass. He tugged me tighter against him with my back braced against the boards.

He was already rock hard behind his pants, and his rigid groin settled into just the right place between my legs. At the contact and the flare of hunger that came with it, a whimper seeped from my throat.

As I rocked against him, reveling in the friction, my head tipped back. Niko branded the side of my neck with his mouth, massaging my thighs at the same time.

Oh, God, he knew how to work me over just right. As

if he'd been created just to get me off, and he was nothing but happy to do so.

A very large part of me wanted to urge him onward, to have him fucking me right against the boards. He slid his fingers along my waist, tracing the top of my leggings, and I knew he'd strip them off me and take me if I let him keep going.

But another part of me, maybe not quite as big but insistent, reminded me that off in the shadowed stands, Rafael was watching over me like some kind of guardian angel himself. He'd be seeing every kiss and every caress.

I had no idea how he'd feel about it. I had no idea how he really felt about me. But after seeing how he'd reacted to my make-out session with Jasper, I was pretty sure those feelings were conflicted.

I wasn't going to give up on a love life just to make sure my bodyguard never got unfairly jealous, but that didn't mean it was kind to rub it in his face.

Dipping my head, I sought out Niko's lips for one more kiss. Then I eased back regretfully. "This is *really* good, but can I ask for a rain check? I've just—I've got a lot on my mind."

Niko cupped my cheek. "Of course. You should never feel like there's any pressure from me."

I grinned at him. "Only to be the best figure skater the world has ever seen."

With another laugh, Niko winked at me. "You've already got that one down pat."

Ignoring the unfulfilled ache between my thighs, I sat down in the stands to pull off my skates. My mind spun with all the things I'd just learned.

There was another problem, one I could never have expected, forming cracks in my partnership with Jasper and our dynamic with our shared coach. I'd solidified the connection with my skating partner... Could I smooth over this lingering tension too?

It was so hard to figure out what was really going on behind Jasper's grouchy front, he wore it so adamantly. But then, I'd never have guessed at the guilt Niko was carrying either.

And obviously neither of them had any idea how far *I* actually was from being an angel.

Maybe all three of us were putting on a sort of performance, not just on the ice. Showing the world what we thought it should see even though that wasn't totally accurate.

Something about that last thought sent a bolt of inspiration through me that had nothing to do with my skating life at all. I sprang to my feet, grabbing my bag.

Yes—yes, that just might work.

And then I could solve the biggest threat looming over me and get back to focusing on the guys who really mattered.

TWENTY-TWO

Luciana

MY NERVES JUMPED ABOUT HALF a mile when Rafael strode into the motel room, only settling when I saw it was him. He shut the door behind him with a thump and a rasp of the heavy deadbolt.

After hearing about the pigeon incident and the gang's unfortunate sighting of me in the woods yesterday, my bodyguard had insisted that we temporarily relocate to a strip motel about a half hour down the highway from Hobb Creek. The rooms seemed to mostly be vacant, the walls scuffed and the carpet musty, but at least the security features appeared to be sturdy enough.

I'd spent the hour since I'd gotten back from practice pacing in front of the dated television set and stewing on the idea that had unfurled during my drive from the arena. I'd whittled away at it until it felt foolproof, but I was still nervous as hell.

If this didn't work, I had no idea what would. And the grim expression Rafael was wearing sent a fresh jitter through my nerves.

"What?" I asked. "Did something happen?"

He sighed. "It's pretty bad. Those trumped-up gangsters are barging all around town looking for you."

I tensed instinctively. "Looking for me how?"

"I saw them openly harassing regular people on the street—pushing them around, demanding to know where 'she' is and what they know about 'her.' Meaning you, obviously. No one over there has a clue what they're talking about. I can't even tell whether the buffoons know exactly who they're looking for or if they're trying to scare someone into tattling."

A shiver ran down my back. "Have they hurt anyone?"

Rafael grimaced. "Not yet, but with tempers running that high… I wouldn't be surprised if they get there soon."

Shit. I sat down hard on the stiff mattress. "It's my fault. If I'd been more careful…"

"They provoked you," Rafael said evenly, though I was pretty sure he wasn't happy about my stunt with the cocaine bags either. "I can't blame you for retaliating."

I dragged in a breath, my fingers curling into the blanket. When I'd first thought about interfering with the gang, I'd assumed I'd have to vanish if they caught on to anything I'd done against them.

But I couldn't leave now, not when they were wreaking havoc against the townspeople because of me.

Not when I'd come up with a plan that could truly end this once and for all.

Resolve wound around the guilt that'd clenched my gut. "We can't let this go on any longer. We have to hit back as hard as we possibly can before they do hurt someone innocent—or manage to track me down."

Rafael gave me a wary look. "Somehow I have the feeling you've already come up with a strategy you're just waiting to get me on board with."

I shot him a tight smile. "My plans haven't been bad so far. Our opponents are just too idiotic to take the hint and realize they're beat. But I think what we really need are some theatrics."

"Theatrics," Rafael repeated with undisguised skepticism.

"Yes." I straightened up, the energy of my brainstorm buoying me up. "We're going to do major damage to their business, *and* in a way that makes me seem way scarier than I actually am. Convince them once and for all that they can't win, that they're better off cutting their losses and leaving town—because the consequences of sticking around would be so awful. And in a way no one would ever associate with the Deadly Rose."

Rafael's tone turned dry. "For the record, I already think you're plenty scary. But what exactly did you have in mind?"

My smile turned fiendish. "I made a list of supplies. That might start to give you an idea."

I tapped my phone's screen to bring up my notes and held it up so he could read it.

Rafael's burgundy eyes scanned the list. He smirked

when he came to the final item and shook his head, his tight black coils swaying slightly.

"You're crazy," he said. "But this… I can see how this could be good. Let's get going. We have some serious shopping to do."

One benefit of Jasper inadvertently ending our training session early was that the army surplus store in the next town over was still open when I parked around back.

Rafael headed down the street to pick up some supplies he'd have an easier time locating, and I sauntered into the unassuming building with my spirits high.

Those pricks weren't remotely prepared for the hell I was about to unleash on them.

The bell over the door jingled as I stepped inside. An old man with low jowls that gave him a bulldog-like look peered at me from behind the register.

"Hello there, miss," he said in a croaking voice that was more bullfrog. "Can I help you find anything?"

I glanced around the shop's cluttered interior, densely packed with shelves of equipment and racks of clothing, mostly in black, brown, and khaki-green. The stuffy air made my nose itch.

I'd rather not give him any more time to think about my planned purchases than necessary. "I'd like to browse for now and see what turns up, thanks."

"Well, let me know if you need a hand. I've got a ladder for the stuff that's high up."

Good to know, since some of those shelves were at least a foot higher than I could reach on tiptoe.

I moved through the aisles, my eyes on the merchandise. Ammunition boxes, canvas satchels, piles upon piles of camo. I shook my head, my mouth twisting to the side in a crooked frown.

No, no, and no. None of this would help me.

I turned the corner around a rack of cheaply made ghillie suits and ran an anxious hand over my ponytail. I'd realized I might not find what I wanted right away, but I'd been hoping I could get everything together quickly.

Who knew how quickly the gang might escalate their anger?

I'd just knelt down to check a stack of boxes along the far wall when the door chimed again. Had Rafael already finished and come looking for me?

I peeked past the ghillie coats and froze with a hitch of my pulse.

Jasper stood at the counter, his broad shoulders blocking my view of the clerk. I let go of the coats, my heart thudding hard in my chest.

If my skating partner saw me here, how was I going to explain my sudden interest in army gear? It didn't jive with my usual style. I definitely didn't lean toward military punk.

If I claimed I was broadening my horizons, would he buy that excuse or get suspicious? Especially if some strange events happened near Hobb Creek shortly afterward…

My mouth had gone dry. I shifted my position, my ears pricked to track his movements.

If he simply never realized I was here, problem solved.

Jasper's brusque voice carried from the front of the story. "Hey. Looking for a parka. Got any in at the moment?"

"Sure, right at the back. We were cleared out a few weeks ago but just got some more in. Preparing for a cold winter, huh?"

Jasper managed to chuckle, a little darkly. "Isn't that what they all are around here?"

His footsteps treaded through the store—right toward my hiding spot. I craned my neck and noticed the rack of heavily padded parkas just five feet away.

Stomach churning, I edged to the side around the other racks. Suddenly I was grateful for the tightly packed stock that made for easy hiding places.

As I sank deeper into my crouch, out of view of the parka rack, a flicker of embarrassment passed through me.

Was I being ridiculous? Maybe Jasper wouldn't think twice about noticing me in here. I could be making the situation so much worse by hiding rather than showing myself like a normal person who wasn't up to anything at all sketchy.

But the possibility that he'd realize my real purpose here gnawed at me deeply enough to keep my legs locked in place. Understanding crept up over me with chilly fingers.

I didn't just want to keep my old life separate from the new one I was building. I was *terrified* of Jasper and Niko finding out who I'd once been.

If they realized the things I'd done, the acts I'd carried

out on Mom's orders… If they knew the world I'd moved in and the people I'd associated with…

How could men like them see me as anything other than some kind of monster?

Neither of them could have blood on their hands—not anything like what weighed on my conscience. They'd never be able to wrap their heads around what I'd been through, what I'd been forced to become.

That version of me had died the second that I'd crossed the Texas border. I was becoming something different now, as well as I could. I couldn't let anything jeopardize the happiness I'd found here.

I couldn't lose the first people who'd really welcomed me in and made me feel like I deserved something more.

Unexpected tears pricked my eyes. I closed them and took a slow, deep breath, praying that the clerk wouldn't call out to me and alert Jasper to my presence.

From the rustling of fabric to my left, I could tell that Jasper was picking up parkas and trying them on. I could even imagine them draping his muscular frame.

It made a pretty sweet visual. Would have been nice if I could have checked it out for real.

I forced my eyes open and pretended to be fascinated by the row of canteens in front of me.

Jasper muttered under his breath, followed by more rustling. "Have you got anything else in the back? The biggest size here is still a little snug."

"What we got is what we got, son."

Jasper let out a long sigh. "Right. Thanks again."

I only let myself relax after I heard the door chime

again with my skating partner's retreating footsteps. That had been way too close for comfort.

I swiveled around—and found myself staring at one of the objects I'd most wanted to stumble on.

A grin stretched my lips, my worries falling away. Reaching out, I plucked the simple gas mask from the floor where it'd tumbled off a shelf. "Come to Mama."

But as I tramped over to the counter with my prize under my arm, my spirits deflated a little. How could I be triumphant when I was living a double life?

As long as I was making plans like this, taking on the criminals who lurked around this town, everything I did and said with Jasper and Niko was a sort of lie.

But as long as the gang kept terrorizing Hobb Creek, I didn't have much choice. So I'd just have to end their reign as fast as I possibly could, whatever it took.

TWENTY-THREE

Luciana

I FILLED my lungs with the chilled air of the rink, closing my eyes as I glided across the ice. Tomorrow was the qualifying round for the competition, and I wanted to be as one with the routine as I could possibly be.

They said if you told yourself something enough times, you'd actually start believing it. So I rehearsed what I wanted to believe in my head.

I was confident in myself and in my skills. I was cool and calm, knowing that I was going to skate well in front of the crowd.

I'd be able to put my troubles with the gang on hold, at least for a couple of days. Thankfully, Rafael hadn't observed anything more frightening since their initial round of harassment in town.

The final pieces of my plan were still coming together

—with a delivery that should arrive tonight. I'd see it through when we got back from Dellville.

There was only one thing I had to worry about right now: my skating partner.

I glanced across the ice to where Niko was discussing leg positioning with Jasper. The vibe between them had relaxed again after Jasper's blow up a couple of days ago, but the younger guy still looked a little tense.

And now that Niko had filled me in on their history, I was noticing little signs I would have simply dismissed before. The way Jasper's gaze lingered on Niko's face when the other man's focus was elsewhere, just a little longer and more intensely than you'd expect from a guy simply paying attention to his coach. The faint hint of a flush that colored his cheeks when Niko patted his upraised leg in approval.

It was like a suppressed version of the markers of attraction that'd revealed his interest in me. Maybe he was even more hesitant to let his feelings show when it was another man, especially if Niko was the first guy he'd crushed on.

Or it could be he was hiding it as well as he could because he assumed our coach didn't return that interest. As far as I could tell, both from watching them and from his comments the other day, Niko was totally oblivious to the signals. Maybe he did see them and was afraid to read anything into them after what he saw as his epic blunder with that first kiss.

So they continued, Niko shooting Jasper a bright but professional smile and turning back to me with a beckoning gesture, Jasper drinking in the graceful planes of the other man's face with his eyes before jerking his gaze away with another trace of a blush. The tension in his shoulders wound tighter.

No wonder he'd been prickly with Niko—and with me intruding on his time with Niko. The guy had followed him all the way around the world after what sounded like a pretty fantastic kiss and now was acting like he didn't want anything from Jasper other than to coach him. That'd be enough to throw anyone for a loop.

And naturally Jasper wasn't going to simply open up his mouth and say something about it.

These men really were hopeless. Possibly it was just as lucky for them that I'd crashed into their lives as it was for me.

I might have brought an unexpected threat down on our heads, as hard as I was working to deflect it, but I could do at least one good thing for them too.

"Are you two ready to try that one again?" Niko asked, smiling at me too.

"Sounds good." I rubbed my hands and checked with Jasper, who nodded.

We set off together, cruising across the ice. At the right spot, we both kicked our legs up in a single flip jump flowing into a spiraling shotgun spin.

My thigh ached with the stretch of holding my leg as straight and high as possible. Jasper matched my movements in perfect synchronization. But as we dropped our skates to the ground with a whirl of motion, he jerked just a little to the side before catching his balance.

Jasper muttered a curse under his breath as we skated back to Niko.

"Remember to let out your breath while you're lowering your leg," Niko said. "That should help keep you steadier."

Jasper narrowed his eyes at our coach. "I think I know how to *breathe*. I'm not quite that inept."

Niko clicked his tongue playfully. "It's not about inadequacies. Anyone can forget the basics in the moment when they're focused on something more complicated."

"I'm not forgetting," Jasper grumbled. "I know what I'm doing. It's just not happening right. How about you figure out the cure for that?"

I caught Niko's wince before he schooled his expression to placid again, and my gut twisted. We *had* to get in sync before tomorrow—all three of us. If Jasper couldn't get his head on straight before the competition, my own nerves wouldn't be the deciding factor.

But I didn't think he'd be able to shake off his uncertainties until we addressed the elephant in the room that they'd both been so studiously ignoring.

I cleared my throat before Niko had to reply to Jasper's snarking and crossed my arms over my chest, looking from one of them to the other. "You know, when a hugely respected skater comes halfway around the world just to coach you, it seems like you could try to listen without biting his head off."

Jasper aimed his glower at me. "I listen. That doesn't mean I'm going to hear anything helpful."

"But you are still here training with him, even though you keep complaining about his coaching." I tapped my finger against my lips. "Did you ever think it's kind of odd that Niko Okabe would have come all this way to shake you out of a slump, like he's got nothing better to do?"

Jasper's posture stiffened a bit, and Niko's expression tightened. I could tell from the awkward smile he shot at me that he suspected where I was going with this, but he kept quiet, not interfering. So far.

"Maybe he was bored," Jasper muttered.

"I guess it could be that," I said, as if I really was thinking it over. "Or it could be the fact that you guys shared that amazing kiss last year right before you fell into your slump, and Niko has spent this whole time thinking he caused the whole problem."

Jasper's face outright flared, blazing nearly as red as his auburn hair. "How did—" His gaze jerked to Niko. "You—"

He couldn't seem to get out more than those few sputtered words.

Niko's throat bobbed with a thick swallow. "Lou," he started, his voice thin.

I shook my head at whatever he'd been about to say, letting the corner of my lips quirk upward in a teasing smile. "You came racing to the rescue like a knight in shining armor because you thought you broke Jasper with that kiss. But he's still been struggling even with your help, right?"

"Jasper's made a lot of progress," Niko said quickly.

"But there's still something off. And as far as I know, you haven't been kissing him anymore since last year, huh?"

"No," Jasper mumbled, looking like he wanted to vanish into a crack in the ice.

"Well, there you go." I held Niko's gaze firmly, aware of Jasper at the edge of my vision. "Obviously he's dealing with a lot of things that have nothing to do with kissing. So you're not to blame. No need to feel like you have to make up for any mistakes. You can go home with a clear conscience and get back to your own skating career."

If I'd thought Jasper had been tense before, it was nothing compared to how rigid his body went at my last comment. Oh, he didn't like that suggestion at all.

But Niko was already frowning, his bright eyes gone momentarily stormy. "No. That's not the only reason— I made a commitment to see Jasper make it back into the competitive circuit. The world's losing out by missing the performances I know he could give, and *he* misses it too."

He paused, flicking a tentative glance toward Jasper. "As much as he might try to pretend he doesn't. I can tell, and I want to watch him shine the way only he can."

"Grouchiness and all?" I prodded.

Niko's expression softened. "That's part of the package, so I'll take it with the rest."

Determination rang through his words… along with unmistakable affection. A triumphant grin tugged at my lips, but I held it in while the two men studied each other.

Jasper's shoulders had come down with Niko's declaration. How many of his spats of temper had spawned from insecurities not just about his interest in Niko but whether Niko would stick around at all? Wanting to push the other guy away first so he could say it was his decision, rather than watch Niko give up on him?

"I wouldn't hold you to that commitment," he said hesitantly.

"I know." Something had relaxed in Niko too, having the tensions between them out in the open. "I want to be here, Jasper."

From the warmth dancing in his eyes, I had the feeling he wanted a whole lot more than that too. But this didn't seem like the time to push my luck that far.

Jasper ran a hand through his hair with a duck of his head. "Well… should we get back to work, then? I'll try to keep the grouchiness to a minimum. And remember to breathe."

The last remark felt like a peace offering. Niko nodded. "Why don't we run through the whole routine from the top? It's easier to get into the zone when you're feeling how it all comes together."

As Jasper and I skated into the middle of the rink for our starting position, I could feel the loosening of Jasper's posture. He caught my eye and offered me a crooked smile.

"You really like to shake things up, don't you, Punk?"

I grinned back at him. "Seems like some things come out better after a little shaking."

"Well, here goes nothing."

His freer attitude seeped into his movements from the first glide across the ice. The sense of his higher spirits buoyed me up too.

We whirled from one move into the next, only getting a little wobbly on that one tricky lift. I salvaged it without outright falling, and we skated on toward the end, but I braced myself after the song shut off.

"That was wonderful," Niko said, back to his usual shiny self. "Just watch your right hand on that lift—you don't want to loosen your grip until she's most of the way down."

To my relief, Jasper tipped his head in acknowledgement without any grumbling or snark. "Right. I can do that." He swiveled toward me. "Let's give it another go."

The same energy carried us through three more run-throughs and some more focused work on specific jumps and lifts. My own chest felt lighter as we soared across the ice.

With our final attempt, I might as well have been flying. My limbs moved like they were one with the music —and with Jasper.

He hoisted me up and around like I weighed nothing at all, and we spun together with perfect balance. There was nothing but perfect control in his grasp as he lowered me, my body adjusting to follow his lead.

I touched down and spun out without missing a beat.

We'd done it. We'd pulled off every part of the routine without a hitch.

Only once, but that meant we could do it again.

When we came out of our ending position, Niko was applauding us enthusiastically from the stands. "Fantastic. You're going to blow them all away tomorrow!"

Jasper beamed back at him with a joy I didn't think I'd seen from him on the ice since he'd performed his old routine on my request. When I threw my arms around him in a hug, he squeezed me back and then tipped my head back so he could steal a quick kiss.

But even with plenty of joy thrumming through my chest, my nerves kept prickling away too. We'd pulled off the entire routine once—and now we had to perform it in front of my first set of judges tomorrow. We might not even make it all the way to the actual competition.

I'd better keep my own head in the game, or I could screw this up not just for myself but for the two men who were starting to mean more to me than I'd have ever imagined was possible.

TWENTY-FOUR

I COULDN'T HELP LEANING BACK against the boards as Jasper and Lou unlaced their skates, my gaze lingering on both of them in turn. My heart had been thumping a little faster than usual ever since Lou had staged her surprise intervention on the ice.

The two of them exchanged a few teasing remarks, looking more at ease with each other than I'd ever seen before. The brightening of Jasper's face sparked something inside me too.

I'd been afraid to insist on talking about that night in Munich in case the subject stirred up even more uncomfortable feelings that would bog Jasper down. But it seemed like the opposite had happened, as if he'd cast off a burden he'd been carrying.

And somehow, Lou had known or at least suspected that would be the case. I knew she'd wanted to help us today, not upset us.

I studied her for a moment as she smoothed a few loose strands back into her ponytail. Why had she decided we needed to clear the air today?

There was something more going on with *her* than she'd said. She smiled at Jasper, but a shadow crossed her face when she was concentrating on her own tasks. For the past few days, I'd increasingly had the sense of a dark cloud hanging over her, and it'd only gotten thicker.

Was she simply nervous about the upcoming competition, or was something more going on?

Jasper gave a spine-cracking stretch that made the muscles in his torso flex in all kinds of ways I could appreciate and aimed another relaxed grin at his partner. "Better not to get too wound up before a performance. You should take it easy tonight. I think a nap is on my agenda."

Lou laughed, but the good humor didn't quite reach her dark brown eyes. "If even *you're* telling me it's good to chill out, I guess I'd better listen."

"You should *always* listen to me, Punk," he said in a teasing tone, and lifted his gaze toward me. He hesitated for a moment, and then the corners of his mouth lifted with another small but genuine smile. "Thanks for everything today, Niko."

My heart just about flipped right over, but I kept my rush of exhilaration under wraps. "That's what I'm here for. Go get your rest. You two are going to stun them all tomorrow."

Jasper lifted his hand in a wave to both of us and loped up the aisle to the exit, his gym bag swaying against his back.

When Lou moved to grab her bag too, I stepped forward. "Hey, before you take off, I have a few more pointers. Since it's your first competition and all."

Lou perked up as if she lived for nothing more than for me to tell her how she could skate better. Which honestly, having seen her in action, maybe she did.

"Sure. What were you thinking? Have I been messing up that tuck position again?"

"No, no, nothing like that." I sat down on the edge of the bench across from her. "Jasper's right about relaxing before a competition. You also want to make sure you're well hydrated before you go on, and you're best off having a solid meal a couple of hours before our performance but nothing too heavy."

I could see Lou making mental notes to herself with each point. "Okay, got it."

"And…" The perfect way to get at the questions I wanted to ask popped into my head. "You should also keep in mind your facial expressions, especially performing in front of the judges."

She cocked her head. "There's something wrong with my face?"

I couldn't hold back a chuckle at her mock-offended tone. "You've just looked a little tense sometimes. Your face should give the impression that everything your body is doing is perfectly easy, no strain at all. It's an… illusion it's always good to convey."

"That makes sense."

I peered at her, watching for a clue about her mood. "Have you been feeling like you're under pressure lately? You know this competition in Dellville is very low-key. Even if something goes wrong, it won't affect your career at all."

Lou shrugged, but I caught a flicker of uneasiness in her eyes. "Oh, you know, it's hard not to be a little nervous when it's my first time performing for an audience."

"Of course. Is there anything else on your mind? You can talk to me about whatever you want, you know."

She gave me a gentle smile that lit me up just as much as Jasper's could. "I know, Niko. Really, I'm fine."

I didn't believe her, but I couldn't see how to push any further without becoming obnoxious. I wasn't her keeper —I wasn't even officially her coach.

She'd share her concerns with me when she felt ready to. I could respect her need for privacy, as much as I wanted to smooth out any strain she was feeling.

A hint of mischief tugged at her lips. "And you didn't figure Jasper needed this pep talk too?"

I raised my eyebrows. "He's been through dozens of competitions much more intense than tomorrow's. It'll be good for him to just get back out there again and remember how much he loves it, but I can't imagine there's anything I could tell him that he doesn't already know."

He did love it—being on the ice. I'd been able to see it in every performance during his high period. That was one of the things that'd drawn me to him to begin with.

"Maybe not about competition prep," Lou said, arching her eyebrows right back at me. "But about other things… You obviously care about him a lot if you came all the way here and put up with all his grumbling just to get him back into competitions. No way did you go to all that trouble just because you felt guilty about a kiss that couldn't have lasted more than a minute."

My throat constricted. "I wouldn't have kissed him if I hadn't already liked and respected him quite a bit."

"Like? Respect?" Lou shook her head in apparent exasperation. "Come on, Niko. He's more than that, right? You've got a thing for him, that for some reason you've been keeping ever so quiet about."

A flush of heat crept up my neck. "It didn't seem… relevant. Jasper's never acted as if he—"

"Jasper can barely seem to figure out what *he's* really feeling half of the time through all his hang-ups," Lou interrupted, the insult tempered by the obvious affection in her voice. "How the heck was he supposed to know that you're interested when he hadn't even seen you for more than a year after that one kiss? Did you really expect *him* to make the first move?"

I grimaced. "Well, I—I didn't want to impose on him."

"Has he ever said anything that made it seem like he's upset about what happened between you two? I didn't see any sign that he was bothered about the kiss today."

"No, we've never even talked about it until now."

She tossed her hands in the air. "Why not? Why don't you go for it to see what could happen?"

I grappled for an answer, my feelings in such a muddle it was hard to tell what was actually accurate. "It's complicated. I'm here to coach him—I didn't want to confuse things. Or upset him again."

"He's obviously not getting upset about it. And I think he was a hell of a lot more confused by you *not* saying how you felt."

Lou tapped me on the chest. "And you're not technically his coach any more than you are mine. There's nothing official tying you together that'd make it hard for him to walk away if he wanted to, right?"

I didn't know whether I should be pleased or frustrated that I couldn't brush off her arguments. "I guess there isn't."

"There you go. That's my pep talk for you. Get out of *your* head, take a deep breath, and tell him everything. I'm not making that part of the confession for you."

I shot her a baleful look, and Lou grinned back so sunnily that I couldn't take any offense. The sight of her gorgeous face sent a strange wobble through my pulse.

My feelings and Jasper's weren't the only ones that mattered.

"You wouldn't have any problem with it if—if something more happened between him and me?" I had to ask.

Lou's snort doused all my worries in an instant. "Of course not. You haven't minded sharing me with him— why should I mind sharing him with you?" Her smile turned coy. "I'd get to see my two new favorite guys find a little more happiness. Sounds good to me."

A swell of affection rose up through my chest and propelled me toward her. I touched her cheek and captured her lips with mine, hoping she could feel just how much I meant the tenderness of the kiss.

"Thank you," I said after, running my fingers over her soft hair. "Apparently I did need a pep talk too."

Lou beamed at me. "Glad to be of service."

She leaned in for one more quick peck and then hefted her bag. "See you tomorrow!"

I watched her go, emotions whirling inside me. They didn't feel as jumbled as they had before.

I hadn't wanted to risk the mostly friendly dynamic I'd established with Jasper… but getting closer with Lou hadn't thrown anything off in our working relationship. If anything, we understood and trusted each other more.

Our hookup and the moments we'd shared since hadn't interfered with her performance, so why would simply talking about the possibilities with Jasper ruin his?

Maybe we could have something special, a deeper bond than I'd dared to let myself hope for before.

I wanted that. I had to admit that fact at least to myself now. I'd traveled around the world to work with Jasper because something about him had caught hold of my heart, and my admiration had only intensified as we'd worked together.

I wasn't going to bring up the subject immediately. He had plenty on his mind already with tomorrow's qualifying round and the full competition I was sure they'd make it to the day after.

But once that milestone in his career return was

over… Then I'd find out just how good things between the two of us could be.

And take the blow if he didn't reciprocate my feelings after all.

TWENTY-FIVE

Luciana

BREATHE IN. Breathe out. In again.

Jasper and Niko had told me to relax before the performance, but that was a hell of a lot easier said than done. My nerves had been buzzing since the moment I'd woken up in the dingy motel room this morning.

I'd kept up my deep breaths every time my heart started pounding a little too fast. Now I was hunkered down on the questionable motel-room carpet, stretching my muscles just for something to do.

I'd be heading out in just a couple of hours so we could make it to Dellville with plenty of time for our qualifying performance. And then... then it would all come down to whether I actually deserved the faith my coach and skating partner had put in me or not.

Imagine how it'll feel at the end if the judges say you're through to the full competition. Not how painful it'll be if you screw things up for everyone.

I was just pushing myself off the floor when the lock clicked on the door. I perked up, expecting the pastries Rafael had offered to grab us from town, but one look at his grim face when he hustled inside sent my spirits spiraling downward.

"What?" I said before he could speak. He hadn't even brought his intended loot—no paper bakery bag dangled from either hand.

Rafael's mouth pulled tighter. "That gang of bozos has stepped up their campaign to find you. When I got into Hobb Creek, there were store windows busted all down main street—including the bakery. They're smashing things up when people can't tell them what they want to know.

My stomach plummeted in the same direction my good mood had gone. "Shit."

"That's not even the worst of it." He rubbed his hand over his face. "One of the store owners tried to intervene, and they stabbed him in the shoulder, bad. The doctor rushed out to help him, but the assholes were shouting about how everyone would pay for it if the cops got called in. I don't know if anyone will dare."

I hugged myself, nausea unfurling from my gut. "*We* can't call the police either—who knows what the pricks will do to the other townspeople. It's not like the cops have managed to get the gang in line before now." I paused. "Why didn't they just come after me at practice yesterday if they're so worked up?"

Rafael shook his head. "It seemed like they're still not

sure who exactly was giving them trouble. The bits I heard, they were carrying on about 'that woman who's been messing with us,' not using your name or anything more specific. Beats me how they haven't put the pieces together when they were already targeting you."

I grimaced. "You did say that they might have been harassing me as a newcomer, not because they had any suspicion I was connected to the sabotage at their hideout. It's not like they're the sharpest tacks in the box."

"Yeah, the idiots might assume it has to be someone who's a long-time resident. They wouldn't figure a new arrival would be invested enough to bother." Rafael sighed. "They don't know you."

His words sent a spike of determination through my veins alongside the thudding of my heart. "No, they don't."

Rafael eyed me. "What are you thinking? Don't we have to head out for your competition soon?"

I glanced toward our pile of supplies, the latest bits we'd received to go with what was already stashed in the trunk of the Grand Marquis. My pulse kept thrumming, images of broken glass and splatters of blood flashing behind my eyes.

How much more damage would the gang do if I let them keep rampaging while I spent the weekend skating?

What if they did finally figure out I was the one who'd messed with their property… and they tracked me down to Dellville? It wasn't just the town under threat but Jasper and Niko—and everyone else who'd be at the competition—too.

A chill swept across my body. No, I wouldn't let that happen.

"We can't put off the plan," I announced, moving to grab the bags in the corner. "It's *my* fault that any of this is happening. The locals shouldn't suffer any more because of what I did."

Rafael frowned. "Are you sure you want to do this? Right before you're supposed to perform—"

"We have to," I interrupted. "We have to end this stupid war once and for all and show them that *they're* the ones who are going to pay. We'll just do it fast."

It'd take a half hour simply to get back to Hobb Creek. We were going to be cutting it so close—and I couldn't rush through the plan without getting every piece in place, or it'd flop and we'd end up worse off than before.

But there simply wasn't any other option. The gang had decided their fate.

Better that I let down Niko and Jasper with a late arrival than bring the wrath of a bunch of rabid wannabe gangsters down on the entire local skating establishment.

Rafael didn't wait to be told again. He grabbed the rest of the bags and rushed after me out of the motel room to the waiting car.

I ducked back in to snatch up my equipment bag, which thankfully I'd already packed for the competition, and heaved that in the back of the car. Rafael dropped into the driver's seat, and I didn't bother arguing about who would take the wheel.

All that mattered was getting to the gang's hideout ASAP.

Rafael turned the key in the ignition, and the car

rumbled to life. "We'll make it work. If those bastards aren't pissing their pants and running for the hills by the time you're done with them, they're certifiably braindead."

I glanced over at him as he hit the gas, with a flutter of warmth rising through the tension that gripped me. We might have had our conflicts since coming to Hobb Creek, but I knew without a doubt now that this man was my rock in the storm, the person I could count on no matter what hell we faced.

He gunned the engine all the way to Hobb Creek, veering around the few other cars on the country highway at a breakneck pace. I pulled on the one piece of equipment I could prepare this far in advance over my head and let the thick fabric of the sort-of poncho settle over my arms. Then I tapped my foot against the floor, my mind leaping ahead to every stage of the not-at-all-beautiful performance I intended to orchestrate just for our enemies.

Rafael only slowed the car slightly when we came around town to where the storage buildings sprawled. He parked behind a warehouse a short distance from the gang hideout where we wouldn't be seen making our final preparations.

I leapt out of the car the second it stopped moving and flung open the trunk. First things first—I tugged on my ski mask and tossed another to Rafael.

"Grab your stuff and get over there."

His mouth twisted. "I don't like the whole splitting up part of this plan."

"It's the only way this is going to work." I shoved the bag with the things he needed toward him. "There's no time to argue about it. Just get as many of them out of the building as you can."

As he slung the bag over his arm, my gaze dropped to the bulge of the concealed holster at his hip. "And remember that I don't want you to shoot any of them—not to kill, anyway. Not if you can help it."

"Yes, boss," Rafael said in a dry tone. "You are definitely not your mother."

I managed a breathless laugh. As he loped off, I stuffed my own supplies into my backpack, getting a whiff of a heady chemical scent that made my eyes water. I tossed the bag onto my back and clutched my fingers tight around the gas mask I'd left in my hand.

With frantic steps, I hustled around the side of the warehouse to where I could see the back of the storage building. A couple of men were standing guard by the rear door, slouched and scowling.

Rafael would have gone around front. I just needed to wait until he—

The first hiss and boom of a firework punctuated his arrival. From my current position, I couldn't make out the parking lot, but the crackle of breaking glass suggested he'd aimed well, right at one of the gang's cars.

We really were making them go through a whole lot of vehicles. This time we'd need to leave at least a few for them to flee in.

"Hey, assholes!" my bodyguard bellowed. "Come get a taste of this!"

More shrieks and bangs reverberated from the roman candles he was carrying. The thugs at the back door looked up with matching expressions of shock and then took off to see what the hell was going on.

The yells carrying from the front of the building suggested a fair number of other goons had stormed out from that doorway as well. Good. Now was the time to make my move.

I sprinted from the warehouse to the back of the storage building. The chaos from up front covered the pounding of my footsteps.

I snatched at the door, already reaching toward my sock for my pins—but the knob turned in my hand.

Ha. The dipshits had left it unlocked, presumably so the guards could easily go in and out. They'd made my job that much easier.

Tugging the gas mask over my mouth and nose, I slipped inside. The hallway was empty, but raised voices filtered to my ears from the front of the building.

No problem. Everything I wanted was back here.

I hauled the big container of gasoline out of my backpack and yanked the cap open. Then I shouldered into the room where I'd found the bags of cocaine last time.

The stacks of crates and boxes still filled the space. I didn't know how much of the stash they had on hand was drugs and how much other was illicit merchandise, but pretty soon it was all going to be ashes.

Breathing through the gas mask with faint wheezes, I splashed gasoline over every stack and then drizzled a train out the door. From the hall, I darted into a couple of other rooms and found another heaped with sacks and more boxes.

Hasta la vista to all of those supplies too.

I doused the second storage room with another trail into the hall and poured a thin line of gasoline all the way to the back door. The fumes would have been dizzying if not for the mask. I'd take the rubbery scent filling my nose instead any day.

Pushing open the door, I tossed the now-empty gas container down the hall and pulled out a lighter. Buh-bye, criminal livelihood!

With one flash of sparks, the liquid trail lit up. Flames shot along the stream of gasoline toward both of the rooms and licked straight under the doors.

In a matter of seconds, the warbling sound of a raging fire resonated down the hall along with clouds of smoke gushing from beneath the doors.

Grinning beneath my mask, I jogged backward a few steps and fumbled in my bag for a tube of special gel that'd been our last acquisition along with the poncho. With a forceful squeeze, I got a big blob of it and smeared it all across my neck, hands, and my face as far as I could reach, pressing beneath the gas and ski masks. I even slathered some onto the fabric of the ski mask itself for good measure.

The cool, slick sensation made me cringe, but I didn't dwell on it. I shoved the tube back into my bag and dashed for the front of the building to reunite with Rafael.

I charged into the parking lot to find him handling the situation there pretty well on his own. Three of the gang members were lying on the ground, moaning and holding various parts of their bodies. Another handful of guys were advancing towards him, but he didn't look worried.

I watched in admiration of his strength as he jabbed one jerk in the stomach and brought a huge fist crashing into another guy's nose, only to toss the loser into the dirt a few feet away.

The few remaining gangsters circled him warily. One glanced back at the building and let out a shout at the sight of the smoke now streaming up into the open air.

A flicker of relief passed through me. Maybe I wouldn't even have to take this last, crazy step. Maybe we'd done enough to have them running scared as it was.

But as that thought passed through my mind, a truck roared down the road with two cars flanking it. They tore into the parking lot and skidded to a stop with a screech of their tires.

A dozen more guys sprang out, all of them clutching pistols or knives. And all of them clearly furious.

TWENTY-SIX

Rafael

IF I'D HAD it my way, every one of the so-called gangsters who'd just torn into their parking lot would have charged toward me. Instead, most of them ran at Lou where she'd emerged from behind the smoking storage building, some twenty feet away from me.

She was both closer to the scene of our main crime, and she must have looked a hell of a lot more vulnerable than I did. The combination of ski mask and gas mask gave her an almost alien appearance, but she was more than a foot shorter than me and slimmer besides, and her feminine curves showed even beneath the black poncho draped over her.

They probably figured they could use her as leverage against me.

Gritting my teeth, I hurtled after them as fast as I could run. If they sent one bullet or blade into her body…

I couldn't let it get even that far. The thought of Lou injured, her petite frame swaying with pain, sent a pulse of fury through my veins. My hands clenched into fists, and my fingers itched for the gun at my hip.

I'd promised her I'd only shoot if I needed to—but our current situation had to count as an emergency. Better if these pricks all ended up dead on the pavement than to let even one of them lay a hand on her.

Lou tensed in a fighting stance, her sharp-edged rings glinting in front of her knuckles. One of the assholes *laughed* at her.

He raised his gun, just a few steps away from her. My hand leapt to my holster. My fingers closed around the grip—

And Luciana Cordova flew into action.

She lunged forward before the guy in the lead could reach her and drove her ringed fist right into his face with a smack that rang across the pavement. As he reeled backward, clutching at the scratches dribbling blood from his forehead, she knocked the gun from his hand with the crack of broken fingers.

As that guy swore and sputtered, Lou was already whipping to the side to slam two other men's heads into each other with a thud that I knew would leave bruises if not concussions as well. They stumbled dizzily while she kneed the next approaching attacker in the groin.

That thug's knees had barely hit the pavement before she was kicking another goon's legs out from under him with a swift sweep of her foot.

Her poncho billowed out around her limbs like an all-encompassing cape, as if she were some strange superhero vigilante. She definitely was a sight to see.

Even as I rammed my fist into one of the guys at the rear of the pack and drove my elbow into another's ribs hard enough to provoke a *crack!*, I couldn't stop glancing at her. And not just to make sure she was okay.

I'd known her mother had trained her in all kinds of fighting techniques. I'd been around for some of those sessions, not to mention a few missions that'd devolved into gang warfare.

But I'd always stepped in to make sure I took the brunt of any attack. Mireya had never pushed her daughter to her limits, at least not in front of me.

It seemed the coldhearted bitch had taught her daughter to fight better than even I knew. Or maybe it was simply that now Lou had something to lose, something she truly cared about.

My heart twisted. She was thinking of those two guys. *Her* guys. Niko and Jasper.

Not me.

But no matter who'd inspired this show of force, she was incredible. A whirling dervish of lunges and blows, leaving her attackers scattering in her wake. Not just fierce and powerful but bringing the same grace to the battle that had always taken my breath away watching her on the ice.

"Jesus Christ," one of the slower guys muttered, easing back from the brawl. "She's fucking crazy!"

Oh, he didn't know the half of it. But she was my kind of crazy, all the way through.

I couldn't have been prouder to be standing here by her side than I was in this moment.

I kneed him in the gut and toppled him to the ground for good measure, but I wasn't sure Lou even needed me for that much. She already had half a dozen guys sprawled and groaning around her, and the remainder had slowed their roll, eyeing her from a careful distance with their weapons drawn.

One of the men still standing had a pistol. I grabbed my own, ready to intervene if he decided that outright killing her was a better option than taking her hostage, but then Lou launched into her final trick.

I didn't even see her reach into her pocket. There was a click and a flash of a lighter by the edge of her poncho—and then the entire specially-treated piece of fabric burst into flames.

My heart stuttered with the urge to dash in and save her from the terrifying scenario she'd just created. But we'd gone over this—she'd protected her skin and hair, she'd read all of the safety measures.

She needed to convince these idiots that they weren't going to win this war, not against her, and for that she needed to pull out all the stops.

The flames sizzled all around her torso as she strode toward the remaining men without a hint of hesitation. Her voice bellowed through the mask, the hollow effect it created making her words sound twice as threatening.

"If you assholes know what's good for you, you'll pack your shit and get the hell out of this town. If I ever — and I mean *ever* — catch you in Hobb Creek again, it'll be your stone-cold corpses I burn. *Do you understand me?*"

The men jerked back when she struck out with her flaming arms, their jaws gone slack, their weapon-arms faltering. I'd bet these imbeciles had never seen anything like this little but potent force of nature before.

"You're all dead men the next time I see you," she growled in calm ferocity. "I'll bury you right where I ice you."

She whipped a fiery blow straight at one of the men standing, and a flicker leapt from her poncho onto his shirt. He shrieked like a baby and swatted at it as he scrambled away from her.

That was the straw that broke the camel's back.

"Let's get the fuck out of here!" someone shouted.

A few of the injured men were heaving to their feet; their colleagues yanked others off the pavement. They fled for the working vehicles like the hounds of hell were snapping at their heels. I noted the damp spots on a couple of crotches where the goons had pissed themselves.

"Fuck, fuck, fuck," one of them mumbled under his breath. Several of the faces had gone sickly white.

One of the guys leaned out of the driver's seat of the truck as he started the engine. "This crappy town is all yours, you freak!"

I enjoyed a brief moment of triumph that was mostly Lou's watching the truck and cars speed out of the parking lot and then groped at my bag for the fire-retardant blanket. The longer Lou let the fire rage on, the more chance—

I didn't even have time to really worry. Lou dropped and rolled on the gritty pavement, pressing her body into the hard ground. The flames hissed as she smothered them, smoke wisping off the special poncho.

The second the worst of them were out, she yanked the poncho right off and stomped on the lingering flares of fire for good measure. Then she chucked her gas and ski masks into the smoldering heap.

She spun around, a grin stretched across her shining face, and swiped at the gel smeared across her jaw and cheeks with her sleeve. "We did it. We fucking did it!"

"You did it," I had to say. "That was fucking spectacular, Lou."

She pumped her fist in the air and bent down to snatch up her cast-offs. "Can't leave any evidence around. Let's get back to the car. I've got to skate! We're going to have to break a few speed limits to get to Dellville in time."

"We will." I silently resolved that I would get her there unharmed and on time, no matter what I had to do. "Don't even worry about it."

But of course Lou leapt into the driver's seat before I'd even loped all the way to the car. She shot me a sassy grin that lit up her dark eyes, and my heart skipped a beat.

As I dropped into the seat beside her and leaned back with her slam on the gas pedal, an undeniable realization sank deep into my gut.

I'd let the cheeky attitude she'd had since she was a teenager, her size, and our age difference lull me into thinking she was still the same girl I'd been protecting for years. But that couldn't have been further from the truth.

She was a woman now. I hadn't let myself see just how confident and capable she'd become. Sure, she was nineteen and technically an adult, and I'd told her I knew all that, but since we'd gotten into town, she'd shown an assurance and sense of strategy way beyond those years.

She was every bit the leader her mother had wanted to mold her into. She could hold her own against forces even I would have avoided tackling.

How could I have still seen her as a victim too vulnerable to take care of herself? How could I have treated her like one, even after she'd made this bold bid for independence?

I glanced over at Lou as she lifted a hand to wipe away a little more gel from her neck. Her eyes gleamed, but there was a distance in them now, as if her mind were miles ahead of us already.

She'd put the situation with the gang behind her. I could tell by her expression that she was entering that realm of grace and balance and beauty, the space in her mind where I could never join her.

It was a place reserved only for skating, for the art that had truly left its mark on her soul. Niko and Jasper might belong there, but I sure as hell didn't.

But God, did I wish that I did.

That was the worst part of the revelation that'd just struck me. In all my refusal to see what was right in front of me, I'd pushed her away, turned down her advances.

I'd known that she'd wanted me, and I'd felt the same desires humming through me every time I looked at her in the past year, but I'd decided I knew best. That I needed to protect her from myself.

As if *I* could possibly be too much for *her* to handle. So totally fucking absurd.

But it was too late to take back the decisions I'd made now. What the fuck could I even offer her? Reminders of the life she longed so badly to leave completely behind?

She'd found something good with two men who understood the most important part of her existence so much better than I did. All I could do now was watch while the knowledge of my mistakes tore my heart out.

TWENTY-SEVEN

Luciana

RAFAEL GLANCED over at me from behind the steering wheel. "That's the arena up ahead. Are you ready?"

I peered at myself in the mirror on the sun visor and smoothed down a few errant strands of my hair that were threatening to escape my ponytail. My pulse was outright thundering now, but I couldn't see anything to be nervous about in my appearance.

Rafael and I had switched off driving halfway to Dellville, when I'd briefly ducked into a service center restroom to scrub the last traces of gel off my skin. The high of my victory over the wannabe gangsters had carried me careening along the highway that far, reveling in the lingering adrenaline and the thrum of the engine, but it'd been a necessary transition.

Because all the rest of my prep I'd carried out while

Rafael handled the Grand Marquis like a race car, weaving through the thickening traffic. In the less busy stretches, I'd squirmed out of my stealth gear and into the skating outfit that was only a temporary costume until Jasper and I saw how this initial routine landed with an audience. While my bodyguard had been cruising swiftly but steadily, I'd tamed my hair into this sleek ponytail and applied some basic makeup.

All thoughts of the other performance I'd put on today had gradually faded to the back of my mind. My routine on the ice called for grace and elegance, nothing like the violent chaos I'd just created.

Some kind of celebration should be in store, but not until Jasper and I made it through the qualifying round and had that to celebrate too.

If we made it through the qualifying round.

The butterflies in my stomach flapped harder. But I said to Rafael, "Now or never."

As he pulled the car into the parking lot outside the big, pastel yellow arena building, I swallowed hard at the sight of the rows and rows of cars already stretched across the space. But the time on the dashboard clock said it was still ten minutes before our assigned performance time.

I'd made it, if only barely.

I grabbed my equipment bag out of the back and hauled ass to the arena doors. I was still several steps away when Niko and Jasper burst out to meet me, Niko's eyes shining with relief but Jasper in a furor.

"Where have you been?" he demanded before I could say anything, raking his hand through his tousled hair.

"You missed our warm-up time. We're supposed to be going on to perform, like, *now*."

"Ten more minutes," I said with a gulp of breath. "Sorry, I didn't mean to cut it so close. I tried to take a shortcut and then we got delayed by an accident on the road."

It was a reasonable enough story, and Niko nodded. "We're just glad you made it."

But Jasper's eyes had narrowed as he looked at my ponytail. "Your hair…"

I frowned. "What?"

He reached over and fingered the strands, tugging a lock over where I could see it from the corner of my eye.

See the brittle, blackened tip where that bit had gotten singed.

Oh, shit.

I fumbled for a reasonable excuse and let out a laugh I hoped didn't sound nervous. "Just a little accident with the straightener. Come on, we've got to get inside and into our skates, or we really will be late."

That spurred my partner into action. A strange cosmetic detail was nothing compared to making it to the competition ahead.

As we all hustled inside, Niko waved to Rafael. "Come with me. You should sit up front for this performance— bring all that moral support."

A hint of a smile touched Rafael's lips. When the two of them split off from Jasper and me, a bloom of warmth filled my chest.

All three of the men who mattered most to me were here together, supporting me as a team. My two skaters had no idea about the trouble I'd gotten involved in, and now that was over. I could really put my past behind me and move forward.

I couldn't have asked for anything more.

The inside of the arena was only a smidgen nicer than the one in Hobb Creek. Along with the other skaters and the judges, there were several dozen onlookers in the stands, but not anywhere near enough to bring news crews. Just a small portion of Dellville's population curious to see the competition all the way through.

As we slipped into the rink area, the pair before us was gliding across the ice. Curiosity tugged at me to check out their routine, but I couldn't afford to give them even a few seconds of my time.

Jasper rushed me onward to the prep area at the base of the stands. I dropped onto the bench and yanked on my skates at record speed.

With each cross of the laces, I breathed in and out, willing my pulse to steady and my mind to clear of everything but my love for the ice.

Images from beautiful routines I'd watched in awe in the past floated through my mind—some of them spectacles put on by the very men who'd helped me reach this moment. Jasper and Niko had taken my breath away so many times.

I could make art like that too. Even if it wasn't a kind of art that could ever hang on a museum wall or be displayed at a gallery, it was art all the same.

But the fact that you had to be there in the moment to see it made it even more special. The beauty was so fleeting, so pure and so brief, that it had to be magic.

Determination wound through my limbs as I knotted the laces. I'd just defended the town I'd made my home and won, and now I was going to win this opportunity for myself and the men I was falling for too.

The song for the pair before us petered out. I looked up just in time to see them in their ending position before mild applause carried through the stands.

As they glided over to the boards, I quickly brushed my fingers over the pocket of my bag that held my childhood lace, for whatever luck it would offer me.

Jasper and I stood up in anticipation of our summons onto the ice. Jasper's shoulders looked stiff, his forehead furrowed.

When a woman with a clipboard motioned for us to take our starting positions, my partner's stance didn't loosen. The tension wound through his body while we skated into the center of the rink, storm clouds gathering in his eyes.

My own nerves had formed a twitching ball in my stomach, but they were as much excitement as anxiety. But then, maybe it made sense that he would be worrying more than I was.

This was my first chance to show the wider world what I could do. The possibilities were endless.

He'd already experienced the highs of success… and the lows of failure. He knew exactly how awful it would feel if he faltered out there.

It wasn't right. *I* knew what an amazing skater he was.

And maybe by working together, we'd find our way to a place where he could believe it again too.

Just before we settled into position, I tucked my hand

around Jasper's neck and pushed up for a quick but tender kiss. When I drew back, he was staring at me with a hint of a flush in his cheeks but the storm clouds parted.

"Lou…"

I tapped him on the chest with a playful smile. "I just want you to know that I can't wait to be your partner—in this and in all kinds of other ways. We're going to make something really beautiful together."

His shoulders came down as an answering smile crossed his lips. "Yeah. Yeah, we will."

We arranged ourselves in our planned poses, my ears pricked for the first strains of our music. When the opening note reached my ears, my heart leapt.

Jasper and I took off at the third beat of the song, a dreamy nocturne that we had both agreed captured the emotion we wanted to evoke in our viewers. In that first moment, I realized he was just a tad ahead of me, not quite in sync. I pushed myself to catch up and wobbled, and my pulse stuttered.

We matched each other as we swept across the ice, every lift of our hands mirroring each other. When we whirled into our first set of spins, I caught a brief waver of Jasper's leg, but he straightened it in less than a second.

Keep breathing. Keep moving. We could do this.

We veered apart and circled back toward each other in preparation for the first—not quite as tricky—lift. Jasper's eyes met mine, and everyone off the ice seemed to dissolve from existence, as if we were the only two people in the universe.

When he hoisted me into the air, the cold air breezed

by my face, stinging my cheeks. But I didn't care. This was what I was put on this planet to do.

I arched my back, letting my arms reach out wistfully, and hoped that my expression conveyed the gentle, heavenly emotions of the music.

Maybe I focused a little too hard on what my face was doing rather than the rest of me. As Jasper moved to lower me back down to the ice, my body shifted, and I sensed in an instant that I'd missed a moment when I needed to adjust my position more.

My weight wasn't even; my balance was off kilter. And Jasper had set his hand a little farther down my hip than was ideal, so I couldn't quite get it back on my own.

With a jolt of panic, I felt myself wobble. I hit the ice at an unsteady angle, already sensing gravity pulling my knee toward the ice.

But I pushed myself against its tug, and Jasper caught my elbow in a move that wasn't technically part of the routine but blended in well enough. I righted myself without outright hitting the ice.

The judges would have seen the awkward landing, even if it hadn't been as bad as it could have been. But as we set off to begin the next series of spins and jumps, I reminded myself that it was over.

We had so much more to show ahead of us, and we were going to knock their fucking socks off like no one else could.

I caught Jasper's eye and shot him a grin, hoping he hadn't been thrown by the error either. His expression relaxed, and he gave me a slight tip of his head just before we launched into our double Lutzes.

We hit the ice in perfect synchronization and whipped straight into the next sequence. With every breath, the pump of our legs felt even more aligned.

I experienced each breath Jasper took as though it were my own, our chests rising and falling together. We were even more united now than when we'd hooked up in the training room.

This was something different, something hovering on a soul-deep level I'd never felt before.

Our jump combo was effortless; our landing without fault. A smile lingered on Jasper's lips—not aimed at me but for the simple joy of the routine.

He was reveling in the art of skating itself, falling in love with the sport all over again. My heart soared at the sight.

This was what Niko had been working so hard for. I hoped he could see my skating partner's expression from his place in the stands.

Our toe loops descended to the ice at the exact same moment. My outstretched hand met Jasper's, and he pulled me close enough that I could feel his pulse hammering.

A twinge of anxiety rippled through me under the swell of the music. This was the lift that'd really given us trouble before. We'd failed in practice more often than we'd succeeded. If we hadn't even pulled off the easier one properly…

I shut out those doubts and gave myself over to the movements. We *had* done it before, just yesterday. We could do it again.

Jasper's fingers squeezed around my hand and against

my thigh. My body soared upward in his grasp to twirl three full times in quick succession.

I followed every shift of his body in time with the peak of the melody. We were still united, still in sync in every way that mattered.

Yeah. We could do this. Watch us now.

I came down at the perfect angle, the tips of my skates' blades connecting with the ice like they were magnets. A whoop of approval carried from the crowd.

We glided around into the last jump-spin combo and twined together in our ending pose. We were both panting for breath, but I could feel Jasper's triumphant grin against my cheek.

Applause thundered through the arena. My own grin stretched so wide my cheeks ached.

We'd done it. We'd recovered and proved just how good we could be.

Jasper took my hand, raising it high towards the rafters. The clapping only grew louder.

My gaze veered to the row of judges with a rush of relief at the smiles on their faces before they ducked their heads to consider their notes.

Jasper nudged me in the arm on our way back to the stands. "You were really something out there, Punk."

I beamed at him. "So were you. I'd say that was a pretty good start to our competitive partnership." I paused with a slight listing of my stomach. "Well, as long as the judges think so too."

Niko didn't appear to have any doubts on that score. Our coach welcomed us to the bench with his face lit up so bright he outshone the overhead lights.

"You two were amazing!" he crowed. "I knew you could do it!"

Even Rafael couldn't completely contain a smile. He studied the judges. "What about their scores?"

"Just a moment." Niko motioned to the judging table. "Look, they're handing them over to the announcer now."

My heart started pounding so hard it drowned out every other sound. The announcer raised his microphone to his lips, but all I heard was the frantic thudding and another round of cheers from the crowd.

Niko grabbed my arm and Jasper's and pulled us both into a joint hug. "You're in! Not that I had any doubts *before* watching you, let alone after."

I blinked at him, breathless. "But—aren't there still some more pairs who need to compete?"

"It doesn't matter," Niko announced gleefully. "Your score is the third highest out of everyone who's performed so far, and there are only five more pairs left. Even if they're all geniuses, you're guaranteed to be in the ten who'll compete properly tomorrow."

He wrapped his arms around us, happiness radiating through our little huddle. "I'm so proud of you two. This is just the start, and it was a fantastic one."

A giddy laugh burst out of me. I hugged him back and then pulled Jasper into an embrace just the two of us. Even after I finally sat down on the bench to swap my skates for my sneakers, the sensation of floating stayed with me.

Rafael leaned over from behind me, murmuring by my ear so that only I could hear him. "I'm going to take a walk around the perimeter. I just want to be sure everything is fine, if you know what I mean. But that performance was incredible, Lou."

I nodded, understanding completely. I couldn't blame him for wanting to be on the safe side after what we'd accomplished earlier today. And a big crowd celebration wasn't really my bodyguard's style.

As for me, I was riding the wave of adrenaline coursing through my veins with nothing on my mind but this first small but perfect victory.

I had arrived, and I was already making my mark.

TWENTY-EIGHT

Luciana

TAKEOUT HAD NEVER BEEN SO delicious in my life.

I dug into a mound of white rice and duck sauce, scooping faster than I could swallow. A veritable feast was laid out between Rafael and me on our little dining table in the bungalow, and all of it tasted like success.

"This was definitely the right choice for a celebratory dinner." I dipped a wonton in soy sauce as it wobbled between my chopsticks. "God, I was starving. Today really took it out of me, I guess."

Rafael only hummed in response, unusually subdued even for the deadpan bodyguard I was used to. I glanced up at him, taking in the distant cast to his eyes and the solemn shadow that'd come over his features.

He'd long since finished his helping of Mongolian

beef. The container sat empty on the coffee table, judging me silently as I chowed down. He hadn't touched anything from the myriad of soups and appetizers I'd ordered.

Now he leaned back in his chair, his mouth setting in an even sterner line than before.

Was he still worrying about our hijinks before the skating competition this afternoon?

I wagged my chopsticks at him. "I don't think we need to worry about that pathetic excuse for a gang ever again. I mean, they wouldn't have cleared out the rest of their stuff from the storage building if they weren't taking off for whatever they figure greener pastures are, right?"

We'd stopped by the old hideout on our way back into town and found the building a burnt-out shell and the parking lot totally vacant other than one car Rafael's fireworks must have done too much of a number on. There'd been no sign of the wannabe gangsters anywhere.

"They're not going to come back," Rafael said brusquely.

His confirmation reassured me but left me even more confused about his mood. I prodded a morsel of duck. "I'm glad that's over with. Now we can live our lives in peace."

All I got in response was a grunt. Where had this new stick up his ass come from? He'd seemed upbeat enough, as much as he ever got, right after I'd skated.

But he'd become increasingly quiet and solemn the whole drive home. I'd thought it was concern about our previous problems, but that clearly wasn't the case.

My stomach ached with all the food I'd stuffed into it and a little apprehension as well.

I set down my chopsticks. "Well, if you're not eating anything else, we'd better pack the rest up. I don't want to gain twenty pounds right before the actual competition."

Rafael got up with a scrape of his chair legs, his attention finally focusing on me. "You're going to be fine tomorrow. Better than fine."

"Oh, yeah?" I said with a teasing lilt as I started closing up cartons. "Then why are you going around like you expect the apocalypse to begin any moment now?"

The corner of his mouth twitched. He gathered up a couple of cartons in a stack in front of him and then simply gazed down at them as if he'd forgotten what he was supposed to do with them.

He lifted his head and met my eyes again. "I'm sorry, Lou."

Say what now?

I cocked my head, trying to hide just how confused I was. "What've you got to be sorry for? I couldn't have gotten through today without you—you had my back every step of the way. You know how much I appreciate that, don't you?"

"It's not… It's not about that." He grimaced as if he was grappling with his words.

My stomach started to sink.

Rafael was normally taciturn, sure, but he spoke his mind bluntly when he did have something to say. What was he so uncomfortable about telling me?

Was he thinking about leaving—going back to Austin to rejoin Mom's operations? Maybe our battle with the small-time criminals here in Hobb Creek had left him missing the bigger thrills of his former career.

He squared his shoulders, and I braced myself for the pain I imagined was coming.

"As much as I said I wouldn't, I've been treating you like a kid," he said. "Like you're a victim—or like you can't make your own decisions. But today showed me just how wrong I was. I should have seen it so much sooner. I should have—"

He cut himself off with a growl, the sound containing so much frustrated emotion that my pulse kicked up a notch.

I shook my head. "It's okay. You don't have to apologize for that. You *have* been watching over me since I was a kid—it makes sense that it'd be hard to shift your frame of reference."

"Maybe. But it shouldn't have taken me so long. If it hadn't..." He let out his breath in a rough sigh. "I've noticed the woman you were becoming in *other* ways for years. You're strong and funny, talented and gorgeous—I can't say there wasn't a tiny part of me that was tempted even when you took your shot when you were sixteen."

My mouth went dry, my heart thumping even faster. "You turned me down."

"I did. I don't regret that—that's a line that should never be crossed. But you waited until you were old enough that no one back home would have batted an eye and gave me another chance, and I blew that one too. I wanted you so badly, but I convinced myself I shouldn't go there, that I'd somehow be taking advantage of you because you couldn't realize what you were really getting into."

As I stared at him in stunned silence, he hung his

head. "That's what I'm sorry about. I rejected you even though you were everything I could possibly want because I was arrogant enough to think you couldn't know what *you* really wanted, and now—now I've obviously lost my chance. I probably shouldn't even be telling you this, but I wanted you to know that you weren't wrong. It was my screw-up."

I swallowed thickly, so much emotion welling up inside me that I could barely breathe.

Rafael had been my first crush and therefore my longest. I'd always wanted him more than any other man I'd met, even after he'd made it clear nothing was going to happen between us.

Well, until I'd blown into Hobb Creek and met Niko and Jasper.

I paused on that thought. Was that why he assumed he'd lost his chance?

But all those old feelings still thrummed through my body, propelling me toward the man I'd loved for so long. I walked around the table, hardly feeling the floor beneath my feet.

"Rafael, I fell for you all the way back when I was thirteen years old. Because you *are* everything I could imagine wanting. Just because I'm falling for other men too doesn't mean those feelings have vanished."

He lifted his hand only to leave it hovering in the air between us, not quite reaching all the way to me. I wrapped my own much smaller hands around it, his solid palm engulfing my fingers.

The warmth of his skin sparked a headier heat right up my arm. But I knew I had to make one other thing clear.

"I *am* falling for Niko and Jasper," I said, keeping my voice steady but soft. "There are other things I want in my life—need in my life—that I never realized before, that I've found with them. I'm not going to give them up."

Rafael's voice came out gruff, but I thought I saw a glint of hope in his burgundy eyes. "I wouldn't expect you to."

I smiled up at him. "And that's exactly why I still need you too, however you're willing to be a part of my life. That's what it comes down to, really. You haven't lost your shot. It's just a question of whether you can handle sharing me with them."

His jaw worked as he considered his answer. "I don't know. A lot of me wants to whisk you away from everything and claim you all for myself. But you're not a woman who can be claimed. I realize that. I'd like—I'd like to see what we could be even with them in the mix, if you want that too."

I grinned up at him with a rush of joy. "Oh, believe me, I do."

I bobbed up on my toes, and thankfully Rafael knew exactly what I was aiming for. He wrapped one brawny arm around me and leaned in to meet my kiss.

His searing heat washed over my body. I sighed into the kiss and tilted my head to angle it even deeper.

For all the hardness of his muscular frame, Rafael's lips were soft as velvet. His tongue slid like a flame against my own.

With each kiss that followed the first, my head spun faster. His fingers trailed over my hair, sparking jolts of pleasure through my scalp.

I matched his passion with my own blazing desire, wanting him more and more with each passing moment. Wanting to savor every bit of the connection I'd believed I was never going to get.

My hands teased up under his shirt to stroke his sculpted back skin to skin. Rafael groaned and kissed me even harder—

And a loud *thump* filtered through the wall from outside in the front yard.

I jumped with a flinch of my nerves, my head jerking toward the door. The passion that'd been flowing through my limbs ebbed with a pang of apprehension. "What was that?"

Rafael's eyes had turned even darker. He strode toward the door, and I dashed after him, my hands balling into fists.

We stormed down the front steps, scanning the yard for any sign of an intruder. In the thickening darkness of the evening, I didn't make out any movement.

Then my gaze caught on a furry form slumped on the hood of the Grand Marquis.

Rafael saw it in the same moment. He held out his hand to ward me off. "Maybe you should go inside."

I shot him a pointed look. "Didn't you just get done saying how I'm a strong woman who can handle myself?"

I marched over, my gut twisting as I made out the details of the tableau that'd been arranged on the hood.

It was a raccoon. Limp and lifeless, its beady eyes glazed, its severed neck leaking blood across the pale blue steel.

And next to its head lay a figure skate with a bloody

blade. The blade that'd been used to cut the animal's throat.

My stomach was outright churning now. "Rafael," I murmured, wrenching my gaze back to him. "We ran the gang out of town. And they didn't even know it was me. They wouldn't come back just to pick on the new girl in town some more."

Rafael scowled at the carcass. "No, they wouldn't. I don't think this is about them after all."

A shiver ran through my body. "We assumed we were dealing with one set of enemies… but it could have been two all this time."

If my latest bloody gift wasn't from the idiotic gangsters, then the doll, the squirrel, and the pigeons hadn't been either. Those two pieces of the puzzle had never really fit together—because they weren't connected after all.

I peered into the deepening night with a deeper chill prickling under my skin.

Whoever was harassing me with unnerving "presents" was someone separate from the gang we'd just run off.

Someone deranged. Someone dangerous. Someone smart enough to play their disturbing tricks without getting caught.

Someone who intended to torment me in every sick way they could, and who wasn't remotely close to stopping.

ABOUT THE AUTHORS

Eva Chance is a pen name for contemporary romance written by Amazon top 100 bestselling author Eva Chase. If you love gritty romance, dominant men, and fierce women who never have to choose, look no further.

Eva lives in Canada with her family. She loves stories both swoony and supernatural, and strong women and the men who appreciate them.

Connect with Eva online:
www.evachase.com
eva@evachase.com

Harlow King is a long-time fan of all things dark, edgy, and steamy. She can't wait to share her contemporary reverse harem stories.